False Witness

False Witness

PATRICIA HALL

First published in Great Britain in 2005 by
Allison & Busby Limited
Bon Marche Centre
241-251 Ferndale Road
London SW9 8BJ
http://www.allisonandbusby.com

A catalogue record for this book is available from
the British Library.

10 9 8 7 6 5 4 3 2

ISBN 0 7490 8235 6

Printed and bound in Great Britain by
Bookmarque Ltd, Croydon, Surrey

Also by Patricia Hall

In the Ackroyd & Thackeray series

And

PATRICIA HALL is the pen-name of journalist Maureen O'Connor. She was born and brought up in West Yorkshire, which is where she chose to set her acclaimed series of novels, including *Dead Reckoning* and *Deep Freeze*, which feature reporter Laura Ackroyd and DCI Michael Thackeray. She is married, with two grown-up sons, and now lives in Oxford.

Chapter One

The explosion blew out the windows of the science lab, showering glass onto a huddle of boys who were taking a surreptitious drag on their cigarettes just below. The sharp crack reduced the class to silence for a dazed second or two, before they broke into whoops and jeers of delight. As the fire alarm filled the whole building with its shrieking siren, eighty teenaged boys, a handful of girls, and their bemused teachers, erupted into the corridors of the Woodlands School and spilled out into the playground.

'Get yourselves into class groups so we can check the register,' shouted a small, determined-looking woman dressed entirely in black who had appeared from the school office with the force of a small gale. What Mary Morris lacked in stature she made up for with sheer strength of personality and she immediately took control of the milling crowd, some of whom by now seemed to be edging towards hysteria. Several of the girls were in tears, clinging to each other for support, and a couple of youths were shoving and pushing each other aggressively and kicking fiercely with outsized trainers amongst the glittering shards of the broken windows.

'Come on, move!' Mary Morris shouted. 'Stay with your class teachers. And *be quiet!*'

She manhandled a shambling, hooded youth almost twice her size in the direction of a pale young man who looked barely older than some of his charges. 'This is one of yours, Mr Manley, isn't it? Come on Craig, help Mr Manley get your group together instead of messing about like that.'

Mary Morris, the deputy head of the special school for disturbed young people, strode around the playground littered with the last wind-blown gold and brown leaves of autumn and an even brighter scatter of discarded crisp packets. Gradually she reduced the milling crowd to something approaching order. Satisfied that the volatile mix of belligerence and neurosis she found herself temporarily in charge of would not now combust, she turned away to meet a heavily built older man making his way down the worn stone steps of the main entrance to the Victorian mansion which served as Woodlands, main building. He was the last to leave, and was surrounded by wisps of smoke as he chivvied a tearful young girl in a bum-freezing mini-skirt and skimpy top ahead of him.

'I think they're all out, Mrs Morris,' he said formally, running a dirty hand wearily across grey hair and creased brow. 'There's a lot more smoke than fire in there, as far as I can see. But I found this one hiding in the cupboard under the stairs, too terrified to move.' Mary Morris took off her jacket and wrapped it around the shoulders of the shivering ashen-faced twelve-year-old, who was hugging herself in apparent terror but seemed incapable of speech. They exchanged a silent glance over her head.

'The fire brigade?' Mary Morris asked her colleague.

'I've called for fire, police and ambulance, just in case.'

'Great. They're going to love us,' the deputy head said dryly. 'Right, let's count them before they begin to bunk off. Are you all ready?' she concluded by raising her voice to a fierce yell, which reduced almost all of the overexcited teenagers, who had already begun to chatter, to something approaching silence again. 'I'm going to call your registers in order, starting with Class 11. Let's hear you loud and clear. We don't want anyone left in there to toast, do we?'

The joke was a lame one but it raised a few nervous grins and seemed to defuse the tension, which had been flickering amongst the assembled crowd like a threatening electric storm. As she began going through her lists of names, the sound of approaching sirens swelled to a crescendo and by the time she had finished a fire engine had swept up the wooded drive towards the main school building, swirling more fading leaves from the avenue of beech trees.

'Now, is anyone hurt?' Mary Morris asked, and when no casualties volunteered themselves she nodded grimly.

'Right. Don't move an inch,' she instructed her charges as she went to meet the first of the fire officers to leap out of the cab.

'There's no one in the building,' she said, anticipating his urgent question. 'Just a little mishap in the science lab, I think, but we thought we'd better be safe than sorry. There's a lot of smoke drifting about in there.'

The fire officer pushed back his heavy helmet slightly as his colleagues ran towards the school to investigate, egged on by ironic shouts and cheers from their youthful audience.

'Do you know what caused the explosion?' he asked.

'I don't,' Mary Morris said. 'But you can be damned sure that I'll find out even if you don't.'

'You're making a bit of a habit of this, aren't you?' the fire officer said, surprisingly mildly.

Deflated now the immediate crisis had passed, the deputy head pushed her hair away from her bright blue eyes, her pale face slightly haggard now and her eyes full of anxiety. She shrugged tiredly.

'They say these things come in threes,' she said. 'But this is number five. Six if you count the headteacher.'

'Aye, I heard they'd arrested someone for that,' the fireman said just a shade more sympathetically. 'Dreadful business.'

'One of our lads is in court today,' Mary Morris said, carefully non-committal. She glanced down the leafy drive towards the school gates where a middle-aged woman in an unseasonably light summer dress stood staring in their direction. 'They've charged him with Mr Graves's murder. I wake up in the morning these days and wonder if I've dreamed it all.'

She shuddered slightly as she looked over the officer's shoulder to where a police car was pulling up behind the fire engine. The woman by the gates had vanished as silently as she had appeared, like a wraith in the slightly misty air.

As two uniformed police officers got out of the car,

there was a murmur of hostility and a few grunting noises from some of the assembled students. Mary Morris glanced at her watch. It was fifteen minutes past three and a couple of mini-buses were already waiting outside the gates, engines idling. Woodlands drew its pupils from a wide area of Bradfield and the surrounding countryside, taking in children whom the rest of the education system had long ago despaired of and discarded.

'I want Miss Smith's science class to stay behind,' she said loudly to the assembled school. 'The rest of you can go home.' Another ragged cheer at that.

'Will there be any school tomorrow, miss?' a tall, thin boy with wild eyes asked avidly.

'You'll all be expected as normal in the morning,' she said firmly as all but one of the class groups began to straggle towards the gates. 'And don't be late!'

She turned to greet the two police officers who were strolling towards her.

'What's this then, Mrs Morris?' the uniformed sergeant asked. 'Some sort of demonstration or what?'

'Oh, I shouldn't think so,' the deputy head said wearily. 'Devilment, maybe. Or just an accident. You'd better talk to Janet Smith over there. It was her science class that went bang.'

'If some folk get their way the whole school'll go bang shortly,' the sergeant said. 'I hear they're talking of closing you down after the last little lot.'

'Over my dead body,' Mary Morris said, and then her fierce expression crumpled into amusement as she realised what she'd said.

'I love these wretched kids dearly,' she said soberly. 'But not to die for.' And her thoughts turned sombrely to Peter Graves, her late boss and a man she had disliked intensely but who had hardly deserved to be struck down violently in his own school grounds and left to die. She glanced past the Victorian house and over the steeply sloping grounds where, beyond the trees, the little town of Bradfield glowed unexpectedly golden in its steep valley. The children still straggling out of the school gates had found little but violence and disruption in their lives down there and now the same malign forces had breached the walls of Woodlands, which should have been a haven for them. Wearily she turned back towards the police and fire officers who were deep in conversation on the broad main steps of the school. This latest disaster, she feared, might well be the school's last.

Her grandmother Joyce was a protest looking for a cause, Laura Ackroyd decided in exasperation as she stared at her computer in the newsroom of the *Bradfield Gazette* without seeing the words on the screen. Laura's mind was a long way from her work and her slim shoulders inside a plain black top appliquéd with a huge cerise flower were hunched in frustration. She had a feature article to finish for the next day's paper and an overlong lunch-hour had put her up against a deadline of her own making.

Irritably she shook herself, tucked a wayward strand of brilliant copper-coloured hair behind her ear and drove her grandmother's demands firmly from her mind. She began to pound out the last couple of paragraphs she needed to complete her piece on Bradfield's latest venture into urban regeneration. Perhaps this time it would work, she thought, as she finished her description: a scheme to put some heart back into those parts of the old textile town which threatened to crumble back into the dark dust from which they had sprung in the nineteenth century. But she was not really convinced herself by the planners' optimism and wondered if she could convince her readers.

Satisfied at last that her own scepticism had not tainted her article, she logged off with a sigh and glanced around the almost deserted newsroom. One day, she thought ruefully, she might make it to some more glamorous corner of journalism. But not while Joyce Ackroyd, ostensibly retired but furiously frustrated politician, made imperious demands like today's on her only relative within a couple of thousand miles.

Laura had driven up to her grandmother's home at lunchtime, disturbed by a somewhat incoherent phone call earlier in the day. Joyce had bequeathed Laura the flaming red curls that were her crowning glory. But as her own hair had faded to near perfect white, the older woman had begun to wonder whether Laura's inheritance was not more a liability than an asset. It was not just the classic redhead's pale skin and green eyes, which had passed down the generations, but the equally uncontrollable spirit that was making for a turbulent old age for Joyce, and, she feared, a troubled life for her granddaughter.

Increasingly confined by her stiffening limbs to her tiny home in the shadow of the tower blocks on Bradfield's most notorious estate, Joyce now had to fight her battles by proxy. Her angry phone calls were legendary and still feared at the *Gazette* and by former colleagues at the Victorian town hall where she had once held sway as a fiery and idealistic councillor. But they increasingly seldom brought her the results she expected. Where she had once been queen she suspected that she was now regarded as little more than an irritant, a bit of grit in the otherwise smooth-running machinery of the town she loved.

Laura had locked her Golf carefully outside her grandmother's bungalow, hoping that she would not find it wheelless or worse within the hour. She had unpacked her sandwich lunch and made coffee before settling down to listen to what was worrying Joyce that sunny autumn morning.

'Come on, tell me all about it,' she said through a mouthful of Marks and Spencer prawn mayonnaise. 'I can always tell when something's up.' Joyce smiled faintly, always cheered by Laura's visits, but today her smile was short-lived and her eyes clouded with anxiety.

'This lad they've charged with the murder of his headmaster,' she said. 'This "juvenile" as they call him – as if that prevents anyone knowing who he is. D'you know any more than the *Gazette*'s printed about the case? Has your Michael let anything slip?'

Laura took a swig of designer mineral water and wondered which of Joyce's questionable assumptions to tackle first: that there might be additional information to be had; that DCI Michael Thackeray might have unprofessionally passed such information on if it existed; or that he was, in any irrevocable way, *her* Michael. With practised skill, she slid between the horns of her dilemma.

'You're not still a school governor up at Woodlands, are you?' she asked. 'Won't you ever give up?' She knew it was one of the offices Joyce had grimly clung to after she had been forced to withdraw from more active politics, but she had thought that, as her health worsened, she had retired from that too.

'It's only a couple of meetings a term,' Joyce said defensively. 'I get a taxi out there and someone generally gives me a lift home. There's not many'll be bothered with difficult kids like that.'

'So you knew the head quite well then?'

'Well enough,' Joyce said shortly and then, spurred by Laura's quizzical look, she allowed herself a grim little smile.

'I didn't vote for him when he was appointed,' she said. 'Too abrasive by half, I thought. But the younger ones thought different, thought he'd knock the place into shape. I was more worried he might try to knock some of those lads *out* of shape.'

'Violent, was he?' Laura said, surprised. It was not an attribute she imagined was ideal for the head of a school for disturbed youngsters who had probably experienced more violence in their short lives than most.

'Aggressive, any road,' Joyce temporised, glancing away. But then, as always, her fierce honesty got the better of her. 'I didn't like the man. Not that I'm saying he deserved to be murdered, mind. Of course not that.'

'So what are you saying, Nan?' Laura persisted, knowing that her grandmother was not a fool and would not even have raised the subject without good reason.

'I had a phone call from one of the teachers there,' she said. 'Said the kids were running wild – I mean wilder than they usually run when anything upsets them. She said that the youngsters were convinced that the police had got the wrong person, that the lad they've arrested, Stevie Fletcher, wasn't the sort of boy who could have done that.'

'A boy at Woodlands?' Laura said sceptically. 'They're none of them exactly saints up there.'

'You know better than that, Laura,' Joyce said sharply. 'You know the lad's black, don't you?' She was very seldom moved to anger by her granddaughter and Laura knew that if she had annoyed her, then her worries were very serious indeed.

'No, I didn't know that,' Laura said. 'Is anyone suggesting that's important?'

'Not outright, no,' Joyce admitted. 'A lot of the Woodlands children are black or Asian. They still seem to rub the mainstream schools up the wrong way out of all proportion to their numbers.'

'Do the kids have anything to go on that they haven't told the police?' Laura said quickly, not wanting to get into that argument, although she knew Joyce had a point. 'They may believe the boy's innocent, or even that he's been picked on, but that's not the same as having evidence to prove it.'

'That's why I wanted you to talk to your Michael,' Joyce said quickly. 'I want to find out just what evidence there is that he's guilty.'

Laura drew a sharp breath at that.

'You know Michael wasn't the investigating officer,' she said. 'I told you he was going away, down to the Midlands to do an internal investigation for another force. He won't be back until this evening. All this happened while he was away and they brought in some officer called Hutton to investigate the murder here. From what I've picked up in the office from our crime reporter it was all pretty straightforward – very quickly resolved anyway. It certainly all happened very fast, the murder and the arrest. I wouldn't have thought the police were in much doubt if they were able to charge the boy so quickly.'

'Maybe it was too quick,' Joyce said. 'Maybe they missed something.'

'And maybe his friends at school are kidding themselves,' Laura said. Joyce's expression hardened at that.

'Mary Morris, the deputy head, isn't a fool,' she said sharply. 'She was my favoured candidate for the headship, as a matter of fact. If she's worried, and she says she is, then you can guarantee there's something to worry about.'

Joyce's lips folded in a thin line and Laura knew that she would not be budged from her opinion. As she finished her sandwiches and made more coffee Laura found herself agreeing reluctantly to mention Joyce's worries to Michael Thackeray when he got home although she knew with absolute certainty that it would be the last thing he would want to hear after an enforced absence which neither of them had welcomed and Laura had positively resented. Finding herself alone again in the flat she and Michael now shared she had found niggling doubts about their future creeping back during long evenings waiting for the phone to ring and lonely nights in the bed where she had grown accustomed to the warmth and solidity of another body beside her own. His divorce was almost complete, she told herself in the cold dark hours before dawn when she woke with a start to find herself chilly and alone. Then nothing should stand in the way of the marriage they planned. But with Michael not there, the doubts still crept in and were driving her crazy.

'I'll let you know what he says,' she said to her grandmother as she prepared to leave, ashamed of the resentment in her voice.

'You're a good lass,' Joyce said. But as she watched her granddaughter get into her car and drive away there were tears in her eyes, not just for the woman she had once been but for Laura and the frustrations which she could see were eating her heart out.

'Drat the man,' Joyce muttered to herself. 'Why doesn't he get on with it?'

Michael Thackeray drove impatiently, knowing that he would be late. He had finished his assignment in Staffordshire at lunchtime but made slow progress back to Yorkshire up a traffic clogged motorway, and it had been four o'clock before he had checked back into his office at the central police station, got up to speed with the pile of files and messages waiting on his desk, and set off again into Bradfield's rush hour traffic. He had one more unwelcome commitment before he met Laura at their favourite pub and he knew he was taking chances as he pushed his car to the limit on the narrow winding lane that led to Long Moor Hospital. Anxiety hung like a lead weight in his chest and his grip on the steering wheel was white-knuckled as he tried to analyse his reaction to the telephone call that had summoned him to Long Moor the previous day. Tethered to meetings as he drafted his report to the chief constable who had asked him to investigate two of his junior officers who were suspected – rightly it turned out – of pocketing large amounts of confiscated drugs from their own police station, he had put off the meeting his wife's doctor had been demanding for twenty-four hours. In his heart he knew he would much rather have put it off for good.

Aileen had been in Long Moor for more than twelve years, so severely brain damaged by her suicide attempt that she was a danger to herself and anyone with whom she came into contact in one of her psychotic episodes. Almost every time Thackeray had steeled himself to visit her he had come away wishing she were dead. Now that he had guessed from the doctor's sombre tone that his unspoken wish would soon be granted, he found himself unexpectedly overwhelmed with grief, not for the unpredictable and often comatose shell his wife had become, but for what she once had been, the lively, beautiful and apparently loving mother of his son.

He turned in through the hospital gates and parked in the almost empty car park. This was one of the few surviving psychiatric hospitals with secure wards, and visitors were rare. 'Long stay', he had concluded years ago, generally meant abandoned by friends and family and Aileen Thackeray, he had to confess, had been no exception. Night was already falling and the tall windows in the old house that formed the core of the institution he had come to dread visiting were already glowing yellow against the dark, stone gables of the mansion. The place was always gloomy, the grounds shadowed by tall trees and the house itself huddled in the lee of a steep hill for shelter from the fierce Pennine gales which often whipped in from the north-west. Tonight it appeared particularly threatening and grim, a place where hope more often died than came to be rekindled, a prison not a refuge.

For a moment Thackeray sat clutching the steering wheel, his broad shoulders hunched, willing himself into a frame of mind to face the medical staff. Nurses and doctors came and went swiftly here, and he knew that few of the current ward staff would know exactly how Aileen had reached the pathetic, bloated, near catatonic state in which he had last seen her a few months before. Yet every time he came near Long Moor he flinched from imagined condemnation in the eyes of everyone he met. And even if that were not real there was always the guilt he carried within himself, lurking like a wolf in the corners of his mind, ready to spring into his consciousness just when he thought he had exorcised the pain and found a tentative sort of happiness again.

He rested his head on the steering wheel for a moment, taking deep breaths. Alive or dead, Aileen would always be with him, he thought bitterly. He had driven her to what she did, destroying her and their baby boy, and very nearly himself in the process. Time did not dim the memories. He could see his drowned son floating peacefully in his bath as clearly now as the day he had found him and run howling from the bathroom with murder in his heart, to find Aileen sprawled on the bed, apparently already dead. And now he knew the doctor was about to tell him that she soon would be gone, that the worry about her failing heart must have become a serious concern for them to have summoned him like this. And he was glad, fiercely glad that he would be rid of her at last while despising the person he had become and wondering how he could inflict himself on his beloved Laura and hope to find happiness with her, carrying this hateful burden with him.

Laura was already sitting in the Malt Shovel at Broadley, a vodka and tonic in front of her, untouched. A cold wind from the bleak moors to the west had driven her off the terrace overlooking the broad expanse of the Maze valley where the evening lights of Bradfield and Milford were just beginning to sparkle amongst the purple shadows of the valley floor. The pub was a favourite of theirs, far enough out of Bradfield for them not to be interrupted by colleagues from the *Gazette* or CID, most of whom preferred the glitz of the modern city bars to the fading charms of a slightly neglected pub on the edge of the Yorkshire moors. Inside, the first log fire of the winter smoked unenthusiastically under the blackened stone arch of the enormous fireplace, and the smell of frying began to waft from the kitchen behind the bar. She had been slightly surprised when Thackeray had suggested meeting here but had not objected. She had hoped to resurrect some of the excitement of earlier meetings here but somehow this evening the Malt Shovel did not feel as welcoming as it usually did, and Laura shivered slightly.

She had gone home to change after leaving the office, swapping her suit for designer jeans and a green sweatshirt, and loosening her hair so that it fell in a cloud of curls around her shoulders. She sipped slowly at her drink, feeling unusually nervous as she waited for Thackeray to arrive. Their relationship was a difficult one, promising more than it ever seemed likely to deliver and tonight she knew that he would undoubtedly be irritated to be quizzed about a case which, if he knew anything about it at all, he would consider firmly closed. She was regretting her promise to Joyce Ackroyd. Her grandmother was far too adept at recruiting her to her crusades, she thought. She should know better by now, especially when her grandmother's concerns threatened conflict with Michael Thackeray.

She saw him come into the low bar before he saw her, ducking through the oak doorway from his solid six foot two and scanning the crowd of drinkers with blue eyes, which were seldom warm, and an expression this evening, which could only be described as austere. But his smile when he saw her was instant as he edged his way through the crowd and her own face lit up in welcome.

'Another?' he asked, glancing at her half empty glass. She shook her head and he turned away, returning in a few minutes with a glass of tonic water.

'Bad day at the office?' he asked, noting the signs of strain around her eyes as he drank in the oval face and the slim figure beneath the loose sweatshirt, a sight that still did unexpected things to his heart rate however familiar it had become. Laura shrugged more lightly than she felt.

'I missed you,' she said quietly. 'How was your trip?'

'Depressing.' He was thinking more of his interview with Aileen's doctor than his investigations in Staffordshire, but the comment would serve for either. 'Bent coppers are always depressing,' he said. 'And even more so when they're young and intelligent but still stupidly greedy. So how has Bradfield been?'

'Equally depressing,' she said. 'You heard about the murder at the special school?'

'One of the thankfully closed files on my desk. Nasty though.'

'Very,' Laura said. 'Ted Grant is ranting fit to bust about out-of-control kids. Or at least he was until they charged this boy. But Joyce...' She hesitated. She always had a lot more sympathy for her grandmother's campaigns than for her boss's, though Joyce's concerns were not what she had intended to burden Thackeray's homecoming with so soon.

'Tell me,' Thackeray said, without enthusiasm. He knew Joyce's potential for taking up lost causes and Laura's for being carried along with them in spite of his own generally more dispassionate reservations. So Laura told him, and as she expected Thackeray's expression hardened as he heard her out without comment. Some of the worst tensions in their relationship had flared when her fierce personal concerns had impinged on his professional ones. She did not want that to happen again, least of all for the sake of a case about which she knew little and a boy about whom she knew even less.

'It wasn't my investigation,' he said when she had finished. 'You know that. From what I've seen of the file it was an open and shut case. The boy has a history of disruption as long as your arm. He'd been expelled from Woodlands after a row with the head. He was seen at the school that night, when he should have been safely tucked up in bed. He couldn't offer any explanation about where he'd been. That's all I can tell you, Laura. You know I can't go into details, even for Joyce.' And if the atmosphere had become unexpectedly chilly Laura could not guess that there was more than one reason for Thackeray's discomfort. DCI Charles Hutton, commonly know as Len, who had been brought in to head the investigation from Thackeray's home town of Arnedale was a man he had more than one reason to distrust, although on this occasion he appeared to have done a competent enough job at clearing up an unpleasant murder quickly.

'You know she won't give up if she thinks you've got it wrong,' Laura said unhappily, hating the distance that had suddenly yawned between them. 'She's still a governor there and knows all the staff, if not the kids. She's taking it very personally.'

'If she thinks we've got it wrong, she should talk to this lad's defence lawyers, not me,' Thackeray said.

'She's been right before,' Laura insisted.

'And I've no doubt she'll be right again,' Thackeray said more gently. He had grown fond of Joyce Ackroyd in the time he had known her. 'But that doesn't mean she's right every time.'

'Open and shut?'

'Open and shut,' Thackeray said firmly. 'Now, do you want to eat here or go back home? I'm starving.' Laura glanced at him sideways and guessed that it was not just food he was starving for.

'A quick bite here and then home?' she suggested with a smile. Sod Joyce, she thought uncharitably. She did not feel like embarking on a crusade tonight when there were much better things to do.

Chapter Three

Peter Graves had not arrived on Bradfield's educational scene like a lamb, more like a raging lion. Flicking through the cuttings in the Gazette's library, Laura soon located what amounted to a manifesto from the new head of Woodlands School that would have gladdened the heart of a modern Gradgrind. There were to be no excuses for poor performance or poor behaviour, Graves had told the Gazette's reporter just eighteen months before. These might be children with problems but at the beginning of the twenty-first century, problems were there to be overcome. He would meet the challenge and so would the children in his charge. He didn't add 'or else' but Laura got the clear impression that it was implicit in everything the man was saying.

The photograph which accompanied the interview showed a tall, gaunt man with a rug-like head of hair, eyes which glinted behind owl-like spectacles, and long almost simian arms which were clasped around the shoulders of two young boys who appeared to be squirming with embarrassment in his clutch.

Laura did not think she would have warmed to the man in life and was not entirely surprised that he had met a premature death. She guessed that either of the lads in the picture could have been a prime suspect for some sort of GBH as soon as the Gazette's photographer had taken his finger off his shutter that day. What was more interesting was that Graves had survived at the school for a full eighteen months, during which time the publicity the place had attracted had become progressively more dire.

Graves had taken up his new appointment at the beginning of the spring term the previous year. An alleged 'superhead' who was being paid over the odds to turn the school around and get some sort of acceptable test results, he had hit the headlines again within a couple of months for expelling six pupils for bringing cannabis into school. The editor of the *Gazette*, Ted Grant's elephantine memory had not forgotten the new head's promises and he was soon wondering publicly in his leader column how putting six young tearaways back onto the streets constituted meeting the challenge of their behaviour. But just in case this view might seem a touch liberal for the self-styled scourge of Bradfield's criminal classes, he concluded that prison rather than mere expulsion was the alternative of choice for Graves's pupils when they stepped out of line.

Laura's skip through the cuttings revealed that there then seemed to have been a period of relative tranquillity at Woodlands, although she guessed that might merely mean that Graves had learned not to expose his activities quite so eagerly to the local paper. The sight of his school paraded in thirty-six point bold type across the front page on a quiet news day must have shaken Graves. And to see it followed up with a carefully orchestrated slanging match between the irate parents of the expelled boys and the increasingly queasy, and well-heeled, local residents, could not have been what the head had expected when he confided his troubles so naively to Ted Grant's crime reporter.

But the period of public calm had ended with a bang at the end of the summer term. Literally. The school's sports day was enlivened by a small but spectacular explosion in the changing rooms as the chair of governors was handing over a modest silver-plate trophy to the captain of the winning team, a tall Asian boy of uncertain disposition who dropped the cup in alarm and promptly burst into tears.

By the time the fire brigade had dowsed the flames and pronounced themselves mystified as to the cause of the fire, and staff and governors and the handful of parents who had made it to the spectators' bench had calmed the pupils down and seen them safely home, the *Gazette* crime reporter had been on the phone to the headteacher again, eager for all the details.

The autumn term had gone from bad to worse. A very

public slanging match between Woodlands pupils and younger children from a neighbouring primary school caused outrage amongst the primary school parents in October, and there was another small fire at the school in November. And the new year had brought no respite with outbreaks of window smashing and book burning in the spring, and yet another incident of arson in May, which could, according to the chief fire officer, have easily reduced Woodlands to ashes if it had not been spotted early by a dog-walker passing by. In October, after a period of relative calm, Peter Graves had been found dead one night in the secluded grounds at the back of the school, struck down violently from behind with a blunt instrument and left to die in a pool of blood.

Laura closed her file of cuttings thoughtfully and rubbed the film of newspaper ink and dust off her fingers with a tissue. She knew from what her grandmother had told her that Woodlands provided some sort of a sanctuary for the most troubled children from a wide area of West Yorkshire. Disaffection and even violence inevitably went with the territory.

But this series of disasters seemed out of all proportion. And she was uneasily aware from the cuttings that as the school's problems had escalated so too had the chorus of discontent from the school's neighbours in their leafy suburb of Southfield, a million miles away in spirit from the inner city estates on the other side of town which had curdled the lives of so many of Peter Graves's young clients. By the summer just gone the neighbours' voices had become shrill and the message well orchestrated by people who knew the right strings to pull to get their own way: for all Peter Graves's ambitions, the consensus was that Woodlands School was out of control and its children running wild. Public opinion was beginning to conclude that it was time for it to close.

At police headquarters, DCI Michael Thackeray was attempting to get to grips with work but it was proving almost impossible to banish the dark shadow of his wife's condition to the back of his mind. He stubbed out another cigarette into his overflowing ashtray and lit a new one, staring moodily out of his office window at the dusty town hall square outside. The rush hour traffic was gyrating at snail's pace around the central gardens where a few Asian elders in white or khaki traditional tunics under heavy coats sat on the benches under the trees engaged in desultory conversation and breathing in the fumes from the traffic apparently without concern. As he had guessed before he even spoke to him, the news from Aileen's doctor had not been good: she might survive months more, but the heart specialist the psychiatrists had called in had not thought this likely. And surgery, in her condition, was not an option.

The shy young Asian doctor who had been waiting for him the previous evening had appeared to expect Thackeray to be devastated by this prognosis and had not known quite how to react to his apparent indifference, indifference being the best face Thackeray had been able to put on the relief he really felt. This must be how a lifer feels as the moment approaches for the prison doors to swing open at last, he thought uneasily. But he was by no means certain, any more than a long term prisoner could be, that the sunshine outside the gates would be as warm and welcoming as it appeared from a distance.

And on top of all that, he was more disturbed than he had been ready to admit to Laura by the doubts she had raised about the murder which had occurred while he had been away. Laura's misgivings nibbled at Thackeray's certainty like a worm in the bud. When he had read about Peter Graves's death in Staffordshire he had called Superintendent Jack Longley only to be told that county HQ had drafted in another detective chief inspector to lead the inquiry into the murder. Slightly affronted that his services were not urgently required, he had distanced himself from brief reports of the investigation in the newspapers and found that by the time he returned to his office, young Stevie Fletcher had been arrested, charged and remanded in custody. He realized now that he might have made a serious mistake in remaining so aloof.

Irritably he walked down the corridor to the main CID office and waved Detective Sergeant Kevin Mower into his sanctum. The sergeant watched his boss cautiously, expert at gauging his moods and not liking the threatening expression around the sharp blue eyes.

'Guv?' he asked tentatively, brushing a hand over his cropped hair. 'Welcome back,' he ventured, feeling Thackeray's eyes swiftly taking in his new suit and silk tie with scarcely veiled disapproval. Thackeray, he thought, masking his own contempt, was a one suit a decade man. But Thackeray made no comment on the sergeant's sharp outfit.

'Thanks,' he said, his tone dry. 'It's good to be back. I take it you didn't warm to my replacement?'

'Know him, do you, guv?' Mower asked cautiously.

'More by reputation than in fact,' Thackeray said. 'I'd left Arnedale before he moved there. He went in as a DI and took over as DCI a few years ago when Les Thorpe got the chop.'

'Ah yes, I remember Les Thorpe,' Mower said thoughtfully. 'As bent as a three pound note.' Both men were silent for a moment, recalling a murder case several years earlier that had exposed Thackeray's past in rather more lurid detail than either man wanted to be reminded of.

'So was this murder of the headmaster as open and shut as the file suggests?' Thackeray asked. 'According to Laura there's already a defence campaign starting up on the Heights on the grounds that we're picking on black kids again and we've locked up the wrong person.'

'Surprise me,' Mower said. 'But as far as I could see DCI Hutton played it by the book. And we were lucky. Stevie Fletcher was seen up at the school by one of his own teachers at the relevant time. And whatever Len Hutton's feelings about ethnic minorities, Gareth Davies, the teacher, isn't prejudiced. I was there when Hutton interviewed him and Davies was tying himself in knots trying *not* to shop the kid. We've not found a weapon but the boy had the opportunity and the motive – or motives in triplicate if you like. He'd been expelled that morning; he claims he was going back to fetch some stuff from his locker, which included the Walkman he said was there, but also a stash of cannabis; and on top of all that there was a can of petrol close to the back door, so we reckon he was planning to torch the place when he'd got his gear out. It's quite possible he was responsible for the previous fires there've been up there. If your head-master stumbled over you in the dark with all that on your mind I suppose you might just hit him over the head with a blunt instrument if the opportunity offered. Panic rather than premeditation, perhaps, but guilty as hell. He had the motive and the opportunity, no problem.'

'He admitted it did he?'

'He didn't admit anything,' Mower said. 'He's only fif-teen and black and seriously mixed up and he had his brief with him the whole time, plus a social worker on occasion. Kid gloves was the name of the game. He says he went back to school determined to break in and pick up his Walkman and some cassette tapes which he'd left behind when Graves threw him out. Said he fell over the petrol can, which was just lying about... I can't see a jury giving much credence to that if that's all his defense amounts to.'

'The forensic people didn't come up with anything else? Bloodstains on his clothes? There must have been a lot of blood around.'

'She really has got to you, hasn't she?' Mower said, risk-ing a faint grin.

'What the hell's that supposed to mean?' Thackeray snapped, his colour rising.

'Laura. She called me and asked all the questions you've just asked. Said her grandmother was up in arms. Naturally

I didn't give her any answers,' he added quickly realising that the incipient storm he'd felt as he came into the office might be about to break.

'Bloodstains?' Thackeray asked again, face like stone.

'Nothing so far on any of the clothes and other stuff forensics took from his room, but he'd have had time to get rid of anything which was badly stained. Which something must have been, given the ferocity of the assault. Other contamination'll be less useful, of course, because we know he's been in the school, in the grounds, close to Graves even, recently enough for hairs or fibres to be quite innocent. It's bloodstains we really need to be sure.'

'He's been remanded?' Thackeray asked.

'Back in court next Tuesday, guv,' Mower said.

'Which just leaves us a few loose ends to tie up?'

'Well, we've not found the weapon and Stevie isn't up for telling us where he got rid of it. And there's still some forensic results to come in. They're looking at fingerprints and DNA on the petrol can and Graves's clothing, examining Fletcher's room in fine detail for bloodstains, his trainers…all the usual stuff. He might have got rid of some of his clothes but drawn the line at his expensive trainers. You never know.'

'So I should tell Joyce Ackroyd you're happy with the investigation?' Thackeray asked, irritably, wondering why he had to justify anything to the old woman on the Heights and knowing that he had no choice.

'With the investigation, guv,' Mower said slowly, as if wondering how far he could go. 'But not the investigator. Hutton's a racist bastard, there's no doubt about that.'

'Ah,' Thackeray said quietly. 'That's a pity. What leads you to that conclusion?'

'Personal experience,' Mower said. 'I couldn't work out why he was being unpleasant to me. I reckoned at first it was just because that's the way he was to everyone. Then Val Ridley told me that he'd been asking if I was a "Paki". She just laughed at him but obviously I was a shade or two too dark for his comfort. My allegedly Cypriot genes showing up, maybe. Then DC Sharif came on duty the next day and it was very clear where Hutton was coming from. He hated having to deal with Omar. Ignored him mostly. And when he did have to speak to him, there was nothing you could lodge a complaint about quite, but he was bordering on the offensive most of the time. If he'd been here more than a week I'd have gone to the super to complain.'

Thackery sighed. It proved endlessly difficult to recruit a police force which was in any way as diverse as the community it had to police, and one racist officer could do immense damage to serious efforts to win a reputation for even-handedness. He knew that Mower, as a Londoner straight from the melting pot, had a more relaxed attitude to race than many of his colleagues and that he should take his worries seriously.

'Did Sharif complain?' he asked.

'No, he keeps his feelings to himself,' Mower said. 'But I could see he was seething once or twice. I don't know what goes on up at Arnedale nick but, off the record guv, Hutton would be a serious liability here in Bradfield.'

'Off the record, I'll make sure that's noted,' Thackeray said. 'But you don't think it affected this particular case?'

'Don't worry,' Mower said. 'I'd have noticed if it had. Believe me.'

Thackeray had his own reasons for relief that the murder had been cleared up so quickly and had no wish to see it reopened or to liaise directly with Len Hutton. As DCI in Arnedale, working with his own former colleagues, Hutton was by now no doubt in possession of far more information about his own past than would be remotely comfortable in a face-to-face encounter.

'Let's hope Joyce's defence campaign doesn't get to hear about Len Hutton's little foibles,' he said. 'They'll put two and two together and make seven.'

'Don't worry, guv,' Mower said, repressing his anger with difficulty. 'I was watching the bastard. I was in on the interviews with Stevie Fletcher and most of the witnesses. It was a clean inquiry, I promise you.'

'I hope you're right, Kevin,' Thackeray said, and Mower wondered whether he imagined a hint of equivocation there.

'So, what else do I need to know about?'

Mower shrugged.

'It was a quiet couple of weeks apart from the mayhem at Woodlands school. No more sign of guns on the Heights; though I'm sure they're still there. A couple of burglaries in Broadley, which could be something to do with Craig Thompson coming out of nick. Val Ridley's looking at that. Otherwise it's just routine stuff.'

'Good,' Thackeray said. 'Let's hope it stays that way for a while.' And this time Mower was quite sure he was not mishearing the underlying weariness in Thackeray's voice.

'How's Laura?' he asked quickly, jumping to a conclusion which was certainly bolstered by the flicker of anger, almost instantly veiled, in Thackeray's eyes.

'Fine,' he said with such absolute finality that Mower decided a hasty retreat was his only defence. But as he closed the door behind him he wondered whether his boss was ever going to do the decent thing for a woman he had once, briefly, fancied himself and who deserved much better than she seemed to be getting.

'Bloody idiot,' he muttered to himself as he returned to the busy CID office. 'He doesn't know how lucky he is.'

Thackeray himself leaned back in his chair for a moment and shut his eyes. He guessed what Mower was thinking and he knew the justice of it. But that knowledge did absolutely nothing to dissipate the depression which muddied his brain and dulled the world to shades of grey. It took an immense feat of will to glance at his watch, realise he was late for his meeting with Superintendent Jack Longley and gather his papers together for the trudge upstairs to the senior officer's room.

Longley glanced up briefly when the DCI came in and waved him into a chair.

'Give me a minute, Michael,' he said, returning to the file in front of him. For a desperate moment Thackeray sat staring at the carpet and considered handing in his resignation there and then.

'Sir?' he said eventually when he realised that Longley had been speaking to him for some time. 'Sorry...'

'Bit gruelling, was it, Staffordshire?' Longley asked, taking in the strain around Thackeray's eyes and his unhealthy looking pallor under the dark, unruly hair.

'I put in a lot of hours,' Thackeray said. 'But they got what they wanted. Two officers have been charged.'

'Unpleasant, though?'

'Two bloody young fools wrecking their careers. Yes, you could say that.'

'Yes, well, you can forget all that now,' Longley said. 'We had our own problems here. A nasty death. Got the entire teaching profession in a lather, that did. Every head's worst nightmare, I imagine, to have one of the little tearaways turn on you.'

'DCI Hutton seems to have wrapped it up pretty quickly,' Thackeray said.

'Well, the lad doesn't seem to have been exactly smart. He seems to have left enough clues to have booked his own date in court, by all accounts.'

'This campaign they're getting up on the Heights won't get far then?'

Longley looked hard at his DCI who seemed to have unaccountably retreated into himself since the last time he had seen him a fortnight previously.

'You soon picked up on that then,' he said. 'Laura Ackroyd, I suppose? Not that she'll get much support from Ted Grant on this one. He's been treating us to a whole series of editorials on the best way to deal with bad boys – lock 'em up and throw away the key being the favourite. The shootings up on the Heights don't help. Drugs and black lads and guns fit together neatly in Ted Grant's world view, of course, and he's not that far wrong.'

'There's not been another shooting?' Thackeray said sharply. 'Kevin Mower said…'

'No, nothing more while you were away, but it's not summat we want to put up with for long, is it? I know no one's been hurt yet. It looks more like someone showing off than anything else, but having a single gun loose on that estate is one more than we need. Now you're back you'd better make finding out who's got what armament up there your top priority. But talk to the drug squad. They're nosing around again and you can bet your life the two things are connected. The dilapidated high-rise estate, officially known as The Heights and generally as "Wuthering" and waiting for the demolition gangs to move in, was where many of the town's criminal families and gangs of teenagers had been housed over the years. It always loomed large in police consciousness, never more so when there was a suggestion that there were firearms in circulation.

Thackeray did not argue. He knew as well as Longley that an occasional pot-shot at an empty flat could escalate with alarming speed into a gang war and leave bodies on the streets.

'Good job Peter Graves wasn't shot,' Longley said. 'Ted Grant would really have done his nut. Any road, as it went, DCI Hutton got a personalised *Gazette* pat on the back when our laddo was charged. One of our new style super-efficient coppers, I think they called him. I don't know whether Hutton slipped him a bottle of Scotch or whether Grant was having a sly dig at you. Take your pick.'

'Ted Grant's no friend of mine,' Thackeray said, trying to contain his anger. 'He's hysterical, bigoted and a bully from what I hear. Just the sort of local paper editor this town doesn't need to have stirring things up.'

'Laura been in the line of fire, has she?'

'Laura's always in the line of fire working for Grant,' Thackeray said. 'But I'm much more bothered about the effect a man like that has on us than about Laura. Ted Grant's a menace.'

'Aye, a similar thought crossed my mind when I had a drink with Charles Hutton after the arrest. "Len" he calls himself, though God knows why. There's hardly anyone left who remembers who the real Len Hutton was.'

'Oh, I wouldn't bank on that. They've long memories in these parts,' Thackeray said, remembering his predecessor's obsession with the roller-coaster fortunes of Yorkshire County Cricket Club.

'Aye, well, I did wonder about long memories at your old nick at Arnedale,' Longley said suddenly, glancing away from Thackeray as he spoke. 'Summat he said I pretended I didn't hear. I'd watch my back with Len Hutton if I were you Michael. He's an ambitious man and ruthless with it, and for some reason he doesn't seem to be any friend of yours.'

'I've not got many friends in Arnedale,' Thackeray said sombrely, realising with a momentary spasm of panic that if and when Aileen died he still had enough enemies there to remind the world exactly how she came to be in Long Moor Hospital in the first place. 'What was it you didn't hear?'

'Summat about you needing to watch out for the traffic cops with breathalysers on the M1. Kids stuff – but it made me wonder what was at the root of it. Come across Len Hutton somewhere, have you?'

'I've never met the man in my life,' Thackeray said.

'Well, he certainly seems to know a lot about you. And none of it to your advantage.'

The editor of the *Bradfield Gazette* vented the gases of his lunchtime pints, adjusted his belly more comfortably over his belt, and narrowed his eyes to help him focus on the woman he mentally described, from long habit, as his "33-year-old flame-haired features editor".

'Doesn't sound as if it'll be worth two pars on page 16 to me,' he said dismissively. 'Teenage nutter brains headmaster? Now that'll be on the front page when he comes to trial, but we won't be wanting any bleeding-heart nonsense about how it was all down to the poor little sod's upbringing when they lock him up and throw away the key. And don't forget we can't name him at the moment as he's a juvenile, though I was thinking I'd get our lawyers to ask the magistrates to waive that, as it's murder. No bloody reason why the little beggar should be anonymous that I can see. But we can't use anything on him before the trial any road, and I can't see that it'll be of much interest after.'

'It wasn't the boy's childhood I had in mind,' Laura said carefully, knowing that she was on a tightrope here if she was to persuade her boss that she should spend time investigating the background to Peter Graves's death for use when the trial of Stephen Fletcher ended.

'It was the headteacher himself I was more interested in. How dangerous is it these days for people trying to help deprived kids, mental patients, all that? You remember the case of the social worker who was stabbed...?'

Laura hesitated, wondering if she had over-egged her pudding. The tension between her view of what a local newspaper should provide and Ted Grant's sub-tabloid excesses stretched between them like elastic always on the point of snapping and if it did break she knew that she was the one who would get slapped in the face. But Ted seemed to have lunched well, which was why Laura had chosen this particular moment to approach him. He belched again and offered what passed for a fatherly smile, although it was one which might have seemed more soothing to a baby piranha than anything warmer blooded.

'Aye, well, there's summat in that, I suppose,' he said grudgingly. 'Why do daft beggars like Graves risk their lives for these little yobbos, that sort of angle?'

'The nationals will all be up for the trial,' Laura said. 'It's as well to be one jump ahead.' She knew that Grant was convinced he could out-Wap Wapping and Canary Wharf combined in the tacky tabloid stakes.

'Don't spend too much time on it, though. If the lad pleads guilty or gets off, the whole thing'll do a belly flop on the day. And don't go running up daft expenses, either. It'll not be worth more than a page, at best, but you might as well get it in the bag now while events are fresh in everyone's mind.'

'Right,' Laura said getting to her feet quickly, not wanting to push her luck, but as she went out of Grant's glass cubicle which overlooked the busy *Gazette* newsroom, he called her back sharply.

'Don't forget to talk to the caretaker,' he said. 'When I was down in the Smoke, I always found it was the caretaker who knew what was going on in a school or college. Sex and drugs and rock and roll, hanky-panky in the showers and nookie on the school trip – the caretaker always knows where it's at.'

If the caretaker isn't in it up to his neck himself, Laura thought as she nodded wanly. There were those on the *Gazette* who reckoned that the brief spell Ted Grant had spent on a London tabloid had been the making of their editor. But they were a tiny minority. The majority shared Laura's view that his determined bid to turn a cuddly and mostly accurate local paper into a pale imitation of the *Globe* was the worst thing that had happened to Bradfield for a very long time.

'We've been burgled more times than I can remember,'

Mary Morris said as she showed her visitor a room of computer equipment which she had opened with no less than three keys. Laura was startled to see that most of the machines were bolted to the worktops and peripherals were attached to long chains.

'Your own students?' she asked.

'Or their big brothers, uncles and cousins,' Mary said wryly. 'Not many have dads. Or not in circulation, anyway. There are advantages to being out here in the suburbs but the school and the neighbourhood can be seen as a bit of a magnet to some of our families, for all the wrong reasons.'

'I got the impression from the cuttings that your neighbours don't love you too much.'

'It's not just a case of not in my backyard, but not on my planet with some of them, as far as I can see. Alpha Centauri wouldn't be far enough away.' Mary Morris locked the computer room door again and led Laura back to her office close to the main door of the old Victorian house, where she waved her guest into a comfortable chair and poured her a cup of coffee. Laura studied the teacher cautiously as she took a sip. Small and slim, with greying hair and a fine-boned face delicately lined around the eyes and mouth, Mary Morris did not appear to have the physical resources for the job she obviously relished. Perhaps it was the shock of recent events taking their toll, Laura thought, but she could sense the tension in her as tight as a coiled spring.

'There's a real head of steam building up in the community since the murder of course. It's "we're not safe in our beds" time out there.' Mary Morris's distaste for the school's nervous neighbours was obvious.

'I'll have to talk to some of them,' Laura said apologetically. 'They're bound to be alarmed by a murder. I've pinned down a few names from the flood of letters they've had in the *Gazette* postbag. The protests about the school are obviously well-organised and co-ordinated.'

'Oh, it's been going on since long before the murder.

That's just the final straw, as far as they're concerned. Mr Oliver and Mr Boston seem to be the public face of the campaign, though when I've had contact with them it's Mrs Boston who's the most virulent.' Mary Morris ran a hand over her grey hair and looked weary. 'This job is stressful enough without having to take on the yuppies of Southfield in high dudgeon as well,' she admitted in what Laura guessed was a rare moment of complaint. 'These are sad, desperate kids. They have to be cared for somewhere.'

'Tell me about your late headteacher,' Laura said cautiously. 'Much lamented, is he?'

Mary Morris stirred her coffee thoughtfully and then shrugged slightly.

'It's no secret that I didn't like the man,' she said with a faint smile. 'Not to put too fine a point on it, I wanted the job, as your grandmother's probably told you. I thought you must be related to Joyce, when you rang. She's been a good friend to this school and I thought there was a chance you'd be that rare bird, an honest hack.'

'I try,' Laura said wryly. She had given up counting the number of times recently she had felt bound to apologise for her profession. 'But Peter Graves? He wasn't much liked then?'

'I don't honestly know anyone who did like him. He was the sort of bully I wouldn't have let anywhere near disturbed children, but the governors seem to have been impressed at the interviews by his gung-ho philosophy. I think some of them really don't know what the problems are here. They imagine a head can suddenly transform these kids' lives and send them off to university with a clutch of A Levels under their belts. They have no idea.' She suddenly seemed to sag slightly in her chair and Laura wondered how difficult Graves had made it for a potential rival on his staff.

'Surely Peter Graves can't have been so unrealistic about the kids?' Laura said.

'No, he wasn't. He was just very good at telling people

what he thought they wanted to hear without actually spelling out the detail. He knew as well as I do that it's a major triumph if some of these kids concentrate long enough to learn to read and write. Most of them have been abused and bullied as small children. Half of them have got undiagnosed learning difficulties. They're angry and frustrated and occasionally violent. They've been in trouble of one sort and another for most of their lives. Some sort of normality is what we aim at. And with most of them we fail.'

Laura glanced around the small office, bright with children's artwork, and thought that with Mary Morris it would not be for want of trying.

'And Stephen Fletcher?' she asked. The deputy head turned away and Laura thought that she glimpsed tears in her eyes.

'Stevie is a sad boy,' Mary said, her voice still firm and unemotional. 'He's quite bright, but no one noticed he was seriously dyslexic early on. And I think there were family problems as well – a succession of 'uncles' who made it very clear they didn't want him around. He's disruptive in class and prone to outbursts of temper. He was thrown out of St Marks about three years ago for persistent assaults on other kids. That was why Peter suspended him this time.'

'An assault?'

'Well, it sounded more like six of one and half a dozen of the other to me, but Peter decided Stevie was to blame,' Mary said. 'He was not a man to let a few facts stand in the way of decisive action.'

'So it was quite likely the boy was angry about that?'

'He stormed out in a fury, sure, but angry enough to come back later and kill someone?' Mary protested. 'I find that hard to believe. I really thought we had begun to make an impression with Stevie. He was beginning to read and write, seemed quite proud of the progress he was making. But if the police are right we must have been deluding ourselves. It happens, particularly when they go back to the gang culture on the Heights every night. They seem to have graduated to guns up there now.'

'Do you think the police have got it right?' Laura asked, cautiously.

Mary Morris shrugged, her expression reflecting a sense of loss and resignation that was almost palpable.

'They say they have evidence. A can of petrol. Fingerprints. A witness who saw him close to the school that night. It sounds as if he came back to torch the place and Peter caught him at it. It sounds about as bad as it could possibly be.'

'My grandmother says that the other youngsters don't think he did it. Is that right?'

'Yes, I think a lot of the kids are more shocked by Stevie's arrest than they were by the murder. They have a fierce sense of fairness, and not to put too fine a point on it they reckon Peter got what he deserved and Stevie's been set up by the pigs – to use their phraseology. I expect that's the story that's taken as gospel on the Heights by now. Your grandmother's well placed to know.'

'You are joking?' Laura said, startled by the deputy head's bluntness.

'No, I'm not,' Mary said, fiercely. ' It's another world a lot of these youngsters live in. You and I can hardly begin to imagine what some of them go through every day. I can't tell you whether Stevie did it or not, if that was what you were hoping. But I know what Joyce and her friends are worried about and what the youngsters are saying on the street. They reckon he's been picked on because he's black. And that's not good news for any of us. And I'll tell you something else that bothers me. These kids don't make friends easily, but Stevie did have one mate he was quite close to. Another black boy called Dwayne Elton. A bright lad, but very disturbed, very volatile. You know there are far more black boys in schools like this than there ought to be? Many of them have just rubbed white teachers up the wrong way. But

Dwayne really does have psychological problems that I thought we were getting to grips with. But he's not been in school since Stevie was arrested and I've not managed to make contact with his family. I don't know where he is or what he's doing and that's not good news.'

'D'you think he might have been involved in whatever went on that night?'

'I should hate to think that anything I said implicated him, but it seems too much of a coincidence to me,' Mary Morris said. 'He may not have been involved, but he may know something about what happened.'

'Have you told the police?' Laura asked, wondering how far Mary would go to protect her pupils.

'I mentioned it to DCI Hutton but he didn't seem terribly interested.'

'An open and shut case, I'm told,' Laura said, thinking unhappily of DCI Thackeray's sceptical smile.

'Something like that. But if you come across Dwayne in your own investigations tell him I'd like to see him, will you, please? He'll curse and swear but when he's worked all that out of his system, he might just slink into school. I think we were beginning to get through to him and I'd hate to see him thrown back to the wolves on the Heights.'

Laura digested this slowly, wondering where this slight, determined woman who was no longer young, got her apparently inexhaustible faith in human potential.

'Do you know who the eyewitness was? Was it one of your unfriendly neighbours.'

'No, it wasn't,' Mary Morris said, her expression sombre. 'It was actually a former member of staff here who'd been up to see Peter Graves himself and was driving home. He's devoted to the kids and riddled with guilt at getting one of them into this sort of trouble, but in the end I think even he thought he couldn't not tell the police what he'd seen.'

'Was not telling the police a possibility then?' Laura

asked, surprised.

'He's a bit far left, is Gareth Davies. Not a warm sup-porter of the defenders of law and order. He was brought up in one of the mining villages where Maggie Thatcher waged her war against the 'enemy within', if you're old enough to remember that. You'd usually be more likely to find him on the other side of the barricades than making a statement to the police. But I think he felt even he had to make an excep-tion for murder. Even Peter Graves's murder. Peter and Gareth never hit it off, of course. As far as Gareth was con-cerned Peter's appointment was a bit like asking the big bad wolf to mind the lambs. And the disrespect was reciprocat-ed with interest. Peter thought Gareth was a woolly-minded leftie more interested in holding the kids' hands than actual-ly teaching them anything.'

'And was he?' Laura asked.

'They both had a point,' Mary said cautiously. 'You can't teach these kids anything until you've persuaded them to trust you. It's a constant balancing act between education and therapy and the stakes are very high. As Peter seems to have found out quite fatally, if the police have got it right.'

'You said a former member of staff. Where is he now?'

'He left,' Mary said. 'You couldn't exactly say he was sacked. More encouraged to resign after a particularly fierce spat about how to treat Dwayne, Stevie's friend who's disap-peared, the one I told you about. Anyway, Peter had pun-ished Dwayne for failing to respond to the fire alarm one day. Gareth was furious. Said it wasn't appropriate and someone should be made responsible for seeing kids like that out of the building if the alarm went off. He raised his fist in the argument and Peter told him to get off the prem-ises if he ever wanted to work with children again. Otherwise he'd get no reference. So Gareth went.'

'Peter Graves sounds like a pretty unpleasant man.'

'Oh yes,' Mary Morris said with feeling.

'What about his wife?' Laura said tentatively. 'I understand they lived here. Is she still around.'

'Oh yes,' Mary said again, and Laura wondered if she imagined the note of faint contempt in her voice. 'One of the perks of the headship is that you get to live in the lodge by the gates. It's been modernised and extended, of course, and Julia's still there. I suppose she's still in a state of shock, but if I'd been her and married to that bastard I'd have been out of there years ago.'

'The marriage wasn't a good one, then?'

'He walked all over her. For some reason she doesn't seem to have ever had a job, and the kids have gone to university apparently. I've never met them. For the year or so they've been here she's just seemed to drift about doing a bit of ineffective gardening and amateur painting and looking languid. It's quite bizarre really. She looks like something out of a pre-Raphaelite painting herself, and about as useless.'

'Do you think she'd talk to me?' Laura asked.

Mary Morris smiled, and Laura did not think she was imagining the malice in her eyes.

'I should think she'd pour her heart out,' she said.

Laura had almost given up and turned away from the door of the Lodge before it opened and a pair of extraordinarily pale eyes peered out through the narrowest of apertures. When she explained who she was, the door was reluctantly pulled back and a willowy woman with milk pale skin and long, straw coloured hair tumbling down her back and into her eyes nodded her into the house's gloomy interior.

Laura had walked slowly back down the tree-lined drive just as the school day ended. She had been quickly overtaken by groups of excited, jostling boys who seemed heedless of her presence as they rushed for the gates where the minibuses, which took most of them home, were waiting. In their jeans and trainers and bright football tops under their coats they looked little different from any other group of teenagers. More worrying, she thought, than the first rush were the handful of stragglers, both boys and girls, who trailed in their wake in a miasma of depression, which was almost visible.

By the time she had reached the gate to the small fenced garden which surrounded the darkly gabled stone lodge, most of the children had gone and the staff cars which had been parked at the front of the building had also begun to pull away. It was as if, with the clanging of the four o'clock bell for the end of school, the old house wanted to expel the noisy intruders which were disrupting its slow decline into senility and restore the tranquillity of a gentler age.

But as Laura had unlatched the gate of the late head-teacher's garden she could see little sign of tranquillity there. The lawn was unkempt, and thickets of overblown roses half smothered the narrow gothic windows and the elaborate porch. In one corner a tangle of litter – crisp and cigarette packets and a disintegrating copy of the *Gazette* – had been blown beneath the hedge and from somewhere beyond that a haze of acrid bonfire smoke drifted across the grass.

Having closed and locked the front door securely behind her, Julia Graves led Laura along a narrow hallway and into a small room at the back of the house which over-looked a shaded patch of garden which the bonfire smoke had shrouded in a dense fog. 'I suppose you want to know all Peter's murky secrets,' she asked. Her voice was as light and airy as her appearance. She wore a loose flowery summer dress of faintly Victorian design and Laura wondered as she sank, billowing, into a low chair and waved Laura into another, whether she had deliberately chosen the style to fit her new home or whether the deliberate whiff of antiquarianism went back further than that. It was like living in a Burne Jones' painting, Laura thought. But close up Julia was not as youthful as she evidently tried to appear. The pale face, with little make-up apart from a trace of pink gloss on full lips, was finely lined around the eyes and mouth, and there were smudges of violet beneath the startlingly pale grey eyes.

'I'm afraid that when the trial is over most of the papers will want to print some sort of background on how the tragedy came about,' Laura said cautiously, but Julia Graves did not seem the least disconcerted at the prospect of having her private life exposed to the public gaze.

She waved a packet of cigarettes in Laura's direction and, when she shook her head, lit one herself with long fingers which trembled slightly as she held the match.

'You have no idea what a relief it is to me to be widowed,' she said as she drew smoke deeply into her lungs as if it were much needed fresh air, her voice still as inconsequential as if she were discussing the prospect of rain. 'If this boy Stevie hadn't swung his blunt instrument to such effect when he did, it might have been me.'

Startled by this unexpected confession, Laura drew a sharp breath which elicited a faintly satisfied smile in return.

'I wouldn't say I'm exactly a merry widow,' Julia Graves said, her voice husky now. 'But when I tell you that my children are reluctant to come home for their father's funeral perhaps you'll realise what sort of a man Peter was.'

'I'm not naive enough to imagine all marriages are made in heaven,' Laura said. 'But isn't that a bit extreme?'

'You have no idea,' Julia said. 'No one can have any idea.'

'Tell me,' Laura said, so Julia Graves did.

They had married young, she said, when both of them were training to be teachers, but she had barely started a career of her own when she became pregnant with their first child and Peter had insisted that she remain at home to look after the baby.

'It was all for the best, I suppose,' she said. 'I don't think I'd have made much of a career woman and it was just about the time that Thatcher began slashing and burning the education system so jobs became harder to find. Anyway, Peter had more than enough ambition for the two of us. He moved onward and upward, a new job every couple of years, promotion here, graded posts there, always on courses to make sure he was on top of the newest theories: child centred education yesterday, back to multiplication tables and desks in straight rows today. Learning standing on their heads tomorrow no doubt if the inspectors recommended it. If they'd prescribed daily doses of the cane he'd have convinced himself it was in the best interests of the kids.'

'Why did he decide to specialise in difficult children?' Laura asked mildly. 'It doesn't strike me as the best career move if you want to do well financially. Shouldn't he have been aiming to be head of a big secondary school? Lots of money in that these days, I'm told.'

Julia Graves laughed, a tinkling sound like water running over stones, although Laura could detect no humour in her eyes.

'Bad career move, that was,' she said. 'In fact he made an almighty mess of the whole enterprise really. He thought the sort of expertise he'd decided to accumulate would be at a premium when they brought in the league tables and all these tests and things. He thought schools would be desperate to help the slowest children catch up with the rest.'

'And aren't they?' Laura asked.

'Are they hell!' Julia said. 'The schools which do well in the league soon get into a position where they don't have to accept the stroppy, difficult kids in the first place, and the rest do their best to throw them out as soon as they can decently get away with it. The schools at the bottom of the league that really get lumbered with the deadbeats are then told they're failing and the only way to shed that little label is to concentrate on the ones who're going to pass their exams and turf out the stroppies as well. Pretty soon, someone like Peter, who's taken all these courses on how to deal with the mad and the bad, finds the only decent job he can get is as head of some sink school in the inner city or at somewhere like Woodlands where the difficult kids have been segregated from the rest.'

'That sounds a pretty cynical analysis,' Laura said. 'Is it yours or his?'

Julia shrugged and drew hard on her cigarette.

'After a few G and Ts he wouldn't have disagreed with much I've just said. Of course, in public it's all about "raising standards" and "bringing excellence to the inner city's casualties." But there's no nimbies as fierce as those who want to keep poor kids, and black kids, and stroppy kids away from their own little darlings who do *so* need to be stretched. And haven't they got it down to a fine art? That's why the neighbours round here are slavering to have this place closed down. Even having children with problems walking down the same street is too much for some of them.'

Laura looked at Julia speculatively. Somewhere beneath that flowery exterior was a much tougher core.

'Were you and Peter always unhappy?' she asked bluntly. Julia laughed again.

'Peter was a bastard,' she said. 'He bullied me and he bullied the children. My first mistake was marrying him. My second was letting him dictate how we lived in those early years when the children were small. That meant that I wasted my chance to make a career for myself so I have very little earning power. Every time I tried to get some sort of further qualifications or training he moved job, onwards and upwards as he used to say, and we moved house, and I had to start all over again. In the end I suppose I gave up. We lived our separate lives. I do some painting, which I love, but there's no money in that. When he moved into special education there was quite often accommodation provided so we didn't have the hassle of mortgages to worry about. I suppose you think I'm a fool to have stayed with him but I think in fact I was just lazy. I made my own world and lived in that and let him get on with his life.'

Laura glanced around the untidy living room where dust lay on stacks of books and flowers reduced to dried up skeletons dropped yellowing fragments on the furniture and she shrugged. A large, brightly coloured abstract painting on the wall looked out of place and Laura wondered if it was Julia's own work. Somehow she felt something more sub-Monet more likely from Julia's brush.

'It's my art teacher's,' Julia said, picking up the question in Laura's eyes. 'Peter hated it, of course, and it's not really my style but she's reputed to be very good. So I hung it in pride of place after Peter was killed and couldn't complain any more. She's the only friend I've made in Bradfield, really.'

'I'm sorry,' Laura said. 'What will you do now?'

'Try to paint more seriously, I suppose,' Julia said. 'It's time I did something for myself.'

'Are you happy with the police investigation into the murder?'

Julia shrugged again.

'How can I be unhappy? They say they have sufficient evidence to charge the boy. It's very sad but the violence is always there under the surface in schools like Woodlands. Every now and again it wells up like lava from a volcano.'

'So you weren't surprised that it should have been one of Peter's pupils?' Laura persisted.

'You don't seem to have been listening to what I've been saying,' Julia said. 'Some of those children have always frightened me. Here by myself now, I lock myself in at night and keep the phone close to the bed. There is so much pent up anger and violence and hatred in some of those kids it positively crackles if you pass them in the street. It can be defused, I think, by some very special people with the time and the patience to devote to them. That wasn't what Peter wanted to do. He wanted to make his mark. They were part of his career plan. I think he saw them as some sort of circus animal who could be coerced into performing as requested. He didn't defuse the violence; he stoked it up, in school just like he did at home. I've had twenty years to watch him do it and he's very, very good at it. Nothing surprised me less than that someone should eventually retaliate: a pupil, one of his staff, his girlfriend, or any one of the hundreds of people he's abused and infuriated over the years.'

'His girlfriend?' Laura said, surprised.

'Sex was a war of conquest with Peter as well,' his wife said quietly. 'He vanquished me years ago and has been looking for new territories on a pretty regular basis ever since.'

'And he had a lover here, in Bradfield?'

'Oh, yes. I can always tell when there's a new one on the go. He has... had I should say, a particularly self-satisfied smirk when he'd got what he wanted.'

'Do you know who it was?'

'No, I don't. I never tried to find out. At least when he had a lover he'd leave me alone, and that was the way I liked it.'

Detective Constable Mohammed Sharif treated Bradfield's most notorious estate with perhaps greater circumspection than it really deserved. He sat in his car, parked on a rise on the edge of the estate that offered a close-up of the flats and the scrubby grassland that lay between them, and a panoramic view of the town in the valley below. He had the windows of the car tight shut and the radio tuned to Radio Bradfield but he could not totally eliminate the worst aspect of the estate, the overpoweringly sour smell in the hallways and stairs which for him – occasional sporadic gunfire notwithstanding – was the worst that the conjunction of the town's poorest families and most neglected housing could achieve. He tapped the steering wheel with long brown fingers and steeled himself to brave the cavernous concrete stairs of Priestley House.

One of the four massive tower blocks had already had to be demolished as it fell into such dilapidation that it threatened to collapse under its own weight. The resultant space had been grassed over by the cash-strapped council and the three other blocks left to slide towards their own inevitable and unlamented end and the redevelopment which was endlessly promised and which for most of the remaining residents could not come soon enough. Local youngsters were doing their best to hasten that day by vandalising every flat which fell vacant and converting others into drug distribution centres with heavily reinforced doors and escape routes cut through the five floor warrens where a handful of families still struggled to survive.

This was not Sharif's home turf. He had been brought up in the cluster of narrow terraced streets closer to the town centre where the Asian community, which had come to Bradfield to work in the now vanished textile mills, still clung together around its mosques and shops with what Sharif, British born and bred, felt was unnecessary defensiveness. For

whatever reason, the Heights had never been Asian territory;
Asian families had either not been offered or had turned down
homes here. A few black families had infiltrated the unpre-
possessing blocks, but so had some of the town's more virulent racists. Even with the protection of a warrant card in his
wallet, Sharif felt vulnerable on the Heights, particularly as he
was on his own and his inquiries were seriously unofficial. He
rested his chin on his hands and kept a dark, wary eye on the
group of teenaged white boys who had just leapt off a passing
bus and were heading in his direction. He was taking a chance,
he thought, and for no very well-thought out reason except a
slow burning anger at the way he had been treated by DCI
Charles Hutton over the course of the last couple of weeks.
Sharif had ambitions. Tall, skinny and very bright, he had
clawed his way from one of the least favoured local schools
into the local university, with little encouragement from
either his teachers or his parents. Their surprise was all the
greater when he had announced his intention of joining the
police force after graduation, although that was nothing to the
incredulity and scorn with which his young contemporaries at
the mosque had greeted his decision. Young men swept along
with enthusiasm for growing beards and taking up aggressively militant poses on street corners had nothing but contempt
for someone willing to don police uniform and pound the
beat around Aysgarth Lane.

But Sharif had persevered, pursuing a stubborn conviction
that there would be no future for him, his family or his community unless they made some effort, and were seen to make
some effort, to integrate into the mainstream of this often
sullenly hostile Yorkshire town. He had ignored the racism
which occasionally surfaced amongst his colleagues, in spite
of the hours they had all spent in race awareness classes during training; he had smilingly accepted being dubbed 'Omar'
instead of Mohammed; and he had doggedly worked his way
towards promotion and eventually a place in CID under a
boss who genuinely did not seem to give a toss what colour he

was. He had found it all the more bitterly insulting to find DCI Hutton gazing at him with barely concealed dislike when he had reported for duty the day after Peter Graves's body had been found, and infuriating to be given the most routine tasks throughout the brief murder inquiry. He did not normally think he was a vindictive person. Revenge was something his generation, as boys certainly, had left to the old men at the mosque who could not extricate themselves from traditional ways. He was British, he thought angrily, by birth, by education, by inclination and most of all through his job which should carry with it a certain respect, not least amongst his own colleagues. When it didn't he felt disoriented at first and furious at last. And he determined to make DCI Charles "Len" Hutton pay for his disillusion.

Once the roaming teenagers had disappeared into the nearest of the tower blocks, giving his car bonnet only a cursory thump as they passed, Sharif squared his shoulders, locked his car carefully and made his way across the muddy grass to the entrance to Priestley House. The supposedly locked security doors swung open at his touch and he made his way cautiously up the stinking concrete stairway – the lifts being, as usual, out of order – and along the walkway on the fifth floor. On this particular level most of the flats were still occupied and someone had made an effort to sweep the concrete clean from the top of the stairs to the front doors. Three doors along he tapped gently on the reinforced glass. The door was held on a chain and a pale face peered out for a second before it swung open and he was hustled inside.

'How are you doing, Julie?' he asked the pallid young woman with straggly blonde hair who followed him through into the sparsely furnished living room. Julie picked up her cigarette from the edge of the coffee table with a hand which trembled, took a deep drag and shrugged. She was wearing tight jeans, a cropped top which revealed her skinny midriff and a pair of stiletto-heeled shoes on which her balance looked precarious before she flung herself onto the sofa.

'Getting by,' she said. 'No thanks to you.'

'You can always call me if you hear anything I might want to know about,' Sharif said. 'You know where I am.'

'Yeah, well,' Julie said. 'I don't hear much, do I, stuck up here with t'baby most of the time?'

'Where is he, by the way?' Sharif asked. He was enough of a Muslim still to feel vaguely uncomfortable alone with a woman and usually when he paid Julie a visit her eighteen-month-old son, a tiny dynamo of wails and screams who careered around the small flat like a caged animal, dominated the conversation and provided a sort of chaperone.

'My mum's taken him out in t'pushchair,' Julie said. 'I thought I'd get a bit of kip, as it goes, and now you bloody turn up.'

'No news of a new place to live?'

'I'm on t'waiting list,' Julie said scornfully. The child's father, whom Sharif had arrested, was serving a six year sentence for causing grievous bodily harm in a drunken brawl and she had applied to be rehoused, in line with the council's policy of not letting high rise flats to mothers with young children. 'I reckon we'll get out of this place by t'time our Brooklyn's drawing t'dole.'

'They'll probably have abolished the dole by the time he's old enough to draw it,' Mohammed Sharif said. 'But they're supposed to be pulling this place down soon. At least you'll get out then.'

'What do you want any road?' Julie asked, lighting a fresh cigarette from the stub of the old one. 'I've nowt for you. I don't get out often enough these days to hear owt interesting, do I?'

Feeling sorry for her after her boyfriend's trial, Sharif had enrolled her as an informant in the hope of getting a handle on the Heights, where faces closed up and doors slammed if he approached residents himself.

'I'm clearing up loose ends after this murder up at the special school,' Sharif said. 'The lad we've arrested lives on the Heights.'

'Stevie Fletcher?'

'Everyone knows who it is, do they?' Sharif asked, unsurprised. Rules to protect the identity of juveniles weren't worth the paper they were written on in a dysfunctional community like the Heights where young villains were as likely to be hero-worshipped by their mates and protected by their criminal families as condemned by an even older generation who could remember when the tower blocks had seemed like a blessed release from the back-to-back slums they replaced.

'He were at St Marks wi' our Darren till they threw him out,' Julie said carelessly. Darren was her younger brother and already known to Sharif. 'Darren reckons he's all right, is Stevie. Thinks you've got the wrong lad. But then he's black, i'n't he, so that figures. Everyone knows you lot blame the black lads for owt and nowt, don't they?'

Sharif bit back a sharp retort. Superintendent Longley and DCI Michael Thackeray might try to run a tight ship but his own recent spat with DCI Hutton proved that Julie's, and her younger brother's assumptions might be all too close to the truth. And it so happened that her own unavoidably absent boyfriend was also black.

'He wasn't arrested just because he's the wrong colour,' Sharif said. 'We've got evidence; you can take my word for that. Is that what people are basing this campaign on, that we've picked on him simply because he's black? Or have folk got something more solid to go on. What's the word on the street, Julie? That's all I'm asking. If there's anyone out there who knows anything relevant, I want to talk to them.'

'I don't know owt about that,' Julie said. 'There's always lads threatening to kill their teachers, or their probation officers, or each other, come to that. Maybe this time someone's actually done it.'

'Is Stevie part of the drug scene?'

'I'm clean, Mr Sharif,' Julie said indignantly. 'How would

I know owt about that?'

Sharif did not altogether believe her but he recognised a stone wall when he hit one.

'Tell your brother and his mates that I'd really like to know anything they can tell me about Stevie Fletcher,' he said.

Julie looked at him knowingly through the cigarette smoke.

'You don't think he did it, do you?'

'I didn't say that,' Sharif said. 'I just said I'm clearing up loose ends. If you hear of any, give us a call.'

'Right,' Julie said. 'Now can I get a little kip before mi mam comes back wi' our Brooklyn. He had me up half the night last night and I'm knackered.'

Sharif spent another hour or so on the Heights, chasing up contacts and listening to the gossip in the estate pub, where his entrance caused a sudden lull in the conversation, and in the single shop which functioned with wire grilles protecting its windows and door, and where he was greeted like a long lost friend by the plump Asian woman behind the counter. But although he picked up a distinct undercurrent of discontent about Stevie Fletcher's arrest, particularly amongst the black youths hanging around the pub car park, he found no one with any real reason for suspecting that the police had got it wrong. He would have to investigate the other avenue that he had in mind, he thought disconsolately as he walked back to his car, and the other avenue led not to Bradfield at all but to Arnedale, twenty miles away, where DCI Hutton had returned to his own nick quite unaware of the fury he had left behind him. As he got out his keys and went to open his car door he saw, without much surprise, that in his absence some one had torn off both the wing mirrors and scratched the single word 'Paki' into the paintwork of the bonnet.

DS Kevin Mower had been out and about on the Heights that morning too and had come to a similar conclusion. But while Sharif kept his impressions strictly to himself, Mower reported back to DCI Thackeray when he returned to police HQ after a quick lunch in the Woolpack.

'It's all froth and hot air, guv,' he said. 'It's not difficult to stir up a bit of paranoia up on the Heights. You know that. I spoke to Joyce Ackroyd but she couldn't give me anything concrete to support this campaign she's involved in. Don't tell Laura, but I think the old lady's lost it this time.'

Mower wondered why Thackeray looked as if he had hardly heard him.

'Guv?' he said.

'Right, Kevin,' Thackeray came back sharply. 'I heard you. I just want to be sure we're on firm ground if some of those yobs decide to torch the Heights on Stephen Fletcher's behalf, that's all. We've had enough mayhem of that sort recently to last Bradfield a lifetime. Keep at it for a bit, will you?'

When Mower had gone, Thackeray sat for a moment, fighting off the waves of panic which were threatening to overwhelm him every time he allowed himself a moment for reflection. His sleep had been plagued the previous night by fragmentary dreams which he could barely remember when he woke but in which he knew that the boy his son might have become played a major role. He ought by now, he thought, be taking him to rugby matches, perhaps watching him play, revelling in his growing prowess as he approached adolescence and became more like himself. The baby boy had been so like him, everyone had said, Thackeray recalled, flinching with almost physical pain at the recollection of adoring grandparents and neighbours, knowing that even then the seeds of the child's destruction had been planted by his own self-centred blindness. If only he had realised that Aileen could not cope, the hours had not been so long, the job so demanding and the escape route so easy...

He was only rescued from his thoughts by the phone, which he picked up automatically, failing to recognise for a second the familiar voice of the pathologist Amos Atherton.

'You wanted a word?' Atherton said. Thackeray wrenched his mind from the tormented past back to present unease.

'Run me through your report on Peter Graves,' Thackeray said quietly. 'I've got people raising hell about persecuted black youngsters and I want to know I'm on solid ground. DCI Hutton's gone back to Arnedale so he's not going to have to face the flak from the lad's friends and supporters on the Heights.'

'Have you found the weapon?' Atherton asked.

'Not as far as I know,' Thackeray said. 'What do you reckon?'

'Oh, I don't reckon, lad, I know,' Atherton said sharply. 'Haven't you read anything I wrote in my report? It was a heavy metal instrument. It left rust in the wounds so probably quite old. Indentations on the skull, two separate areas of fracture, and similar bruises on the neck and shoulders. Someone went for him with a great deal of force, probably from behind. A savage attack, make no mistake. Either of the two blows to the head would have killed him. A hammer, possibly. The blunt end of an axe, but you'd expect some cutting injuries with that. Certainly something heavy.'

'Left-handed? Right-handed?' Thackeray asked, his mind on autopilot now.

'Right-handed I'd say, and inflicted by someone much the same height as Graves, about five eleven, certainly not taller, possibly a bit shorter. The blows came from the back rather than above. If he was standing up when they were inflicted, of course.'

'Anything else come back from forensic tests?' Thackeray asked.

'Nothing of interest,' Atherton said. 'Graves was pretty healthy for his age. He'd eaten a meal that night. No alcohol in the blood. No drugs, prescription or otherwise. He could have lived to a ripe old age if someone hadn't decided his time was up.'

'Any sign that he put up a fight?'

'Some abrasions on the knuckles of his right hand. Could have been inflicted when he fell or maybe he fought back briefly and hit his assailant. But once the head injuries were inflicted he would have lost consciousness pretty quickly. He wouldn't have put up any resistance after that.'

'Someone hated him,' Thackeray said. 'Or was determined not to let him witness whatever they were up to up there?'

'Oh, aye,' Atherton agreed. 'I think you can be pretty certain of that.'

Laura walked slowly back to her VW, which she had parked under the overhanging trees not far from the school gates. She had not had any lunch and she was getting hungry and there was a cold wind from the hills which made her hunch her shoulders inside her fleece. But she still glanced up and down the road curiously. Southfield was a suburb of Bradfield which she did not know well, and one of the few which had succeeded in hanging on to the prosperous middle classes, most of whom had fled to Ilkley and Harrogate or the villages of the Yorkshire Dales long ago.

The substantial houses and leafy avenues sprawled high above Bradfield on one of the seven hills which surrounded what had been the industrial heart of the town. These solid Victorian villas had once housed mill owners in fresher air than had ever penetrated the back-to-back cottages of the bleachers and spinners, weavers and finishers crammed into the valley below. The tree-lined road reminded her of the street where she had her own flat on the north side of town. The difference was that these houses were detached and set in extensive gardens and had not, as far as she could see, been subdivided into flats.

The Woodlands children had disappeared by now, most of them driven off in the mini-buses to the edges of the town where the estates sprawled out beyond the remaining semi-derelict mill sites and the hangar-like barns of commercial redevelopment or to the western slopes where the blocks of flats at the Heights reared up against the backdrop of the Pennine moors. Laura wondered how the council had gained access to the old house which formed the core of Woodlands school without infuriating the neighbours in the first place.

As she took stock of her surroundings she suddenly became conscious of being watched. She turned quickly and realised that an elderly couple were standing by the gates of a house fifty yards down the hill from the school with suspicion in every inch of their demeanour.

With her car keys in her hand she strolled towards them.

'Boston, Neighbourhood Watch.' The male member of the pair, who had barked this information at Laura, was a short, bristling man, in a blazer and flannel trousers, with the ruddy complexion and dry sandy-grey hair of an Englishman exposed too long to the sun. At his side stood a sturdy grey-haired woman in gardening clothes, clutching a trowel and with an expression of deep distaste in her faded blue eyes.

'We always keep an eye on the children as they go home,' the woman said, her voice harsh with dislike. 'You never know what they'll get up to, do you? Little devils.'

Laura tried out a smile, to which the couple seemed particularly impervious, and explained who she was.

'A terrible thing, this murder,' she said tentatively.

'What do you expect?' Mrs Boston snapped, clutching her trowel like a weapon. 'Little thugs like that. Something dreadful was bound to happen in the end. We're just pleased that it didn't involve any of the neighbours. And now we've got reporters...' Her expression made very clear that she regarded journalists as only marginally more acceptable than young criminals.

Her husband glanced at her slightly anxiously.

'Not that we're saying we're glad he's dead...,' he said.

'It's just that, as you know, there's been a lot of trouble at the school. The community is understandably worried.'

Laura nodded cautiously.

'Aren't you involved in the campaign to have the school closed?' she asked. 'Perhaps you could tell me a bit about that for my article?'

'Of course we can,' Mrs Boston said, her eyes lighting up, evidently realising that a reporter might serve some useful purpose after all. She unlatched the wrought-iron gate and waved Laura through with her trowel into the immaculate front garden where beds of red, white and blue radiated patriotism alongside the neatly scalped grass.

She followed the Bostons down the side of the house to a terrace where a table and garden chairs were arranged to catch the late afternoon sun filtering between the tall trees at the bottom of the garden. A motor-mower was parked in the middle of the lawn, the grass half cut. While Mrs Boston hurried away to make tea, her husband settled Laura into a garden chair and went into the house to find her a selection of leaflets which the Close Woodlands School Campaign had produced.

'The *Gazette* has hardly given us any coverage, you know,' he said morosely when he returned. 'Yet the feeling in the community is running very high. If the place is attracting vandals and arsonists at the rate it is, who's to say when they'll turn their attentions to the rest of us?'

'People can't sleep at night with the worry,' Mrs Boston said, dropping a laden tea tray onto the table in front of Laura with a bang. 'It was never meant to be more than a temporary stopgap, you know, the use of Woodlands as a school. They moved in when the original building was burnt down. That was fifteen years ago now, and there's still no sign of them rebuilding. The council gave itself planning permission, of course. Absolutely outrageous. I don't know how they got away with it. And the number of children has gone up and up.'

'Of course, that was before Alicia and I came to live here,' Boston said. 'We faced a *fait accompli*, as it were, and no one else seemed terribly bothered about it then.'

'But the type of children has just got worse and worse, hasn't it Ferdy?' Mrs Boston said, passing Laura her tea. 'Bigger, noisier, more foul-mouthed. The language is just disgusting. And most of them our coloured friends, of course. We spent a long time in southern Africa, so we know them well.'

Laura took a mouthful of tea and tried to swallow her distaste with it. There were times when adopting an objective stance, as a good reporter should, came bitterly hard.

'Lowers the property values of course, something like that on your doorstep,' Boston added. 'You can't have a round of golf these days without some nosy fool at the club asking about the latest outrage in your road. Damned embarrassing, that.' As he sipped his tea his face became even more suffused with fury and Laura began to feel faintly concerned about his health.

'But if it was already here you must have benefited from the lower house values when you bought this place,' she objected mildly, casting a slightly envious eye over the mellow stone and gleaming windows of the house behind them.

'That's not the point, is it?' Mrs Boston snapped. 'We don't feel safe here any more. No one does. It's just not something you want in a neighbourhood like this. It's not appropriate. There are a lot of elderly people here, retired people who came up here for peace and quiet after working hard all their lives. I'm nearly eighty myself.'

'You certainly don't look it,' Laura said with automatic politeness. 'Are you getting any joy from the council with your campaign?' she asked.

'You really need to talk to our chairman, Mark Oliver, about that,' Boston said. 'He was planning to talk to the council again this week. He's not let them rest since the murder. That was really the last straw. He lives about six houses down on the other side of the road. The Pines, the house is called. He's not one of the old duffers like me. Made his pile young, Mark has. Lots of energy. Lots of contacts. He's the one who got the campaign up and running, it has to be said. You won't catch him in at this time of day, though. Works long hours, Mark. But always finds time for the community if the cause is good.'

'I'll track him down,' Laura said. 'You don't know where he works, do you?'

'Some big company in Leeds,' Mrs Boston said, a note of disapproval in her voice. 'I'm not sure what it's called. You could ask his wife, I suppose. She's sometimes around during the day, when she's not at the tennis club or nipping off to shop at Harvey Nichols.'

Laura smiled faintly as she picked up her bag to leave. Campaigning was obviously creating strange alliances around the Woodlands School.

Chapter Six

'Off the record, you said?' David Mendelson looked quizzically at DCI Michael Thackeray over his pint of Tetleys, wondering why his friend appeared so stressed. Thackeray was staring at his glass of mineral water as if it held the secret of the universe and he had lost the ability to drain the vital elixir.

'You don't mind, do you?' he asked quietly. He had arranged to meet Mendelson, who worked for the Crown Prosecution Service, as the two of them made their way home: Mendelson to his wife Vicky, who had been Laura Ackroyd's best friend since they had been at university together, and the three young children Thackeray so bitterly envied them, and Thackeray himself to the flat he shared so uncertainly with Laura.

'I don't want to make waves officially,' Thackeray said. 'But Laura's grandmother is involved in this defence campaign which seems to be taking off for Stephen Fletcher and I need to be one hundred per cent sure we've got it right.'

'Well I can't give you one hundred per cent, but I can give you about ninety-nine,' Mendelson said. 'What's up? Don't you rate your colleague from Arnedale?'

'I hardly know him,' Thackeray said. 'But the lad's black and Kevin Mower noticed a certain, shall we say, coolness between DCI Hutton and anyone with more than the lightest of suntans.'

'Ah,' Mendelson said thoughtfully. 'I didn't know that might be a factor.'

'You see why one hundred per cent might be good?'

'Bradfield needs a racist police scandal like it needs a hole in the head,' Mendelson said. 'I'll go over the papers again tomorrow but it looks a reasonably solid case to me. Motive is pretty obvious. The lad must have hated Graves. Opportunity isn't in doubt. He was seen at the school and doesn't deny being there at the relevant time. He even admits he intended to break in to get his stuff out of his locker, which incidentally included his stash of cannabis, which would probably have made him even more afraid of being caught. And his interview statements are all over the place – he saw Graves, he didn't see Graves, he was on his own, he had a mate with him, although if that's true he refuses to say who it was. It's true there's not much forensic evidence, although as you've probably heard they've just confirmed his fingerprints were on the petrol can they found up there. But we don't have the weapon yet and he won't tell us where he's disposed of it. He's probably chucked anything incriminating in the canal. Even the kids are getting wise to DNA matching now, but something may still turn up. But as far as DCI Hutton's concerned he seems to have played it all by the book. The lad had a solicitor with him and a social worker, but still chose to make some pretty ambiguous statements. If I'd been Hutton I'd have charged him and I think we'll get a result.'

Thackeray nodded, finally picking up his glass and taking a sip of the effervescing water.

'Even so, it does seem to me that there were a few leads which were never followed up and which the defence may exploit if they find out about them. Which they will.'

'Laura hasn't been digging around the case, has she? Has Joyce convinced her that there's a miscarriage of justice on the cards?' Mendelson asked shrewdly and knew from the closed look on Thackeray's face that he had hit home.

'Come on, Michael,' he said. 'Your job and hers were never going to be very compatible. I thought you'd learned to live with it.'

Thackeray shrugged, and ran a hand across unruly dark hair, blue eyes veiled.

'Maybe,' he said. He took another sip of his drink and tried to wipe Laura from his mind.

'Where did the lad get the can of petrol from?' he asked quietly. 'We don't seem to know that. It's not that easy for a young tearaway to go to a garage and fill up a petrol can without someone noticing and asking questions. And there was more than one set of fingerprints on that petrol can. Has anyone tried to find out whom they belonged to? And what about Gareth Davies, who seems to have had more than enough reason himself for losing his temper with Graves? We know he was there that evening. Can he prove that he didn't hang around and see Graves again later? Did anyone bother to ask?'

'You want to reopen the investigation?'

'Not officially,' Thackeray said. 'Just a few discreet inquiries for a start. There might be something on petrol station video records, if we ask around. Not many people buy petrol in cans these days. Certainly not fifteen year old lads.'

'If they haven't wiped the tapes,' Mendelson said sceptically. 'I know the arrest was quick but not that quick. But you're right in one sense, of course. We're obviously going to get a lot of hassle over this boy. I'd be happy to see the case strengthened if it goes to court, which may be what happens as a result of your inquiries. So long as you're aware of that possibility. That won't please Joyce Ackroyd and her friends. Or Laura, maybe.'

'There's more,' Thackeray said. 'Amos Atherton raised another doubt in my mind, coming to it fresh,' he said. 'He reckons Graves's assailant was about the same height as he was himself. But when I asked Mower about Fletcher, he said the boy's unusually small for his age, only about five three or four whereas Graves was getting on for six foot. I've asked Amos to look carefully at the angle of the blows and let me know if that makes sense. He's not likely to come up with anything conclusive, of course, but it might be interesting.'

'Fine,' Mendelson said. 'Let me know what Amos says formally. There's no reason not to be cautious at this stage. He'll only be remanded when he comes to court again next week.' He glanced at Thackeray across the top of his glass. They had got to know each other well since Thackeray had come to Bradfield to take over CID a few years previously but Mendelson never felt that he had ever totally conquered the deep reserve with which his friend cloaked his private life.

'How is Laura?' he asked tentatively, wondering whether another rift in that relationship was responsible for the dark circles under Thackeray's eyes and the ever more haunted expression.

'She's fine,' Thackeray said.

'And the trip to the Midlands? Did that work out well.'

'As well as arresting and charging young coppers can ever go,' Thackeray said, his expression hardening. 'Bloody fools.'

'Right,' Mendelson said. He nodded at Thackeray's glass. 'Another?' he asked, but Thackeray pulled a face and got to his feet.

'I'll keep you in touch,' he said. 'Laura's cooking. We've hardly seen each other for weeks…' His voice trailed away and Mendelson knew better than to pursue it. There was a hard core to Thackeray he wondered if even Laura would ever be able to breach.

'You must both come round for a meal soon,' he said. 'We've hardly seen you for months, never mind weeks.'

'That would be good,' Thackeray said although his enthusiasm seemed muted and Mendelson's sense of anxiety increased. Thackeray had met Laura Ackroyd at his house and both he and his wife had long hoped that the relationship would last. But there were times when his optimism ran thin. He got to his feet.

'Let's keep in touch on this Graves case,' Mendelson said. 'It might get tricky if a head of steam builds up on the Heights. But Michael, you are sure you're not pushing this just to keep Laura happy?'

'Let's just say that my motives may be mixed,' Thackeray said as he turned towards the door.

Soon after seven that evening, Laura unloaded her supermarket bags in her small kitchen, poured herself a vodka and tonic and went into the bedroom to change out of her suit into a brilliant green shirt and a calf-length black skirt. She loosened her hair from the long plait she had constrained it in all day and shook it loose around her shoulders. If she was going to annoy Michael Thackeray, she thought ruefully, she had better sugar the pill.

Thoughtfully she began to slice root ginger, garlic and lemongrass into paper-thin slivers, and put water on for rice. Thackeray's time-keeping, like most policemen's, was erratic but he had seemed, for him, as enthusiastically committed to a Thai curry at about eight as he would ever be, so she reckoned her preparations were not too premature. But she was well into her second V and T by the time Thackeray let himself into the flat with his key and slipped his arms around her as she put her wok onto the gas. She leaned back to kiss him and then wriggled free of his roving hands.

'Later,' she said. 'Let me concentrate on this. You know how easy I find it to burn the oil and ruin the whole damn thing.' He kissed her neck and smiled faintly. They both knew that Laura would be the first to admit she was not a natural cook, but as he himself aspired to little more than bacon and baked beans and an occasional steak, legacy of years spent working long hours and living alone, she did not let her shortcomings oppress her. An attempt at a Thai curry was better than anything he could offer.

They ate companionably enough at the small dining table against the living room window which gave an uninterrupted view across the town in the valley, where skeins of bright lights and the shimmering glitter of moving traffic made a fairyland of what by day was merely a dusty grey urban blur punctuated by the odd church spire and surviving mill chimney. Laura could see that Thackeray was making an effort, but she knew his heart was not in it, and she became edgy herself as she tried and failed to penetrate his increasingly sombre mood.

After they had finished, Laura flung herself into a chair

beside the big Victorian fireplace which she had filled with a golden collection of leaves and dried grasses and began to tell Thackeray how she had spent her day.

'I went up to Woodlands school today,' she said. 'Ted Grant wants me to do a backgrounder for use after the trial.'

Thackeray looked at her sceptically.

'I wonder who put that idea into his head,' he said. 'It could be twelve months before the boy's convicted.'

'If he ever is,' Laura said with her sweetest smile. 'There's a hell of a lot of hostility up there in Southfield. It's deeply depressing. I spoke to the people campaigning to get the school closed down. They hate the kids, really hate them, mainly because a lot of them are black, as far as I could work out. And then there's Graves's wife who seems to have been bullied for years. Really, if you're looking for motives for the murder the place is littered with them and your man Hutton seems to have barely scratched the surface with his inquiries.' He listened without comment and without enthusiasm, knowing that Joyce Ackroyd's concerns might drive a wedge between them which could be even more damaging than usual. When she had finished he sighed. Laura knew the risks she was taking and was not surprised when Thackeray responded with muted anger.

'Laura, I can't reopen the case without very solid evidence that we've got the wrong person. You know that. The boy was there when he shouldn't have been, up to no good; he hated Graves; he was known to have a violent temper. My advice to you is to do your background research, by all means, but don't get carried away by the campaign on the Heights. There's all sorts of motives for that which have very little to do with justice for Stephen Fletcher, believe me. Joyce is a very old lady and maybe her judgement isn't as good as it used to be.'

'She'd be furious if she heard you saying that,' Laura said, irritated herself now. Somehow Thackeray's homecoming from Staffordshire was not turning out as she had anticipated and she did not quite understand why.

'I saw David Mendelson on the way home,' he said. 'He's handling the case for the CPS and he seems entirely happy for it to go ahead. The boy will be remanded for another week when he comes back to court. David's perfectly happy with what we've produced in the way of evidence – though I certainly shouldn't be telling you this.'

'I bet you didn't know that Stephen Fletcher's best mate has gone missing?' Laura said. 'Mary Morris said she told the police he hadn't been in school since the murder and she's not been able to track him down, but she doesn't think the police did anything about it. One more thing they didn't seem very interested in.'

'I'll mention it to Kevin Mower. He's tidying up any loose ends for me, but seriously Laura, I don't think there's any mileage in this campaign Joyce is launching. Just because it's a black lad doesn't mean it's a miscarriage of justice, for God's sake.' His tone had become unexpectedly cold and Laura flinched slightly but she still pursued her point.

'You have to worry about a black boy being arrested so quickly...' Laura persisted, an obstinate expression in her eyes which Thackeray recognised only too well.

'You're asking me to question what a colleague's done without a shred of hard evidence to cast doubt on his judgement,' Thackeray protested. 'And suggest the arrest might be racist? You are joking?'

'It's not as simple as it looks,' Laura said. 'What struck me talking to people was how many of them absolutely detested Peter Graves. His colleagues, his wife, most of the kids.'

'If the Crown Prosecution Service is happy, there's nothing I can do.'

'In just one afternoon I've spoken to at least three possible suspects, people who really hated Graves and who never seem to have even been questioned properly in the original investigation,' Laura said, knowing the treacherous waters might close over her head now.

'You're suggesting that what happened was a premeditated murder which by sheer coincidence happened at the same time as a little tearaway was trying to torch the school? Come on Laura, how likely is that?'

'Did you know Graves had a girlfriend?' she flung back, working on the premise that the sheer weight of doubts in her own mind might move him.

'Personally, no. But I didn't investigate the case. I was away, remember?'

'I don't know who she was but it opens up all sorts of possibilities. And he spent some time that evening with a teacher he had virtually sacked?' Laura persisted.

'That I do know about, but so what? He had enemies? I should think it goes with the territory, just as it goes with mine. Have you ever thought how many people might like to bump me off? All those villains I've put away?'

Thackeray's words brought her up short and she knew that she was not going to get any further. He did not often discuss the risks of his work, but they were there, like an undertow beneath the choppy waters of their relationship and she had sometimes wondered, lying awake on dark nights when he had not come home, whether it was that element of unease which years ago had sent Michael's marriage so catastrophically onto the rocks.

'I won't give up, you know,' she said mutinously, getting up and beginning to clear their abandoned dishes from the table before flinging herself onto the sofa beside the fireplace and opening the day's *Gazette*, to which she had made no significant contribution herself.

'Did I say I expected you to give up?' Thackeray said moving across to sit down beside her and taking the paper out of her hands. He slipped an arm around her shoulders and pulled her towards him. 'When did I ever expect you to give up? You're the most obstinate person I know, with the possible exception of your grandmother. If you weren't I wouldn't even be here, would I? You are pig-headed to a fault.'

'You've never heard of that saying about pots and kettles, I suppose?' she murmured, before his wandering hands distracted her from anything else.

'I really missed you,' he said, at last.

'You seemed depressed last night,' she murmured, feeling guilty now that she had persisted to the point of a row so soon after his return.

'The trip was depressing,' he said. It was an answer which barely touched the surface of his anxieties but the rest he clamped down tight, most of all the call he had taken from the hospital on his mobile just as he arrived home. It was from the doctor he had seen the night before and warned him that they might soon have to move Aileen to the Infirmary for specialist treatment. The young doctor had sounded anxious and Thackeray guessed that the beginning of the end might be closer that either of them had anticipated. He had sat in the car for a few moments gazing down the street of Victorian houses seeing nothing but a grey haze out of which floated images from his past: the laughter of a happy baby, the speck of a skylark high in the blue sky over the summer moors where they had calculated Ian must have been conceived, and Aileen herself as a radiant bride with all the hope of the world in her shining eyes. How had it all gone so wrong, he asked himself? And how could he make it work a second time around as Laura wanted without his fear of the past tearing him apart?

He kissed her again and she responded, as he knew she would, with growing passion. But later, in bed, after he had lost himself briefly in her body, he turned away to sleep with the bitter taste in his mouth of trust betrayed and confidences not shared.

Chapter Seven

The office of da Silva and Sweetman, Solicitors, was behind a small shop front on Aysgarth Road, the main artery into the town from the north and the bustling heart of the Asian community. Squashed between a halal butcher and a green-grocer, whose display of mangos and ladies' fingers nestled companionably up against the potatoes and runner beans, the solicitors' door stood open to the street when Laura arrived and slid into an unexpected parking space just outside. Inside a young Asian woman in green and gold shalwar kameez was tidying up the reception desk.

'I was hoping to see Jenny Sweetman,' Laura said. 'I haven't missed her, have I? I got held up in traffic.'

'She's in but she's trying to catch up wi't paperwork,' the receptionist said with the Yorkshire accent of a Bradfielder born and bred. 'Who shall I say?'

The paperwork, piles of it on the desk and every available surface, was very evident when Laura was admitted to one of the offices at the back of the reception area, but the woman half concealed behind the desk stood up and held out a hand with a welcoming smile as Laura walked in.

'Come in, come in,' she said. 'I've heard all about you, read a lot of the stuff you've been writing in the *Gazette*. What can I do to help?'

'It's a change not to be regarded as some sort of nasty smell,' Laura said wryly, thinking of the reception she'd got from Alicia Boston. 'Reporters are never flavour of the month.'

'Lawyers who represent folk the establishment doesn't like much get the same sort of treatment,' Jenny Sweetman said with a grin which implied she enjoyed the challenge.

'Like lads who bump off their headteachers?' Laura asked.

'Ah,' the lawyer said, sinking back into her chair and half disappearing behind a pile of files, leaving only a pair of dark, intelligent eyes fixed on Laura's. 'You know you can't use this boy's name, don't you?'

'And you know Stevie Fletcher's name's common knowledge around the town, I expect?' Laura said. 'Don't worry. We won't commit contempt of court but there's a campaign going on and we can't ignore it. It must make your job more difficult if he's anonymous like this, mustn't it? Searching for witnesses and so on?'

Jenny Sweetman was young, dark-haired and bubbly and, Laura guessed, not much more than five feet tall, making up in effervescence what she lacked in height. She pushed her files carelessly to one side the better to concentrate on her visitor.

'It's never easy,' she said. 'And I think it's in his own interests if we ask for his name to be released next time he's in court. It might jog someone's memory who could help his defence. At least people are already realising that young Stevie looks like being the next awful miscarriage of justice. The only thing that surprises me is that it's happened so quickly. Par for the course would be for him to rot in jail for ten years before anyone noticed that the police had made a major cock-up again.'

'Tell me about it,' Laura said. 'But all I've met so far are a lot of people convinced he didn't do it but without a shred of evidence that seems to cast doubt on the police line.'

'Well, the shreds are still a bit thin on the ground,' Jenny Sweetman said. 'But I reckon they'll add up to serious doubts before long.'

'Tell me more,' Laura said.

'Better than that,' Jenny flashed back getting to her feet. 'I was due to see his mother this morning before she goes to work a late shift at the infirmary. Come with me and judge for yourself what's going on here.'

She picked up a bulging briefcase from the side of her desk and swept out of her office, leaving Laura to follow slightly breathlessly in her wake.

'Lock everything up carefully at lunchtime, Shamilla. Ben's in court all day,' she told the receptionist. 'Ben da Silva's my partner,' she explained to Laura as they left the office and stood for a moment allowing the crowds of mainly Asian shoppers to swirl around them. 'We're kept pretty busy in an area like this. Your wheels or mine?'

In the end it was Laura who manoeuvred her car into the traffic and ground down into the town centre and then up the long hill to the Heights, where Stevie Fletcher's mother lived on the fourth floor of Holtby House, one of the dwindling number of residents who were waiting anxiously for the final redevelopment plan to begin at last. As they got out of the car Laura glanced guiltily towards the line of elderly people's bungalows where her grandmother lived. She knew she would not have time to call in on this trip.

They had parked in a littered car park to one side of the block, watched by the straggle of youths who habitually kicked balls around and monitored the comings and goings of the estate through cold and narrowed eyes, and Laura locked her car carefully. She gritted her teeth as she followed Jenny Sweetman up the concrete staircase unusually reeking of disinfectant rather than urine this morning and out onto the long walkway eighty feet above the ground which gave access to the highest flats. The lawyer knocked on a door and gave Laura a smile of triumph as someone inside began to release the bolts and locks which was the normal level of security required for safety in this shattered community.

'Good, she's home,' Jenny said as a tall black woman opened her front door and included Laura in a cautious smile of welcome.

'I know I'm not a perfect mother,' Doreen Fletcher said when her guests were seated in her sparsely furnished but scrupulously clean living room. 'How can I be when I have to work all the hours the good Lord sends? And boys are difficult to raise these days, you know?'

'Do you have other children, Mrs Fletcher?' Laura

asked, glancing around the tidy room and taking in the array of school photographs on the sideboard.

'Older,' Doreen said. 'They all left home now. Stevie was the youngest, and always the most difficult. He was a hard baby, hard toddler, hard right through to his teenage. And then he got impossible for me. I didn't want him to go to Woodlands, you know? I wanted him to stay in normal school but in the end they expelled him so we had no choice. But to be fair to those teachers, I think Woodlands was doing him good. At least until the new head came. Him I did not like.'

Doreen glanced at Jenny who nodded her approval.

'I think you can tell Laura what you really think,' she said. 'I think it might help Stevie.' Doreen nodded, her dark eyes full of tears..

'Mr Graves, he was a strange man. I thought he would be good for the boy. I thought he was a strong man and that is what my boy needed. Not having a father here, you know? Not enough discipline. But in the end I began to think he was all mouth, that man.'

'My grandmother's a governor at the school,' Laura said slowly. 'That's not all she thought. She was afraid that Peter Graves would hit the boys.'

Doreen Fletcher looked at her for a moment before replying.

'If my grandmother had heard you say that she would say that Stevie was not hit enough,' she said. 'That was the way in the West Indies in the old days. Spare the rod and spoil the child, you know? I didn't hit my children. Not if I could help it, anyway. And she would have blamed me for that. But Stevie was not a violent boy, more obstinate, deter-mined to go his own way, from being a little boy. It wasn't that he didn't really want to learn anything, more that he needed to be encouraged more than most. But there was no violence until he got to St Marks where he met some racist youth who made his life a misery. Then he became violent.

He fought back.'

'Sounds as if he had good reason,' Jenny Sweetman said. 'Did the racist youth he was fighting with get expelled too?'

Doreen shook her head.

'Thought not,' her lawyer said. 'But Graves didn't use violence, as far as you know?'

'Stevie said that he shouted and threatened but nothing happened beyond that.'

'Sounds wonderful,' Laura said, sarcastically. 'Was he a racist?'

Doreen shrugged.

'Stevie didn't say that, but it's there in most people isn't it? Woodlands is full of black boys. How come it's always black boys who end up there? Are the white boys all saints or somet'ing?'

'But Mrs Fletcher, the police seem quite convinced that Stevie is the person they're looking for in connection with the murder,' Laura cut in. 'They say they have evidence. What makes you so sure he's innocent? That the head-teacher didn't perhaps push him beyond endurance just like the boy at St Mark's seems to have done?'

Doreen Fletcher glanced at her lawyer again, who nodded in encouragement.

'The police, they came here looking for evidence. Men in white suits in his room for a whole day, taking things away in bags, asking questions, but I don't believe they found anything, you know? They didn't look as though they found anything to me.'

'They do tests. It takes time to find what they're looking for, but I've not been told they've found anything significant here,' Jenny Sweetman said quietly, and Doreen Fletcher shrugged helplessly.

'His friend came to see me after they arrested Stevie,' she said slowly. 'Dwayne came to see me. He told me that he was with Stevie that night. Mr Graves had thrown Stevie out that day for being awkward and he'd left his Walkman in school.

He wanted it back in case it got stolen so they planned to get into school late that night and bring it home. That's what Dwayne told me, though Stevie won't say anything when I go to see him. Nothing at all. Dwayne says they didn't see the headmaster that night. They heard him but they didn't see him. And if they didn't see him, how could Stevie have hit him and killed him. I believe Dwayne.'

'Have the police spoken to Dwayne? Do they know he was with Stevie?' Laura asked.

'He said he hasn't spoken to the police. I think he's very frightened they will lock him up too. And he thinks Stevie has kept quiet about having someone with him that night,' Doreen Fletcher said. 'Stevie seems to be more interested in protecting Dwayne than helping himself.'

'Have you told the police Dwayne was there?' Laura asked, and was not surprised when Stevie's mother turned away.

'I don' want to get another boy into trouble either,' she said quietly at last.

'And Stevie's said nothing? You think Stevie's trying to keep his friend out of trouble because Dwayne is the guilty one? He killed Mr Graves?'

'I don't know what Stevie's doing because when I go to see him he won't tell me anything,' Doreen said, her voice breaking slightly. 'He's just withdrawn into himself, you know? It's as if someone has put a lock on his mouth. And now Dwayne has disappeared. No one has seen him for a week. So what can we do? Miz Sweetman, can you tell me? What can we do?'

DC Mohammed Sharif was working on his own time when he drew up in the broad main street of Arnedale, and parked a hundred yards from the police station. Most days of the week the parking space he had found would be occupied by one of the stalls of the open-air market which was Arnedale's main attraction for the scattered population of the surrounding villages and farms. Cattle and sheep auctions had been held there from time immemorial, which explained why the Georgian fronted stone premises were set so far back from the road, leaving the castle to dominate the town with unrivalled defensive views. But such country pursuits had now been banished to a modern auction mart on the edge of the town and the centre of Arnedale was left to the shoppers and tourists who flooded into it most days of the week to buy fruit, veg, cheeses, crockery and household goods and clothes at knock-down prices in a slow-moving, sharp-eyed procession.

Sharif sat in his car for a moment watching the passersby, very aware that there were few if any black or brown faces amongst them. It worried him that his own community clung so ferociously to the familiar narrow terraced streets of Bradfield although he understood why they stayed. Only the most prosperous Asians, it seemed, gained sufficient confidence to move out of the town and then mainly to well-protected and secure large houses not too far away. Few of them had reached Arnedale, and he became unsettlingly self-conscious as he joined the shoppers on the pavement and wove his way determinedly through the jostling throng to the nick. He felt like a dark presence from a different world even though he had discovered that there was at least one other Asian in the town. That was the reason he had come.

The desk sergeant glanced at him impassively and without enthusiasm when he presented himself in the front office of the police station.

'I wondered if I could see DC Achmed, if he's in?' Sharif asked. The sergeant said nothing for a moment although Sharif thought his face became marginally less friendly than before.

'That'd be Hussain Achmed, would it?' he asked eventually.

'That's right.'

'Aye well, you'll be out o'luck then,' the sergeant said. 'He's gone, has our Hussain, and I can't rightly say that I know where you'll find him now. Likely not in Arnedale, any road.'

'Gone?' Sharif said, feeling slightly ridiculous. He could feel the eyes of a second officer, ostensibly burrowing into a filing cabinet at the back of the reception area, glancing continually in his direction and the feeling was not a comfortable one.

'Moved to another nick, you mean? Transferred?'

'No. I don't mean that,' the desk sergeant said. 'He left the job a couple o' weeks ago, did Hussain. Left Arnedale, an'all, as far as I know. You'll probably find him in Bradfield, won't you? Back with his kith and kin.'

A snort from the officer at the back of the room was quickly stifled but Sharif could feel the hostility of the two men now, lapping around him and threatening to choke him. He pulled his warrant card from his pocket and slapped it down on the counter in front of the sergeant.

'Bradfield CID,' he said sharply. 'I need to talk to him about a case.' He had to hope that this claim to official status on a strictly unofficial visit would not filter back to Sergeant Kevin Mower. The desk sergeant hesitated for a second before pulling the phone towards him, his eyes openly unfriendly now.

'I'll see if CID have got a forwarding address,' he said. 'You'd have saved yourself a journey if you'd phoned first.' But after a brief conversation, he came up with nothing useful from whoever picked up the CID phone.

'You'd have better luck at county,' he said dismissively. 'They'll likely know where he's at. Or DCI Hutton might have some idea. D'you want me to contact him for you?' His hand hovered over the phone again and Sharif knew this was a challenge he couldn't risk accepting.

'Do you know why he left?' he asked, knowing he was wasting his time as the sergeant's eyes became opaque and he shrugged.

'I'm not privy to CID shenanigans,' he said.

'I'll try my luck with county then,' Sharif said and turned on his heel, conscious of two sets of unfriendly eyes boring into his back as he went back down the stone steps to the wide crowded pavement outside.

He walked back down the main street like a panther, alert to hostile threats from any quarter. Like most young Asian men of his generation, born and bred in Yorkshire but still not wholly accepted, he had developed a sixth sense for danger. Here, he knew, it was unlikely to be overt. This was a quiet country town unlikely to harbour any physical threat in broad daylight, not like Bradfield or Leeds at night when a football crowd on the rampage or the wrong pub turning out at closing time could threaten an explosion of extreme violence within seconds if your face didn't fit. Here, amongst the shopping crowds, there was nothing more than a slight hardening of expression, or a surprised sideways glance, as he strolled back to his car. Here he was no more than a stranger in his own country and he had got bitterly used to that.

He hesitated as he was about to put his key into the door lock when he realised he had parked almost opposite the shop-front of the local weekly paper, the *Arnedale Observer*, with its window full of glossy pictures of local events, from weddings to a pony gymkhana and a sheep dog trial. Dodging the traffic, he crossed the road to study the display and then, after a moment's thought, opened the door to find himself in another reception area with a blonde young woman behind the counter with a smile more sympathetic than he had come to expect in Arnedale.

'Can I help you?' she asked. 'D'you want to put an ad in the paper?'

'Well, I could do that, I suppose,' he said. 'But I'm not sure it would work. I'm trying to find someone who used to work in Arnedale and seems to have left recently. You don't have a phone book I could look at do you? That would tell me where he lived, maybe. You can never find one in a phone box, can you?'

The girl looked dubious.

'What was he called, this friend of yours?' she said.

'Hussain Achmed,' Sharif said. 'You don't know him, do you? That would be a coincidence.' He smiled encouragingly and found an answering glimmer of sympathy in her blue eyes. He did not correct the assumption of friendship although in fact he had learned of Hussain Achmed's existence in CID quite by chance when chatting to a detective from Leeds who knew him.

'He was Asian?' the girl said and in spite of the redundancy of the remark Sharif missed the hesitation that often came as people banished the word 'Paki' before it could slip from their lips.

'I did know him, actually,' she said to his surprise. 'Well, I didn't know him, to speak to, like, but there's not many Asians in Arnedale, are there, so he stood out a bit? He's a policeman, a detective, right? I used to see him around.' She grinned. 'He was nearly as good-looking as you,' she said.

'Impossible,' Sharif said happily. 'But that would be him. He doesn't seem to work here any more. You don't know anyone who might know where he's gone, do you? I really need to get hold of him quite urgently.'

The girl pondered some more, twisting a strand of hair around her finger as she thought in a way which set Sharif's heart beating faster.

'He had a girlfriend, I think,' she said eventually. 'I saw him a couple of times in the Bar Med in Sheep Street. It's the only half trendy place in Arnedale, so you see everyone who's not married in there if you hang about long enough. He was definitely there a couple of times with a girl.'

'An Asian girl?' Sharif asked cautiously, seeing a whole new cultural abyss opening up in front of him.

'No, a girl called Mandy Collier. She was at my school, a

couple of years ahead of me, tall, blonde, very slim. Quite a looker, right.'

'And d'you know where I might find Mandy Collier?' Sharif asked.

'Oh yes, she works just over the road in the solicitors' office at the top of the old post office building.' She pointed Sharif to a Victorian pile not unlike the police station. 'If you can't find out what you want to know from Mandy, come back and I'll have another think,' she offered expansively. 'In fact if you hang on until the Bar Med opens, right, we could likely find some other people who might know where Hussain went. He was quite popular, was Hussain, even though he didn't like being called Saddam when all that was going on. It was only a joke, know what I mean? No harm meant?' Sharif nodded impassively, knowing only too well how many insults were regarded as only a joke.

Five minutes later he was sitting in his car deep in thought. He had not intended to spend his entire day off in tracking down Hussain Achmed, and he had been entirely thrown by the news that he had left his job. When he had called the Arnedale nick from home earlier in the day a female officer had simply told him that Achmed not available. Had that been simple carelessness, he wondered, or a defensive response because Achmed had left the job in acrimonious circumstances. He thumped the steering wheel in frustration and decided he had no choice but to continue the hunt. If Achmed had worked for DCI Hutton and had left in a hurry he suspected that it could be for much the same reason that he had fallen foul of Hutton himself. The man was a racist bully and he needed to be stopped.

It was coming up to lunchtime and Sharif was pretty sure that Mandy Collier would take some time out from her reception duties. Tall, blonde and slim, and quite a looker, he thought, as he watched a procession of mainly male, portly and unattractive professionals make their way in and out of the old post office. She shouldn't be difficult to spot, he convinced himself, but it took half an hour of waiting. Then a young woman in a dark business suit and pink top emerged and he had no doubt. She was, he thought, a cracker. He locked the car again, crossed the road eagerly and fell into step beside her.

'Mandy?' he asked. 'Sorry to bother you but I'm a friend of Hussain's and I've lost touch...'

The young woman stopped and turned towards him with a furious expression contorting her flawlessly made-up features.

'A mate of Hussain's, are you?' she snapped. 'What makes you think I know where he is? He didn't tell me he was going, did he? He just fucked off without a bloody word, didn't he?'

Sharif flinched slightly at this onslaught.

'Tell me about it,' he said. 'I really need to talk to him.' Mandy Collier hesitated for a moment and then shrugged.

'Buy us a drink then,' she said. 'I've had a bad morning with those bastards in there.' She glanced at the tall stone building she had emerged from and stuck out a pink tongue in the general direction of the top floor. Then she offered Sharif a brilliant smile.

'It wasn't really owt serious with Hussain,' she said. 'Here today and gone tomorrow with a little Muslim girl he could take home to mum, he'd have been. I knew that, really. But it would have been nice if he'd let me know he was leaving, right?'

Sharif ushered her into the crowded bar of the Bull where most of the tables were taken up by lunchers tucking into roast beef and two veg' with gusto. He fought his way to the bar with sharp elbows, ignoring the scowls of the elbowed, and bought Mandy an alcopop, and an orange juice for himself. They found a corner in the crowd face-to-face, not the most suitable place for the conversation he had in mind, he thought, but probably the best he was going to be able to manage. The animated chatter all around them was, he hoped, sufficient to prevent anyone overhearing them.

Mandy took a swig from her bottle and gave him an appraising look.

'Are they all as fit as you down in Bradfield?' she asked.

'How do you know I come from Bradfield?' he countered.

'All you Pakis come from Bradfield,' she said, obviously oblivious to the fact that he might find the epithet insulting.

'Did Hussain?' he asked. She looked startled.

'No, he didn't, as it goes. He came from Leeds, I think. At least he worked in Leeds before he came up here.' She looked at Sharif shrewdly.

'You don't really know him at all, do you?' she asked. 'Who are you, exactly?'

'I'm a copper, just like him,' Sharif said. 'I only knew of him by reputation – the Asian who had got into CID in Arnedale. It was regarded as quite an achievement. I wanted to talk to him about what it was like up here only to find he's left the job. It was a bit of a surprise, that's all, and I wondered what went wrong.'

Mandy glanced around the crowded bar for a moment before moving closer to Sharif and lowering her voice.

'What usually goes wrong, I think,' she said. 'He didn't get on with his boss.'

'Mr Hutton?'

'Yes, I think so,' Mandy said. 'I was completely pissed off when he went off without saying anything, but I wasn't right surprised. He'd been fed up for as long as I knew him.'

'D'you know where he's gone?'

'Not exactly, but I think he once said he had family in Bradfield. I just assumed he's gone back to Leeds but maybe not.'

'Not as a policeman he hasn't,' Sharif said. 'They actually said at the nick that he'd left the job, so he couldn't just have moved to another division.'

'No,' Mandy said, draining her bottle and waving it

hopefully at Sharif. He ignored the gesture. 'He'll have gone back home to his mum, then, I reckon. I don't think he liked living on his own much. He was like a fish out of water in Arnedale, to be honest I felt right sorry for him. He didn't seem to have any mates at all.'

She glanced at Sharif's half-drunk orange juice.

'Course, he was like you. Didn't drink. It's a bit of a party-pooper, that, know what I mean? I can give you his mobile number if you like. He's got it switched on but he isn't answering my calls. You might have better luck.' She pulled her mobile out of her bag and located a number which Sharif wrote down.

'Thanks Mandy,' he said. 'I'm sorry he mucked you about.'

'Oh, I'll survive,' she said cheerfully. 'I'd not like to have seen my dad's face if I'd taken Hussain home. Know what I mean?' And with a grin she insinuated herself into the crowd of drinkers and was gone.

Chapter Eight

'So did you give the Close Woodlands Campaign short shrift? That's what I really want to know,' Laura asked. She was sitting in a huge office on the first floor of the Victorian town hall, facing the admirably uncluttered and well polished desk of councillor Jeremy Waite, holder of the education and leisure services portfolio for the town council.

Waite ran a hand across short spiky hair and smiled at his visitor. He was, Laura guessed, a year or two younger than she was herself, fashionably dressed in pale shirt-sleeves and silk tie, with a Paul Smith jacket over the back of his chair and evidently with both eyes and hands firmly fixed on the ladder of advancement in new Labour politics. Laura smiled to herself as she remembered her grandmother's description of the councillor as a jumped up little pipsqueak, though she suspected that Jeremy Waite was in fact a rather more formidably smooth operator than Joyce could imagine from her vantage point of old-style municipal politics.

The councillor sighed dramatically as if about to explain the obvious to a rather dim fourth former.

'What you're forgetting is that it's always been intended to move the school out of Woodlands. It was only a temporary expedient to move it in when some little bastard set the old buildings on the Heights alight. Unfortunately, my predecessors' chronic inability to get a new building off the ground has meant the long delay which is now annoying the residents of Southfield so much.'

'So you will close it?' Laura said.

'I didn't say that,' Waite said, with exaggerated patience. 'What I've already done is set up a task force to look at the best way of dealing with these very difficult children. My own instinct is to get them back into the mainstream. I don't think it does them any good being segregated like that.'

'So if you did decide to do that, what would happen to Woodlands?' Laura asked. She was sure that Waite would not have underestimated the significance the future of a highly desirable plot in an exclusive suburb would have for the council's finances. But to her surprise, the councillor's eyes did not light up with quite the avaricious gleam she had anticipated. In fact they clouded slightly.

'The complicating factor is that we don't own the land,' he said. 'We leased the house, at pretty disadvantageous terms, I may say. But I suppose they were in a blind panic back then, with a smoking ruin on the one hand and a gang of disaffected kids with nowhere to go on the other.' Waite's expression made it clear that he personally would have found a more appropriate solution to the problem had he not been in short pants at the time.

'So there's no financial advantage to you in closing the place down?'

'Serious disadvantage, as it goes,' Waite said. 'We're going to have to house the kids somewhere when the lease expires. And that's going to cost'

'Which is when? The lease, I mean?'

'Oh, it's got another couple of years to run,' Waite said airily. 'There's no great rush about any of this. I told the campaigners that they'd have to wait until our task force reported before we even began considering alternatives. But in the long run they'll get what they want anyway. There's no chance the lease will be renewed. So I can stroke the voters of Southfield without actually giving anything much away.'

'The property's too valuable now, I guess, for anyone to want to renew the arrangement,' Laura said.

'Absolutely.'

'So who owns it?' she asked.

'Oh, I don't think I can discuss that,' Waite said. 'Commercial confidentiality and all that.'

'You know, I suppose, that my grandmother's a governor of Woodlands,' Laura said cautiously. Waite nodded equally warily.

'I heard she was making waves about the murder at the school,' he said. 'She's not doing anyone any favours, you know? We need that sort of publicity in this town like we need a hole in the head. It damages business confidence. It's bad enough getting a headteacher murdered without allegations that we've managed to lock up the wrong black lad for it as well.'

'I'm not sure that PR for Bradfield is top of Joyce's list of priorities if we really have got the wrong person locked up,' Laura said tartly.

'Well, it should be if she wants to see this town regenerated. That won't happen if all we get is bad publicity about bad lads and decaying estates and racial tension and all the other stereotypes we get lumbered with.'

'She also says that the majority of governors didn't want Peter Graves appointed in the first place,' Laura said, irritated by Waite's tone as much as by what he said. 'He wasn't the right man for the job. He was a catastrophe waiting to happen, in fact.'

'Well, they would say that, wouldn't they?' Waite shot back sharply. 'They're the sort of people who've turned a blind eye to the mess the schools are in for too long. This town had one of the worst sets of results in the country five years ago. Gradually we're pushing them up. We need heads like Peter Graves to drag us into the new century.'

'He was your candidate then?' Laura hazarded.

'As it goes, yes, he was. I thought he'd shake Woodlands up and that's what it undoubtedly needed.'

'My grandmother would disagree,' Laura said.

'I'm sure she would. I'd have thought you'd have had more sense than to get mixed up with these old Labour dinosaurs more than you have to,' Waite said. 'They're the ones who got us into this mess in the first place. You should know that. Your editor tells me you're one of the *Gazette*'s high flyers.'

'Does he now,' Laura said, astonished that her name

might have come into any conversation between Jeremy Waite and Ted Grant at all, still less that it might have resulted in an unprecedented compliment to her professional skills.

'We must have lunch some time,' Waite said smoothly, getting to his feet and slipping into his jacket, and eyeing her with what Laura suspected was less than professional detachment. 'You'll have to excuse me now, though. I should have been at a meeting of the cabinet three minutes ago.' Laura raised an ironic eyebrow at that, not yet quite used to the new streamlined council, with its cabinets and portfolios and business plans, within which Waite obviously flourished.

'Sounds quite governmental,' she said.

'Good,' Waite said, with a thin smile. 'It's intended to. Keep in touch. But don't get carried away with these campaigns in the *Gazette*. As far as I can see, they're all sound and fury with not a bit of substance between them.'

Laura had taken the call from her grandmother just as she was logging off her computer at the end of a long day. Concerned more than irritated by her somewhat abrupt invitation to come up to see her, she drove up the hill to the Heights and parked outside Joyce's bungalow.

Joyce came to the door to meet her, looking strained.

'What's happened?' Laura asked.

'I can't believe it,' Joyce said. 'I've just had Mary Morris on the phone. The poor woman's distraught. They had the inspectors in a month or so ago, and according to Peter Graves and Mary, the word privately was that there would be a good report. There were a few problems but nothing that couldn't be sorted out, which I could have told anyone who was interested myself. Now the draft version's arrived on Mary's desk and apparently they've put it down as a failing school: ill-disciplined, poor teaching, bad management, the lot.'

'That won't do their campaign to stay open much good,' Laura said dryly.

'It can't be an accident, Laura,' Joyce said, her eyes blazing with outrage. 'Someone's nobbled the inspectors. What they're saying simply isn't true. I may be getting on a bit, but I'm not a complete fool. I've known that school for years and in spite of Peter Graves's antics, it's doing a good job. The inspectors have been got at. There's no other explanation.'

'Oh, come on, nan,' Laura said, aware of the tears in her grandmother's eyes but unable to hide her scepticism. 'That's a bit too paranoid, even for you. They're a national organisation. How could they be nobbled.'

'No, they're not, not really,' Joyce said. 'They farm the contracts out for each inspection. The Woodlands job went to the local lot, the lot they privatised at the town hall. What's to stop Jeremy Waite and his so-called cabinet getting at them, telling them a bad report would be very useful just now?'

'I think it's farfetched,' Laura said, doubtfully.

'But you'll look into it?' Joyce insisted. 'It's a month before the thing will be published officially. Plenty of time to get it changed. If only I wasn't stuck here with these wretched knees of mine I'd do it myself.'

'Have you got a copy of the report?' Laura asked, unwilling to make any promises but knowing that if she did not go through the motions Joyce would be inconsolable.

'Just what I jotted down from my phone call with Mary,' Joyce said, handing Laura several sheets of paper covered in her precise handwriting.

'I'll see what I can find out,' she said. 'But I very much doubt the inspectors will talk to the Press.'

'They won't even talk to Mary, from what she says. The chief inspector's away somewhere and no one else will comment, apparently.'

'I'll see what I can do,' Laura said, feeling helpless.

'And what about the murder?' Joyce went on, her anger building. 'Have you persuaded your Michael that they've got a serious miscarriage of justice on their hands?'

'Not quite,' Laura said. 'But there's one thing you might put feelers out on the estate about, though. Stevie Fletcher's friend, a lad called Dwayne Elton, hasn't been to school since it happened. According to his mother he was with Stevie that night.'

'Elton?' Joyce said. 'There's a family called Elton used to live in Brontë House before they pulled it down. I don't know where they've gone now. I'll talk to one or two folk and see what I can find out. Do you think he's a witness Stevie needs?'

'He's either a witness or an accomplice,' Laura said dryly. 'Which may be why he's disappeared.'

At the end of a working day when Sergeant Kevin Mower had found DCI Michael Thackeray inexplicably morose, all he had wanted was a workout at his gym, a shower and a curry, in that order. Instead he found himself driving irritably out of the town centre and into the narrow streets around Aysgarth Lane to park outside a café apparently patronised exclusively by Muslim men. He found Mohammed Sharif sitting at a table close to the steamed up window with another Asian who looked rather older than Sharif, and where Sharif was clean shaven and short haired and in his usual jeans and leather jacket, his companion appeared unkempt, with an incipient beard and a slightly grubby *shalwar kameez*.

'Sarge,' Sharif said. 'Thanks for coming. This is Hussain Achmed who's just resigned from CID in Arnedale a couple of weeks ago.' Mower hoped he did not register his surprise too overtly but his stomach lurched uncomfortably.

'Hi,' he said non-committally. He glanced at the two men's half empty glasses of fruit drinks. 'Can I get you anything?' he asked, and when they shook their heads he turned away to buy himself a tea and give himself time to think. There was only one reason he could think of for

Sharif engineering this meeting and it was one he definitely did not want to explore. Tea in hand, he joined the other two detectives at their table and waited for Sharif to explain.

'Our friend DCI Hutton,' Sharif said without preamble. 'You won't have forgotten him, any more than I have. Hussain's thinking of taking action against him for race discrimination.'

'Jesus wept,' Mower said. 'What do you want me to do about that? It sounds to me like a real can of worms.'

'I want to act as a witness for him,' Sharif said, his face set. 'You know how Mr Hutton behaved when he was in Bradfield. The man's not fit to be in the job.'

'I passed my exams two years ago,' Achmed said. 'And still he gives me all the crap jobs, no responsibility, no respect. You can put up with the jokes and the lack of co-operation but when your career's on the line it's too much.' Mower could see the anger in his dark, tired eyes.

'Were you in Arnedale long?' he asked, playing for time.

'A year,' Achmed said. 'I moved up there from Leeds when the CID vacancy came up. It looked like a better bet than waiting for a job in Leeds where everyone in CID looked like staying forever with their wives and their kids and their mortgages. At least I could move easily, not being married. I jumped at the chance, to be honest, but I might as well have stayed in uniform for all the real detective work I got from Hutton. I was stuck in the office most of the time, doing office-boy jobs, treated like muck.'

'But you two knew each other? Compared notes?' Mower was still trying to make sense of the relationship between the two disgruntled younger men.

'No, no, I moved up from Leeds to a bedsit in Arnedale. I went to school in Bradfield but I joined the job in Leeds. We never met before. It wasn't till Sharif belled me that I realised I wasn't on my own after all as far as Hutton was concerned. He'd been at it in Bradfield too.'

'DC Sharif thinks so,' Mower said non-committally.

'I know so,' Sharif said, angry himself now. 'And this looks like a chance to stop the bastard.'

'It won't do your career any good,' Mower said flatly. 'Hussain here seems to be out of it, so he can make as many waves as he likes, but if you want to get any further in the job, attacking a senior officer in public isn't the way to do it.'

Sharif stared at Mower for a moment with a mixture of anger and disbelief.

'I thought you were on my side,' he said at last. 'You saw what Hutton was like.'

'I know exactly what Hutton is like. I got a taste of it myself. And I've passed the message on. But quietly.'

'I'll talk to Mr Thackeray about it,' Sharif said. 'Our DCI,' he explained to Achmed. 'He's backed me every way he can since I made it into CID. He's one of the good guys.'

'Are there any good guys?' Achmed asked, his face twisting in anger. 'I don't think so.'

'He may be a good guy but he won't like you getting involved with what's gone on in another nick,' Mower said sharply. And especially not in Arnedale, he thought to himself. He foresaw nothing but trouble if DCI Hutton discovered anyone from Bradfield CID getting involved in complaints against him. As for Thackeray, whatever the justice of the young Asian's case, Mower knew with absolute certainty that he would be deeply unhappy with Sharif's – and potentially his own – involvement, for all sorts of complex reasons of his own.

'Have you talked to the Police Federation about this?' he asked Achmed.

'They'll back me. They think it's constructive dismissal – make it impossible to function in your job so you end up resigning,' Achmed said.

'Well, I can't tell you not to go ahead. But I think you both need to think very, very carefully about what you're getting into,' Mower said. 'Especially you, Omar. It could get very messy.'

He left the two of them simmering over their fruit juice and drove himself thoughtfully back into the town centre. He knew how deeply entrenched prejudice still was in parts of the police force, in spite of years of effort to eradicate it, and he sympathised completely with the victims of DCI Hutton's bullying. But his first loyalty was to Michael Thackeray, who had stood by him more than once when his own future had looked bleak. Thackeray would welcome conflict between Arnedale and Bradfield like an outbreak of plague, he thought. But given Hussain Achmed's outraged determination to get even, he could not see an easy way of preventing it.

Chapter Nine

Laura tracked Gareth Davies down to a tall, gabled Victorian terrace house close to the old industrial heart of Bradfield. A narrow strip of garden shaded by an overgrown laburnum tree, its pods still rattling forlornly in the chilly wind, separated the front of the house door with its stained glass inset and fading paintwork from the pavement. There was no gate and rubbish had blown in and piled up in a matted heap in the corner of the tiled porch.

At first she thought there was no one at home. As she waited she studied the miscellany of posters taped to the front window, advertising a range of events from a long-out-of-date demonstration against the Iraq war to a meeting of an ecological group concerned about the contamination of food by pesticides. After a fourth push on the doorbell she was about to turn away when she heard faint movements inside.

She pressed the bell-push one more time and waited until the vague shadow behind the coloured glass materialised into a small wiry man, with untidy brown hair and beard, who looked as if he had just pulled himself out of a deep sleep. He listened impassively while she explained who she was and what she wanted.

'So what's your interest in Stevie Fletcher?' he asked when she had finished, fingering a yellowing bruise on one side of his face. 'The *Bradfield Gazette*'s not exactly well known for its altruism where black kids are concerned.'

'Don't tar us all with the same brush,' Laura said sharply.

'Who are you, then? A female Clark Kent ready to put it all right? As if!' The man's expression remained deeply sceptical.

'Don't get me wrong,' Laura said quickly. 'My interest is partly professional. I do want to write about the case. But it's partly personal too. My grandmother's one of Woodlands' governors and she's extremely unhappy about the boy.'

'Aren't we all?' Davies said, his eyes unfreezing marginally. 'And especially me. I know Joyce Ackroyd, though. A
woman after my own heart. If you're Joyce's granddaughter,
you'd better come in, I suppose.'

He led her down a narrow hallway and into a living room
which stretched from the front of the house to the back. It
was comfortably if shabbily furnished, but what brought
Laura to a standstill in the doorway were the paintings which
were hung on almost every inch of wall and were stacked
against the walls and furniture. They were huge abstract can-
vasses which swirled in a riotous blaze of movement and
colour.

'Who said painting was dead?' she asked, stunned by the
spectacle. 'Are they yours?'

'My wife's,' Davies said, without obvious enthusiasm.
'She has an exhibition coming up in London. She's collecting things together for that.'

'She's very good,' Laura ventured. She could not think
where she had seen something similar before.

'So people say.' The artist's husband was evidently not
her greatest admirer. 'I'm the equivalent of tone deaf where
pictures are concerned. Folk music's more my scene.' Laura
forbore to ask how a man so immune to what was obviously his wife's passion in life had come to embark on marriage
with her.

'She might make an interview for my feature pages some
time,' she said neutrally. 'If you let me have the details of the
exhibition.'

'I'll tell her when I see her,' Davies said, as off-hand as if
talking about an acquaintance whose path seldom crossed
his own.

'But it was you I came to see,' Laura said quickly. 'Mary
Morris at Woodlands told me that you were the person who
saw Stevie Fletcher at the school the night the head was
killed.'

Davies flung himself into one of the sagging armchairs

covered with a worn but brilliant blue plush throw and groaned faintly. Laura noticed that his fingernails were bitten to the quick and tried hard to repress a slight shudder.

'I wish to God I'd never gone up there that night,' he said. 'It was a complete waste of time as far as I was concerned, and then I saw Stevie walking up the hill as I drove away. Of course I didn't realise it was significant until the next day when I heard about the murder on the local radio. I couldn't believe it.' He glanced away from Laura and began to gnaw on one of his already bitten nails.

'What couldn't you believe? That Peter Graves had been killed or that Stevie might have done it?' Laura asked.

'I don't want to be quoted on any of this,' Davies said sharply. 'Is that understood? I'm not even sure I should be talking to you before the trial. I've been told I'll probably have to appear as a witness.'

'Well, I might ask you to reconsider that when I come to write something,' Laura prevaricated. 'But that probably won't be until after the trial anyway. There are legal restrictions on what we can publish beforehand. We can't even identify Stevie at the moment. But OK, for now, let's talk off the record.' She took her tape-recorder out of her bag and placed it on the arm of the chair between them and switched it on. Davies glanced at it suspiciously but then shrugged slightly.

'You have to understand what a bastard Peter Graves was,' he said.

'I'm beginning to,' Laura said dryly. 'People keep telling me precisely that.'

'These are kids who've had everything go wrong for them. They've been abandoned, abused, impoverished. They're insecure, frightened, angry and sometimes mentally ill. I went into that sort of teaching to see if I could alleviate some of that. I know that's regarded as a bad career move these days: you don't get brownie points from the government or much cash in your pocket at the end of the day for devoting yourself to the rejects in the system. And it's getting worse, of course.'

'In what way?' Laura asked.

'Oh, you know. If kids don't or can't fit in they're being thrown out of primary school in case they damage the league table results. By secondary school they're written off by the mainstream, so for me going into special education seemed like the right thing to do at the time. Someone's got to try and put the pieces together again. And then along comes someone like Graves who doesn't actually give a shit for the kids. He's actually out to make a name for himself out of their problems, clambering on their backs, writing articles, expounding theories, getting himself onto committees, telling the powers that be what they want to hear. Yuck.'

Davies shifted irritably in his chair, felt in the pocket of his jeans and pulled out an evil looking pipe which he began to stuff with tobacco from a tin.

'It doesn't sound like a meeting of minds, you and him,' Laura said.

'He was just biding his time for an excuse to get rid of me in a way which wouldn't have the union on his neck. Stupidly I gave him the chance he needed and was out on my ear the same day.'

'You threatened him?' Laura asked.

'We got into a very public row over a boy who I think is verging on the schizophrenic. I didn't hit Peter, as it goes, but I raised a fist and that was enough. There were too many witnesses around. I knew I'd blown it.'

Gareth Davies stared moodily at one of his wife's paintings on the opposite wall for a moment before applying a match to his pipe and puffing furiously to get it going. Laura drew back to avoid the clouds of pungent smoke which drifted in her direction but it was obvious she was not in the company of a man who felt it necessary to apologise for smoking in his own house.

'It's terrifying how one moment of madness can muck up a perfectly normal life,' he said. He continued to puff energetically for a moment and Laura waited until the silence lengthened intolerably, but Davies evidently did not feel willing to expand on his regrets.

'This was Dwayne Elton, was it? The boy you were arguing over?'

'That's right,' Davies said, surprised. 'He's a lad with serious personality problems, the last kid you should rant and rave at because he's not obeyed some arbitrary rule. Graves was an insufferably stupid man.'

'But it was Stevie you saw that night, not Dwayne. Not the two of them, maybe?'

Davies looked at Laura, evidently horrified.

'Just Stevie,' he said. 'He was walking up the hill towards the school, and happened to be right under a street light as I passed. There was no mistake.'

'You wished there could have been?'

'Damn right I did,' Davies said bitterly. 'I could see all the preconceptions being confirmed in that bloody policeman's mind as I was making my statement: black lad, single parent, expelled from school, violence, arson, murder, you name it, that bastard Hutton had it all clicking into place almost before I'd opened my mouth. I wish to God I hadn't had to. And if your grandmother can find anything to clear the boy no one will be more pleased than me.'

'Why did you go to see Peter Graves that night?' Laura asked. 'Were you trying to get your job back?'

'That was one of the things we discussed,' Davies said, glancing at the bowl of his pipe as if the glowing embers would extricate him from the situation he hated.

'And was he sympathetic?'

'Let's just say he listened to what I had to say.'

'Will Mary Morris re-instate you now she's in charge?' Laura asked.

Davies looked at her sharply through the smoke from his pipe and smiled faintly.

'If you're looking for a motive why I might have bashed

Peter Graves over the head myself, you're barking up the wrong tree,' he said. 'I'm sure it crossed Chief Inspector Hutton's mind too, before I dropped sad Stevie into his lap, but it's a non-starter. Graves was alive and well when I left him in his office. In fact I think he was expecting another visitor, as it goes. He lives on the site so he often sees people at school in the evenings. One thing you couldn't accuse him of was not working hard enough. He spent far more time in his office after school hours than he ever did at home. It was just a pity that so much of that hard work was so bloody pernicious.'

'So how did you convince the police that you couldn't have killed him?' Laura asked, genuinely curious.

'Oh, that?' Davies said. 'His wife saw me drive off, apparently. She hovers around that lodge like a ghost a lot of the time, which on this occasion was lucky for me. Anyway, she saw me go and called him by phone for some reason. I was back here at nine thirty and at nine thirty Peter Graves was alive and well and slagging his wife off down the phone.'

'With Stevie Fletcher by this time allegedly lurking in the bushes somewhere outside the school clutching a can of petrol? Did you see him carrying the can, by the way?'

'No I didn't,' Davies said vehemently. 'And that's what makes me think the police have got it wrong. As far as I could see Stevie Fletcher wasn't carrying anything at all.'

'You told the police that?'

'Of course I did. They went on and on trying to convince me I was mistaken, but I wasn't. He didn't even look furtive, come to think of it. He was just marching up the middle of the pavement, as if he hadn't a care in the world.'

'You like Stevie?' Laura hazarded, aware that Davies's expression had softened as he talked about the boy. He glanced away but could not entirely disguise the pain he evidently felt.

'I do like Stevie. He's a bright lad, a bit volatile but he's fine if he's handled sensibly. He shouldn't be at Woodlands at all, of course, and if he was white he wouldn't be. Some of the white teachers in mainstream schools haven't a clue about handling black lads. It's a bloody disgrace the number of them they expel.'

'That's what his mother says,' Laura said thoughtfully. 'Was Peter Graves a racist?'

'Not overtly,' Davies said. 'But then he was far too canny to do anything politically incorrect.'

'But?' Laura prompted.

'Yeah, there was a but with Graves,' Davies said, knocking quantities of smelly black debris from his pipe into an ashtray. Laura wondered what colour his lungs were.

'It's difficult to put a finger on it,' Davies went on. 'There was just a feeling that he despised some people. Certainly black and Asian kids. But other people as well, actually. I certainly fell into that category. He once said I was "one of those hippy Sixties idealists who had mucked the country up." I quote.' Davies grinned unexpectedly. 'I wasn't born till 1963, for God's sake. A bit late for the Beatles, though I have to admit that unlike Bill Clinton, when I got around to it, I did inhale.'

'Me, too,' Laura said cheerfully.

But as she got up to go she heard the front door open and close. She was aware that Davies had clenched his pipe hard between his teeth as the living room door opened and a woman in a long black skirt and loose burnt orange shirt of some silky material came in.

'My wife Ella,' Davies said as bright, dark eyes beneath a tangle of wild black curls flashed hostility first in Laura's direction and then in Gareth Davies's. He explained who Laura was and she was granted another hostile stare.

'Don't let me get in your way,' Ella said dismissively. 'I only popped in to pick up some books for my class this evening.'

'Ella...', Davies began, but she had already gone, slamming the living room door behind her and running up the stairs two at a time.

'I'm sorry,' Davies said. 'Things have been a bit difficult since I lost my job...'

'I'll get out of your way,' Laura said. 'But I just wanted to say that my grandmother's trying to launch a campaign to help Stevie Fletcher and his mother. Can I tell her she can get in touch?'

'It's the least I can do,' Davies said sombrely. 'I'm having nightmares about what I've done to that kid.'

As Laura got into her car, she was surprised to see Ella Davies follow her out of the front door and slam it behind her. She glanced at Laura for a moment before coming over to speak to her through the open window.

'I hope these campaigners don't think they can implicate Gareth in what went on up at the school that night,' Ella said grimly.

'It sounds as if Julia Graves has got him off the hook,' Laura said neutrally.

'Bloody Julia,' Ella said unexpectedly, and suddenly Laura made the connection.

'You're her art teacher,' she said.

'For my sins,' Ella said. 'At least I've weaned her off the Christmas card tat she was working on when she first came to my class at the college.'

'She's got your painting in pride of place at the lodge,' Laura said, able to place the swirling abstract with its companions now she had seen more of Ella's *oeuvre*. 'Shows some taste, I guess.'

'Bloody hell, I must go up there and persuade her to lend me that for the exhibition,' Ella said abstractedly. 'I'd almost forgotten she'd got it. She had it stashed in her studio for ages out of Peter's sight. Peter wasn't a fan of my work, as it goes.'

Laura drove home thoughtfully and to her surprise discovered Thackeray's car already parked outside the flats. As she walked up the steps to the front door, she hesitated for a

moment before putting her key in the lock, half aware of
something moving in the garden at the side of the tall
Victorian house, but when she scanned the overgrown rho-
dodendrons and viburnums which formed an impenetrable
jungle between the neighbouring gardens she could see
nothing and hear nothing more.

Thackeray was slumped in an armchair reading that
afternoon's *Gazette* when she walked in. He glanced up as
she dumped shopping in the kitchen and flung her jacket
onto the bed. She came up behind him and kissed him on the
neck.

'You're early,' she said superfluously, unable to judge his
mood.

'I was just reading your grandmother's opening salvo,'
he said. 'She's called a public meeting to set up a defence
committee for this boy Fletcher.'

'Yes, I know,' Laura said. 'I told Ted Grant to get someone else to cover it as it's so close to home for me.'

'Too bloody close for me, too,' Thackeray said.

Laura drew back, stung into anger with an abruptness
which surprised them both. 'I'm not Joyce's keeper,' she said.
'You know she'll do what she likes.'

'Like all the Ackroyd women,' Thackeray said, and the
anger was evident in his voice too.

'What's that supposed to mean?' Laura demanded.

'Kevin Mower mentioned the other day that you'd been
picking his brains about the case while I was away. That's
not on, Laura. You can't abuse your position like that.'

'What position would that be, Chief Inspector?' Laura
asked in a silkily sweet tone that should have warned
Thackeray that he had gone too far.

'You know what I mean. It puts me in an embarrassing
position, Kevin in an impossible one.'

'Oh, sod that, Michael. You know what this is about. It's
too important to let that sort of claptrap get in the way of
the truth. If that boy didn't do it...'

'If that boy didn't do it the jury will have the opportunity to acquit him.' Thackeray's face was cold and closed now but Laura was too furious to notice.

'And we all know how often it doesn't work like that if the accused just happens to be black. The more people I talk to about this case, Michael, the more convinced I am that it's all wrong. Stevie Fletcher is just too convenient an answer. There are all sorts of leads which don't seem to have ever been followed up by your colleagues.'

'Then tell his lawyer. But leave me and Kevin out of it. It's not our responsibility now. It's down to the CPS and the defence.' Thackeray recalled Superintendent Longley's chilly disdain when he had raised doubts about the case out of what he now regarded as misplaced loyalty to Laura and Joyce.

'There are things the police don't seem to have passed on to the defence,' Laura said, knowing that the accusation was a dangerous one with Thackeray in his present unreceptive mood. 'I thought they were supposed to share their evidence.'

'Only if it's relevant. Get his lawyer to talk to the disclosure officer,' Thackeray said. 'It's Jenny Sweetman, isn't it? She knows how it works, Laura. It really doesn't need your input.'

'You think I'm wasting my time?'

'I didn't say that.'

'No, but you meant it,' she snapped.

For a second they looked at each other in mute incomprehension until they were interrupted by Thackeray's mobile. He listened for a moment before thanking the caller abruptly and ending the call.

'I'm sorry,' he said. 'I'll have to go out again. Something urgent's cropped up. Don't wait up for me. I may be very late.'

After he had slammed the door behind him Laura stood at the window and watched him get into his car and drive away down the hill without a backward glance. She unclenched her fists and dashed a tear from her cheek in irritation, wondering what it was which had frozen Thackeray so completely that he had not even offered her the briefest kiss on leaving.

'Damn and blast you,' she said aloud, and with her eyes blurred, she was still unsure whether a slight movement she noticed in the shadows outside the window was merely the cat from next door or something else as she drew the heavy curtains closed.

Thackeray drove into town much faster than he ought to have done and parked in a no-parking zone outside the infirmary. He went quickly through reception and made his way in one of the huge lifts to Ward 7. As soon as he had made himself known, a senior nurse led him into the ward where half a dozen patients, hooked up to the complex machinery of modern medicine, lay in semi-darkness, most of them either unconscious or asleep, it was impossible to tell. He barely recognised Aileen. Her hair, still as fair as it had always been with no sign of grey, had been scraped back from her broad forehead, and her face was an unhealthy putty colour, with touches of blue around the mouth and nose. Her eyes were closed and she seemed oblivious to the monitors and drips and tubes to which she was attached, and to the nurse and doctor who were busying themselves around her bed. Thackeray's attendant nurse signalled to the young woman doctor, who turned towards him. She was a slim Asian woman with dark circles under her eyes and what Thackeray suspected might be a permanent frown of anxiety.

'Mr Thackeray,' she said, shaking his hand. 'I'm glad you could come so quickly. We're very worried about Aileen at the moment. She's had a severe heart attack, I'm afraid. We're doing our best but I'm not completely optimistic about the outcome.'

Thackeray swallowed hard, knowing his furious wish to

pull Aileen away from all this machinery and let nature take its course would shock these women to the core.

'Is she conscious?' he asked.

'She has been, but she keeps drifting away,' the doctor said. 'You're welcome to stay with her for as long as you wish. There's no more that we can do at the moment but of course she is being closely monitored by the nursing staff. They'll call me if there's any change in her condition.'

'You know she's been a sectioned patient at Long Moor for years?' Thackeray asked.

'Yes, of course, we've been fully informed about her problems. She's very very weak now, so there shouldn't be any difficulties for us in treating her at the moment.' The doctor glanced at Thackeray with a weary sympathy that he found almost intolerable to bear. 'I'm sorry,' she said.

When the medical team had moved on Thackeray slumped into the chair beside Aileen's bed and gazed at the woman who was technically still his wife, although his divorce proceedings were nearing their conclusion. Her podgy arms lay outside the bed coverings and her night gown, pulled well down to allow space for the tubes and wires which linked her to the life-supporting machinery around her, exposed soft billowy breasts, a half revealed nipple flat and blue against the white skin. The ties of the oxygen mask through which she breathed distorted her face and her eyes were closed, flickering occasionally. She was, he thought, a complete stranger, with no trace left of the slim, attractive young woman he had married all those years ago. He supposed that the hospital would not have notified Aileen's parents as he was still technically her next-of-kin and he realised, with horror, that this was something he would have to do himself, indeed should probably have done by now.

Aileen's parents had moved away from Arnedale some years before and he knew that he might have difficulty finding their address and phone number. They were the two people he had perhaps least wanted to see in the dozen or so years since Aileen's suicide attempt and their last meeting across a hospital bed where their daughter's life had also hung in the balance. Then, Thackeray, consumed with grief for his son and a cataclysmic anger with himself and Aileen, had hardly bothered to conceal his wish that she should not recover. And she had not recovered in any meaningful way, and he had suffered the anger and reproach of two sets of grandparents for the loss of their golden grandson entirely alone. He thought for a moment that Aileen's breathing had become more laboured and glanced around in panic for the nurse before he decided that he must be mistaken. He sighed. This latest turn of events, he thought, would revive all that bitterness, all those memories, not so much for him, who had hardly known a day since Ian's death without regret, but for those who had perhaps come to accept if not forgive what had happened.

He was not really aware of how long he had sat watching Aileen's bloated frame rise and fall gently beneath the covers until the duty nurse approached softly and put a hand on his shoulder.

'There's been no change, Mr Thackeray,' she said. 'If I were you I'd go home and get some sleep. It's gone midnight. You can come back as early as you like in the morning.'

Thackeray rubbed his knuckles across his eyes wearily. He knew the nurse was right, but even the prospect of getting to his feet seemed too much for him. With an effort he pushed himself upright and made his way like an automaton through the sleeping hospital and out again through the main doors. He crumpled up the parking ticket which jeered at him from his windscreen and sat at the wheel for a moment with his eyes closed. He wanted Laura desperately, and yet could not bear to burden her with this ugly detritus from a past which still tormented him with shame and guilt. Sometimes he dared to believe that Laura was his future and he did not want these two conflicting worlds to touch. In any case, he assured himself as he started the car and turned south out of the town centre towards his own flat, he had things to do at his own place.

Although he had shared Laura's flat for months now, he had not yet sold the small utilitarian apartment in a modern block which he had bought when he first came to Bradfield to work. He opened the front door and was greeted with the musty smell of stale air and a hall light which had ceased to function. Had he paid the last electricity bill, he wondered, as he tripped over a pile of post inside the door. He gathered it up in the dim light from the communal landing and to his relief found that the living room light responded to the switch. He dumped the letters on the dining table, put the kettle on in the kitchen and hunted through the cupboards for a tea bag, sugar and a can of evaporated milk. That done, he fumbled through the jumble of documents in the drawers of a small desk under the window and eventually found an address book in which he had jotted his parents-in-law's new address near Newcastle.

He glanced at his watch. It was twelve-thirty in the morning. Ring now, he thought, and they would be able to set off early and perhaps be in time to see their daughter alive. Leave it until daybreak and they might be too late. With reluctant fingers he dialled the number and waited patiently for the phone at the other end to rouse someone from their bed. How many times, he wondered, in his career had he been the bearer of unbearable tidings. It came with the territory. He should be inured too it by now. But this was different. This was personal and it hurt almost as much as that other time he had had to tell his father-in-law the worst news possible.

'Duncan?' he said, when the phone was finally picked up at the other end. 'Duncan, it's Michael. I'm sorry to wake you but I thought you'd want to know...'

Duncan Mackie listened to what Thackeray told him in a silence which continued for some time after his son-in-law had finished speaking.

'I'll tell mother in the morning,' he said at last. 'She'll want to be there, I know that.'

'If you need me to find you somewhere to stay...?'

'No, that won't be necessary, I shouldn't think,' Duncan Mackie said, his voice as unemotional as Thackeray remembered it had always been, even when he had directed the most bitter accusations his way, quiet, steely and devastating. 'We'll make our own arrangements,' he said.

'Do you have my mobile number?'

'Aye, I think we have that.' And he hung up without anything in the nature of a farewell.

Thackeray flung himself into the single armchair and gazed around the bare and dusty room in despair. The craving for a drink which had tormented him all evening was at its strongest now and he was thankful that there was no alcohol in the flat and that it would be almost impossible to buy any as late as this. Even in his desperation he balked at slinking into a nightclub and drinking himself into oblivion in public. He drank his half-cold tea and replayed the evening in his mind, wondering how he could face the Mackies across Aileen's bed if they happened to be there at the same time as he was himself. Best to avoid that if possible, he thought. Best to check their movements before he went back to Ward 7 himself. Best to slink away like a whipped dog rather than face those accusing eyes yet again across the wreck of their daughter probably breathing her last. He put his head in his hands and pressed his eyes hard to keep the tears back.

'Ian,' he whispered aloud. 'How could I have not have noticed what was happening? How could anyone have been so blind?'

Laura got up late the following morning. Thackeray had not come home at all the previous night which was unusual although not completely unprecedented since he had ostensibly moved in with her permanently. He still had his own place and sometimes used it if he had been working so late that he decided not to disturb her. Fortunately she was not due in the office until ten as Thackeray's absence meant that he had not set the alarm for its customary seven o'clock call. She had slept badly, falling into bed after too many vodka and tonics and reaching out in the night into the empty space beside her. She cursed herself and Thackeray roundly as she stood up and a thumping headache cut in. She was still standing in the kitchen nursing a mug of black coffee when the phone rang.

'This is Mary Morris at Woodlands School.' The voice was piercing and full of anger and Laura held the receiver away from her ear to protect herself.

'How could you do that? How could you betray a confidence like that?' Mary went on with hardly a pause for breath. 'I thought we could trust you. I thought you were different, but it turns out all reporters are bastards just as I suspected.'

'Just a minute,' Laura said, irritated by the headteacher's tone. 'I've absolutely no idea what you're talking about.'

'Come on, Laura,' Mary said. 'Don't tell me you don't know about it. I've just been talking to your grandmother. She's just as appalled at what's happened as I am, although she seems to think you couldn't be involved...'

'Involved in what?' Laura interrupted, trying desperately to collect her scattered wits. 'What on earth am I supposed to have done?'

'You mean you don't know that your so-called education reporter at the *Gazette* has got hold of the inspectors' report and is planning to put it in today's paper? Joyce told me that she'd told you what was in the report. She thought she could trust you too?'

'I haven't been into the office since mid-afternoon yesterday,' Laura said carefully, keeping her temper in check. 'I've no idea what's been going on there. And I'm certainly not responsible for what our education person gets up to.'

'He rang me this morning, Martin something-or-other, wanting to confirm the details, all that stuff about unsatisfactory teaching and learning, slack management, a failing school and all the rest of it, and I know you knew about it because Joyce said she told you. So how else did he find out? If that's splashed all over the *Gazette* before we've had chance to talk to the inspectors about it, we're done for. It's just the excuse they've been looking for to close us down.' Mary Morris's torrent of words trailed away as the implications of what had happened, which Laura knew were only too credible, seemed to overwhelm her at the other end of the line.

'I'm on my way into the office now,' Laura said, glad that Mary could not see her still in her pyjamas, pale-faced and hungover, her unruly hair tangled and unbrushed. 'I'll see what I can find out for you. The first edition doesn't go to Press until midday. But I promise you, wherever Martin Bates has got his information from, it wasn't from me. I haven't spoken to Martin for days.'

'Oh, come on Laura,' Mary said with bitter weariness now. 'How else could he had got hold of the details?'

'I don't know, but I think you should do a check on your enemies before you start accusing your friends,' Laura said sharply. 'Joyce did tell me about the report. She also told me that it was very different from what you'd been led to expect and persuaded me to try to find out why. That's as far as it's got so far. It's not the sort of thing I can investigate overnight.'

'But you can get it into your paper overnight, can't you?' Mary came back quickly, though her voice was calmer now and Laura wondered if perhaps she could detect the beginnings of a hint of doubt in it.

'I could, if I wanted to, but that was the last thing on my mind,' she said.

'Laura, someone's out to get us,' Mary said, and there was a definite note of appeal there now.

'Oh, yes,' Laura agreed. 'Someone's certainly out to get you, and they don't seem too worried about the methods they use.'

'You don't think the murder...?'

'I think that's a bit farfetched as a conspiracy theory, even for some of the nimbiest of your neighbours,' Laura said. The coffee seemed to be having an effect at last and her headache was subsiding from pneumatic drill mode to drum-and-bass thump. 'But think about who else can have had sight of that report, will you? Call me later at the office, say about eleven-thirty, and I'll let you know exactly what's going on there. In the meantime say nothing to anyone, especially not reporters. I'll see if I can show you I'm the exception that proves the rule that a lot of them are as trustworthy as a fox in a hen-house.'

What puzzled Laura as, half an hour later, she drove into the *Gazette*'s car park and slid the Golf into a space next to Ted Grant's shiny new BMW was that she had never classed Martin Bates as one of the foxes. Pale, slim and serious behind fashionably tiny oval spectacles, with cropped blond hair and an unassuming smile, he was one of the graduate trainees who had recently joined the paper in the same way that she had some ten years earlier. Straight from his journalism course, he appeared to be taking his responsibilities almost too seriously.

Still feeling only precariously in charge of her faculties, she slipped into the newsroom and took stock as she hung up her jacket by the door. Most of the workstations were occupied at this time in the morning by her colleagues, all of whom seemed totally preoccupied with the words on their computer screens as the clock ticked towards the first dead-line of the day.

The door to Ted Grant's cubicle was firmly closed and she could see through the frosted glass that he was deep in conversation. At this time of day, it was probably with the production editor who was responsible for the final shape of the news pages which had been kept clear for the morning's latest stories. Their discussion of the shape of the day's paper, and in particular the front page splash headline, should keep them occupied for some time yet, Laura thought thankfully. Grant would not be best pleased to dis-cover that she was attempting to scupper what was undoubt-edly a good story.

She walked slowly over to Martin Bates, whose fingers were flying over the keyboard in front of him, his eyes on the screen, oblivious to anything which was going on around him. For a moment she stood behind him, reading what he was writing and feeling increasingly sick as she realised that Mary Morris's worst fears were true. Suddenly becoming aware that he was being watched, Martin spun round in his chair.

'Oh, hi,' he said. 'I was hoping you'd be in this morning. I wanted to pick your brains about this story I'm doing about Woodlands School. Ted said you'd been up there recently. When I rang them I got short shrift from the act-ing head. A real dragon, she sounds. Have you met her?'

Laura took a deep breath before she replied. She did not want to antagonise Martin who was, after all, only doing his job. At his age she would have been just as pleased as he evi-dently was to have an exclusive leak land on the desk. On the other hand she guessed both he and the newspaper were being used in an increasingly unpleasant political game and if that was so the *Gazette*'s readers needed to know about that too.

'Yes, I heard that you'd got hold of the inspectors' report,' she said. 'In fact, I was accused of breaking a confi-dence to give it to you.'

'You knew about it?' Martin asked, evidently surprised at this turn of events.

'Only off the record. And only yesterday afternoon,' Laura said. 'I assume someone's given you the whole draft?'

'Well, yes,' Martin said uncertainly, obviously thrown by her use of the word draft. 'It came in the proverbial brown envelope. No indication where from.'

'But you've checked it's genuine?'

'The inspectors wouldn't comment, said the top man was away. But they were obviously furious that it had leaked. Said we should wait for the final version in four weeks time.'

'So who would comment?' Laura asked, and was surprised by the answer.

'I spoke to Councillor Jeremy Waite.'

'Ah, yes, our esteemed holder of the education portfolio.' Laura made sure that Martin did not miss the scepticism in her voice. 'And who happens to be very keen to see Woodlands closed down, though he daren't quite say so publicly yet. What did he say about this alleged report.' Martin glanced down at his shorthand notebook on the desk beside him.

'He said that if it's accurate, he would have to think very carefully about what steps to take next at Woodlands,' he said cautiously. Then his voice trailed away as he realised the implication of what Waite had told him and a look of anxiety eclipsed the excitement with which he had greeted Laura.

'*If* it's accurate? But he didn't confirm that it was accurate?' Laura asked quietly. Martin shook his head.

'No,' the reporter said. 'He said I must confirm it with the inspectors. And they're saying nothing.'

'You must get confirmation,' Laura said urgently. 'Mary Morris says it's a travesty of what she was told would be in it. The whole thing could be a fake, a put-up job by people who want the school closed. They seem to be ruthless enough and they know very well how mud sticks. Even if the final report is less damning the damage may well have been done by then.'

'Oh, hell,' Martin said, his face crumpling like a disappointed schoolboy who has been told he has been dropped from the football team. 'What d'you think I should do?'

'Does Ted want to use it today?'

'Front page lead,' Martin said miserably.

'If it's a forgery you'll cost the paper a fortune in libel damages and Ted'll have you on your bike so fast you won't have time to pick up your P45,' Laura said flatly.

'Help!' Martin said faintly.

'Look on the bright side,' Laura said with her best attempt at a motherly smile. 'If it *is* a forgery and you can prove it is, that's an even better story. And I can think of at least two groups of eminently respectable citizens who are clever enough, and hate Woodlands enough, to try it on. But first you'll have to tell Ted that you can't get any corroboration and he'd best not run it today. OK? Emphasise just how expensive it might be if you get it wrong. He'll buy that, though he won't thank you for it. Then get in touch with those inspectors and push them harder. They won't want a scandal around their work, if you put it to them that way. And if they confirm that what you've got is not what they wrote, you're on your way to the real villains.'

'Is it often like this?' Martin asked faintly, glancing in the direction of Ted Grant's office.

'Not every day,' Laura said cheerfully. 'Go on. It's not as bad as having him discover tomorrow that we've libelled a school full of angry teachers.' Although when she had returned to her desk and logged on to her own computer, and caught the roar of rage from the editor's office which had evidently greeted Martin Bates's bad news, she wondered if she had been right. If nothing else, she thought, she owed Martin a large drink after work tonight.

DCI Michael Thackeray had slept as badly as Laura in his own chilly and unwelcoming bed and had got to work just as

late. One of the unexpected side effects of his edgy relationship with Laura had been that the nightmares, which had
plagued him for years, had receded and eventually released
him for weeks and sometimes months at a time. He might
not have absolved himself for the death of his son, but it
seemed that some god in which he no longer had any faith
might finally have stopped tormenting him.

But not the previous night when he had found himself
struggling against tangled bedclothes which had metamor-
phosed into demons he had thought long buried, and then
pacing around his room in the early hours craving a drink
that might dull the agony with its treacherous promises of a
lasting peace. As the morning light filtered through the curtains he had wondered how early he dare call Laura and try
to patch together a truce. But as he had watched the minute
hand of his alarm crawl round to seven he knew that he had
nothing to offer her that he could not have offered the night
before, and nothing, with Laura in her present mood, was
not worth talking about. And with all the tension between
them he could not even begin to imagine how he could tell
her about Aileen's sudden deterioration and the emotions it
had stirred. Eventually he had switched off the alarm and
dozed back into an exhausted sleep.

When he finally arrived at work, he sat at his desk for a
good ten minutes, smoke drifting in a cloud around him as
he lit one cigarette after another and stubbed them out half
finished. When the phone on his desk eventually rang he
considered not picking it up but then forced himself to
respond and listen to Superintendent Jack Longley demanding his presence in his office with an unaccustomed touch of
steel in his voice. When he presented himself upstairs,
Longley waived him into a chair and gazed at him for a
moment in some astonishment.

'What the hell's happened to you?' he asked. 'You look
like death warmed up.'

'I'm fine,' Thackeray muttered, not wanting to encourage

any speculation on his private life. 'What's the problem?'

'DCI Charlie Hutton's the problem,' Longley said. 'I've had him blasting my ear off for half an hour already this morning about the apparent shortcomings of Bradfield CID in general, which he seems to lay at your door, and about Kevin Mower in particular. Neither of you, in his view, seem to have any place in his ideal police service. Specifically he wants to know if either of you sent an officer snooping round Arnedale looking for what he described as a useless effing Paki officer who was lucky to get away with resigning before he was sacked.'

'What?' Thackeray said explosively. 'What the hell is that all about?'

'You don't know?'

'I have no idea,' Thackeray said. 'I've not sent anyone to Arnedale. It's the last place I'd want to stir up trouble.'

'Quite,' Longley said dryly. 'I told Hutton it was a bit farfetched. But what about Mower? Is he up to something on his own account? Something he hasn't got around to telling you about? I heard on the grapevine he didn't think much of Hutton. Thought he was a racist and you know that's a touchy subject with him, particularly since he lost that Indian lass he fancied. Or is this something to do with the Graves case and the campaign to get the lad we've charged off? Is Mower unhappy with the result? Does he think Hutton got that wrong?'

'He certainly didn't like Hutton or what he reckoned were his prejudices,' Thackeray admitted. 'But I can't see him running round the county trying to even up that score. He's not that stupid. And anyway he seemed to think Hutton played it by the book with Stephen Fletcher, said he couldn't fault the interviews – and you can be pretty sure he'd have complained to me if he'd been unhappy about it.'

'The CPS is satisfied with the evidence?' Longley asked.

'They've asked me to chase up a few loose ends. Nothing significant, I don't think,' Thackeray said.

'Aye, well, let me know if anything changes. And see if you can find out who's pissing DCI Hutton off. We really don't want to waste time on turf wars of that sort. We've enough on our plates as it is.'

'Sir,' Thackeray said and turned to go, leaving Superintendent Longley still wondering why his mind seemed to be only half on his job.

Laura picked up the phone on her desk.

'Princess?' said a voice which she half recognised. 'A call from the past. Ye've not forgotten me?'

Laura smiled in spite of herself.

'How could I possible forget you, Fergal? How's it going?'

'Ach, ye ken what they say about local papers,' Fergal Mackenzie, the editor of the *Arnedale Observer* said in his inimitable and, she suspected, carefully cultivated Scots brogue. Laura could imagine the mischievous gleam in the eyes of one of the hairiest and most irreverent men she knew. 'In the good old days it used to be hatch, match and dispatch. These days it's feuding, fornication and fraud.'

'You're having a good time, then?'

'Terrific,' Mackenzie said and Laura knew he meant it. She had briefly occupied the editor's chair in Arnedale herself when the company which owned the *Observer* and the *Bradfield Gazette* had decided that it was time to drag the dull and sycophantic little newspaper into the modern world, not least because Mackenzie was unearthing scandals in the town that the *Observer* had seen fit to ignore on a freelance basis and winning readers for his free sheet. Fergal Mackenzie had almost died for his pains and Laura had watched the way he had modernised and sharpened the Arnedale paper in the following few years with some satisfaction after she had turned the permanent job down and he had taken over the vacant chair.

'So, what can I do for you?' she asked.

Mackenzie seemed to hesitate for a moment which was unusual for him.

'Are ye still with Prince Charming, Princess?' he asked. 'Your deeply dour detective?'

Laura felt herself hesitate for a second and knew that Fergal would not miss the beat.

'Just about hanging in there,' she said truthfully. 'Why do you ask?'

'It may be nothing,' Mackenzie said. 'I bumped into some of our local CID in the Bull the other night and ended up matching Scotch for Scotch with the DCI long after closing time.' He laughed. 'He thinks he's got a head for it.'

Laura had no doubt that Fergal the professional Scotsman could hold his own with any Yorkshireman when it came to his national drink.

'And?' she asked quietly.

'Got a bit garrulous, he did, and bent my ear for at least an hour,' Mackenzie said. 'He's a deeply racist bastard, by the way, which is something I'll be following up if I can. He seems to have just got rid of his only Asian detective and I want to find out exactly how that happened. But he also told me he's just spent some time in Bradfield, which he seems to regard as some sort of multiracial hellhole, and that's how your man's name came up. He obviously didn't realise I knew you and your inspector Thackeray.'

'What's his problem?' Laura asked, her mouth slightly dry.

'Oh, I think Charlie Hutton has a lot of problems,' Mackenzie said thoughtfully. 'Not least wanting to be called Len in honour of some long dead sporting hero. A wee bit sad, that. But I think the relevant problem in this case is ambition. He wants your man's job and he's picked up something about what happened to him in Arnedale which leads him to think he can get it by blowing Michael Thackeray out of the water.'

Laura drew a sharp breath.

'Any idea how he's planning to do the blowing, exactly?'

'He was getting a wee bit garbled by that stage in the conversation,' Mackenzie said. 'But he obviously knew what had happened to his family and that he'd been a bit too fond of the hard stuff.'

'Michael's lived all that down long ago,' Laura said, wanting to believe it.

'Well, something seems to have set the *tricoteuses* of Arnedale off again,' Mackenzie said. 'They're gathering round the guillotine and Hutton knew far too much about what happened when your man's wee bairn died. Either he's been digging or someone else has been dishing the dirt for some reason of their own. Either way, I'd tell your man to mind his back, if I were you. Hutton's a nasty bit of work.'

'Keep me in touch, Fergal,' Laura said, feeling sick.

'You know I will, Princess,' Mackenzie said. 'Take care.'

The *Gazette* had appeared that afternoon without the story which Martin Bates had hoped to write about the Woodlands school's inspection report. But by mid-afternoon Laura knew that her efforts to protect Mary Morris and her staff had been futile. Ted Grant was not a man who ever disguised his displeasure and she heard him heading in her direction long before he had threaded his way through the close-packed desks and dropped a sheet of paper unceremoniously onto her keyboard.

'So how come these beggars can get away with it, then?' he asked, his face still flushed after his lunchtime session and his eyes alive with fury. Laura picked up the bright blue leaflet with a sinking feeling in her stomach. It was the latest barrage in the Close Woodlands School Campaign's war of attrition against the school and claimed in block capital letters that the Ofsted inspectors had decided that it was a 'failing school'.

Laura glanced up at her boss, whose large and steamy presence kept a barely supportable distance half an inch from her shoulder.

'They're taking a chance, aren't they?' she said. 'And it'd be very interesting to know how they got hold of this unconfirmed report, wouldn't it? The same way we did, I suppose. A plain brown envelope. Someone's playing some very nasty games with those kids.' And Mary Morris was probably on a hiding to nothing in trying to keep her school alive, Laura thought, as Ted continued to breath heavily down her neck.

'I'll get the bloody thing confirmed,' Ted said angrily, spinning on his heel. 'I'll talk to the effing inspectors myself. Martin!' His bellow across the newsroom made Martin Bates visibly jump in his chair and turn a pale and anxious face towards the eye of the tornado which seemed to be bearing down on him.

'My office!' Grant yelled and Bates scuttled to the glass cubicle ahead of his boss.

'Bastard,' Laura muttered to herself as she glanced again at the leaflet Grant had left on her desk. Issued by the Campaign it included no address, merely the name and phone number of Mark Oliver, whom she already knew lived in Woodlands Road. Glancing cautiously at Ted Grant's now tightly closed door, she dialled the number.

'Mrs Oliver?' she asked when a woman answered. She identified herself. 'I'd like to come and talk to your husband about the Woodlands Campaign,' she said in her least threatening tones. 'Would some time this evening be OK?' Without apparently giving the matter much thought, Mrs Oliver agreed on her husband's behalf. Laura could hear a TV on in the background and wondered what Mrs Oliver did with herself all day.

Left to her own devices in the empty office at the end of the day, without enough time to go home before her appointment, Laura trawled the Internet to find out more about the property company which she had already discovered from the Land Registry owned the Woodlands site. A call to the headquarters of Freeland Properties in Leeds had confirmed the bare facts but she had met the stonewall of an unhelpful public relations executive when she had tried to find out how long Bradfield's education department's lease on the property lasted. The education department's Press office had proved just as unhelpful.

An Internet site offering company profiles was more revealing, and she printed out some details of the company's financial performance for future reference. As she scrolled down the screen, she became more alert. A link to the site of a business magazine provided the snippet that Freeland might be in some sort of financial trouble. What effect would that have, she wondered, on its plans for the valuable Woodlands School site?

By six o'clock she had compiled a small file on Freeland

Properties and she tucked it thoughtfully into the bottom drawer of her desk. As she slipped into her jacket she glanced at the phone. Michael Thackeray had not contacted her all day and she guessed that he would still be in his office, less than half a mile away but at the moment separated by a chasm which felt as deep as the Grand Canyon. She desperately wanted to tell him what Fergal Mackenzie had told her about his colleague in Arnedale, but she didn't think he would welcome that sort of news at work. She hesitated for a moment, her hand on the receiver, and then shrugged wearily. There were times when she wondered whether their turbulent affair would ever navigate into calm waters. This time, she thought, she would leave it to him to make the first move towards a reconciliation. It was time he made up his mind where he thought they were going.

Sergeant Kevin Mower had also spent a large part of the afternoon wondering where Michael Thackeray was heading and, even more urgently, whether he wanted to follow him there. The DCI had called him into his office as soon as he had returned from his meeting with Superintendent Longley that morning and explained what he wanted him to do.

'The lad could have nicked the petrol from a lockup or a shed, guv,' Mower objected, reasonably enough. 'It's not the sort of thing he would have risked buying from a garage. Nor would any arsonist, when you think of it.'

'So it's a long shot,' Thackeray said. 'But it's only ten days ago, so the garages may well have hung onto their video tapes.'

Mower knew that there was no point in arguing with Thackeray in his present intractable mood but by the time he had drawn a blank at the third garage of the half dozen which lay on a direct route between the Heights, where Stevie Fletcher lived, and Southfield where Peter Graves had been killed, his anger had crystallised into something close to a burning resentment for the time he was wasting. The wild goose chase he was sure he was on could only be the fault of Laura Ackroyd, he thought uncharitably, as he drew up at garage number four, an extensive forecourt on the main road out of town to the west.

But this time he struck lucky as the manager pulled a jumble of tapes from a shelf.

'The camera's been on the blink for a week,' he said. 'Otherwise we'd have taped over anything as old as that. We don't get many people filling containers these days. It's not as if many people run out of juice and carry a can in the boot like they used to do. It's only the lawnmower trade. Here, there's the 24th – was that the day you mentioned?'

Mower nodded. That was the day Graves had died.

'What about the day before, and the day before that? Are they still there?'

The manager banged half a dozen tapes down on the counter.

'D'you want to take them all away to look at? I'm just going off duty.' Mower picked up the tapes ungraciously. At least they were dated, he thought, but they threatened him with hours of unproductive viewing of fuzzy images as an endless stream of motorists had come and gone over several days and nights.

He drew another blank at the final two garages on his list, and went back to police HQ to run through the slim haul he had been given, stopping for a large Scotch on the way to what he knew would be a boring few hours in front of a video screen. It was more than an hour before he struck gold: three customers had each filled a plastic can with petrol on the couple of days before the murder, and although the figures at the pumps were hardly recognisable, thanks to the garage's focus on car registration numbers in case drivers did a runner, he had ill three legible number plates to run through the police computer.

'Well, there's a turn-up,' he said when the answers to his vehicle checks also came up on his computer screen. The owner of one of the cars, a dark-coloured Volvo estate, was a Ferdinand Boston of Woodlands Road, Southfield.

'Now I wonder why you went so far afield to get your lawnmower petrol,' Mower muttered to himself as he made his way back into the deserted CID office to put the relevant tape away safely and pick up his coat, congratulating himself on a job well done.

But before he could leave the office, the phone on his desk rang. He picked it up reluctantly, anxious to get away, but was soon listening to the desk sergeant at the main entrance to police headquarters with a mounting sense of excitement.

'I'll be right down,' he said. In the front office he found an anxious-looking young woman and on the counter in front of her a loosely wrapped plastic parcel.

'She found it in her garden under the hedge,' the sergeant said. 'Picked it up before she realised what it was, but had the sense to wrap it up before she brought it in.'

'And you are?' Mower said, lifting the parcel carefully and peering at the heavy hammer it contained.

'Susan Richards,' the woman said. 'I couldn't get down here any sooner because I had to find a babysitter for the kids. My husband works nights, you know, and...'

'Whoa, Mrs Richards,' Mower said. 'Let's start at the beginning, shall we? Where did you find this exactly?'

'Well, I was telling you,' Mrs Richards said. 'I was just tidying up the front garden after my husband had cut the hedge before he went to work. This was lying wedged behind a bush. It was already getting a bit dark so I picked it up and took it into the light. To be honest, I thought it might be useful. Then I realised what was on it. I was nearly sick.'

Mower nodded. He had little doubt that Susan Richards' instincts were right and that the brown stains on the hammer had been made by blood. He took down the details of where she lived with her husband and two small children. He knew that the road of semi-detached houses was one which lay on the direct route from Southfield to the Heights.

'D'you think it's...it's...?' Mrs Richards looked even sicker as the full horror of what she might have found sank in.

'We won't know that until it's been examined by the forensic scientists,' Mower said with uncharacteristic gentleness. 'That'll take some time. In the meantime, we'll get in touch with you tomorrow and have a good look under your hedge in the daylight, if that's OK?'

'Oh, yes, of course,' she said, flustered now.

Mower nodded at the uniformed sergeant and carried the parcel carefully back up to CID.

'Bingo,' he said before he called Michael Thackeray's mobile number without success. He hesitated for a moment, drumming his fingers on the desk and then shrugged, deciding that the call of an evening out took precedence over a hunt for his boss. But he pulled his coat on again with a faint smile. 'Perhaps there is some mileage left in this case after all,' he said to himself as he closed the office door.

Laura drove slowly up Woodlands Road that evening, past the firmly closed gates of Woodlands School. Glancing in the direction of the darkened building, she winced as she noticed that someone had unfurled one of the Close Woodlands Campaign's bright blue banners the length of the gateway. There seemed to be no shortage of money to fund this campaign, she thought, recalling more ramshackle protests on the less prosperous side of the town which had frequently met with a less ready reception at the town hall. Her grandmother would have something succinct to say about that, she thought wryly. Joyce was never one to miss a political cue.

She slowed down as she passed the Bostons' immaculate front garden, where she glimpsed Alicia carefully pulling across her heavy sitting room curtains, and finally drew up outside The Pines a couple of houses further up the hill on the other side of the road. If she had thought the Bostons' house desirable, the size of the Olivers' took her breath away, though it's full extent was carefully shielded from the road by ten-foot hedges of closely clipped Leylandii cypress.

She had to get out of the car and press a buzzer to gain admittance to the broad sweep of a gravel drive where two gleaming Mercedes convertibles, his and hers, she assumed, were parked side by side close to the portico. This was a house which would look more at home in Beverley Hills than on a Yorkshire hillside, she thought, as she surveyed the pan-tiled roof, the immaculate white stucco and the wide windows still protected by half-closed blinds which must have been pulled down against the late sun.

As she stood admiring the sheer chutzpah of the place, the front door opened and a tall man in his early forties, fair hair fashionably close-cropped, dressed in Armani jeans and Gucci loafers, stood looking at her impassively from the top step.

'Miz Ackroyd?' he asked. 'Come in. We're having a drink on the terrace. Will you join us?'

He led her through a light and airy hall to another door at the back of the house which gave onto a terrace shaded by a vine-clad pergola from which bunches of apparently ripe grapes hung at head-height. An outdoor heater kept the chill of the autumn evening at bay and the whole back garden was lit by discreetly concealed lights. Beyond there was a lawn as smooth as the Centre Court at Wimbledon, a swimming pool with its own changing room and bar area glittering like a holiday hotel on some Costa or other.

'Can you eat them?' she asked, nodding in astonishment at the grapes, but Mark Oliver shook his head with a faint smile.

'They're not often sweet enough. We're too far north. But they look nice. Remind us of holidays in Positano. This is my wife Serena, by the way.'

He waved in the direction of the woman who was sitting

in a cane chair next to the table and close to the heater, a slim, deeply tanned, blonde figure in trousers which Laura suspected were Nicole Farhi and coveted as soon as she saw them. She was holding a glass in a hand seriously weighed down by gold and reading *Hello* magazine, to which she quickly returned.

'Pimms?' Oliver asked. 'We're making the most of the last hint of dry weather, pretending it's still summer, really, though if you're cold I can turn the heater up.'

'I'm fine,' Laura said as she accepted a glass, heavy with orange and cucumber slices, mint and a striped straw, and drank deeply while she settled herself in a cane chair and took stock. Mark Oliver was nothing if not relaxed as he took his ease at the end of the day, she thought, and she wondered if her suspicions about his anti-school campaign could possibly be justified. She pulled the blue leaflet out of her bag and put it on the table.

'As I told your wife on the phone, I'm writing about the school and its problems,' she said. 'I've already spoken to the Bostons about the campaign but they advised me to have a chat with you too. I suppose what I really want to know is why you're all so keen to get the place closed down when the council says that it will only be here for a few years now in any case. What's the hurry, Mr Oliver?'

Oliver put his glass down and refilled it from the glass jug on the table before replying. His face was friendly enough, Laura thought, but his blue eyes were as chilly as the ice cubes in the Pimms and the tanned face had fine lines around the eyes and a deep frown mark between his brows.

'I suppose you think we're all selfish nimbies,' he said.

'I want to put your side of the argument,' Laura protested, hoping that she sounded more sincere than she felt about the obligations of her trade.

'Well, our side of the argument is what you'd expect,' he said flatly. 'This is an exclusive neighbourhood, property prices should be rising fast, and while that nest of young thugs stays, they won't. Call us selfish if you like, but I've yet to meet a house owner in any price bracket who doesn't want their property to appreciate.'

'But the school's going soon anyway, Councillor Waite says. Why the hurry?'

'Because it's getting worse, isn't it? Quite apart from this latest horror – the murder. Serena will tell you. Won't you darling?'

Hearing her name his wife glanced in Laura's direction for a moment.

'They swear at you as they go past,' she said, without enthusiasm, almost as if reciting something she had learnt off by heart. 'I even had something thrown at the car a week or so ago. Dented the paintwork on the bonnet. They're little hooligans, quite frankly. Jailbait.' She turned back to her magazine with a shrug of a silken shoulder.

'We've had nothing but trouble since the new head took over,' Mark Oliver said. 'Police cars and fire engines screaming around at all hours of the day and night. If they'll burgle and vandalise the school, which is supposed to be doing its best to help them, who's to say what they'll burgle and vandalise next? It's not so bad for people like us. We've got the security pretty well sussed here.' He waved a hand at the security lights above them and the burglar alarm box high under the roof.

'State-of-the-art, that is,' he said. 'It's people like the Bostons I feel sorry for. They came up here for a quiet retirement and they get an offshoot of Wuthering dumped on their doorstep. That's really why I agreed to help them.'

'You know the site will be redeveloped when the school moves out? A block of flats or half a dozen executive homes up there don't bother you?' Laura asked.

'Not the sort of flats they'll be putting on that land,' Oliver said. 'It must be worth three or four million.'

'There are flats and there are luxury apartments,' Serena Oliver broke in unexpectedly. 'I don't imagine they'll be filling many of the Woodlands flats with DSS scum.'

'Is that what they've got planning permission for?' Laura asked.

'Yes, I think so,' Oliver said, uncertain for a moment. 'I think that's what Councillor Waite told me.'

'Did you get any encouragement from Councillor Waite and the education people when you went to the town hall?' Laura asked.

Oliver took a long drink of his Pimms and nodded.

'He was very helpful,' he said. 'But he wasn't making any promises. He's not the right party for this area of course, so he has to watch his back, but I've been to see our own councillor as well. He's very sympathetic, says the building was never properly designated for educational use, so in theory they're in breach of their own planning guidelines. That's probably the line we'll follow up next.'

'You must have been very pleased to hear about the school inspectors' report,' Laura said.

'Yes, that was very useful, wasn't it?' Oliver agreed with a self-satisfied smile. 'No more than we suspected of course. Those kids are running out of control.'

'How come your organisation got an advance copy?' Laura asked. 'The school told us it wasn't due to be published for another month.'

'Ah, well, we have our sources,' Oliver said. 'As a journalist you'll know that I'm not going to reveal those.'

Laura hesitated, but then realised that she faced a brick wall with that line of questioning, so changed tack, trying to keep the atmosphere light.

'So would you say that your campaign is going as well as you would like?' Laura asked.

Oliver glanced at his wife who returned his smile.

'Oh, yes, I think you can quote me on that,' he said. 'I think the next meeting of the education committee will be very interesting indeed.'

Laura finished her drink and got up to take her leave.

'Can you give me your mobile number so I can get in touch more easily next time?' she asked.

'Of course,' Oliver said getting to his feet and waving her back into the house. He took a card from a walnut bureau in the hall and handed it to her. 'That's the number here and our mobiles,' he said.

'And work?'

He took the card back and scribbled another number on the back.

'I'm out of the office a lot but you can always leave a message there if you need to,' he said easily as Laura tucked the card into her bag, wondering why he had not simply given her a business card as well as a personal one.

She drove away from The Pines in a thoughtful mood and as she passed the school noticed that Julia Graves was frantically pulling at the banner which had been attached to the gate. Laura stopped the car and got out.

'Let me help you,' she said. Julia was wearing an old cotton smock splashed with multi-coloured paints. She glanced down and shrugged, running a hand smeared with more paint through her hair.

'I was painting,' she said distractedly. 'It takes my mind off things... just passing the time really. A friend just dropped in. Then I heard someone fiddling around out here and thought it must be some of the kids.'

'Grown up kids,' Laura said. 'I've just been talking to some of them down at The Pines. They're like spoiled brats on a beach trying to keep the best patch of sand for themselves.'

'Oh yes,' Julia said. 'They're all of that. There's so many grown-up brats around, aren't there? Snatch what they want. Grab and snatch. She's not having it back, you know? She's taken too much already.'

'Sorry?' Laura said, bemused by the turn the conversation had taken.

'Ella,' Julia said. 'She's not having it back. Her painting. She can't just come round here demanding something she's sold back again, can she? Fair exchange, I call it, don't you?'

'Are you all right?' Laura asked, mystified by this sudden outburst and concerned at the wild look in Julia's eyes. Julia nodded vigorously and glanced away up the drive where the falling leaves shifted slightly in the breeze.

'I'm fine,' she said unconvincingly. 'I did hope my daughter would come, but apparently not.'

'I'm sorry,' Laura said helplessly.

'They'll pull the old house down, you know. When the lease runs out. Of course, it's in a very dilapidated state. The council's never spent any money on it. They'll probably put up some monstrosity like The Pines instead. It's a shame, isn't it? Quite apart from the kids, I mean. It's such a lovely old place. I love painting it. I must finish that...'

She trailed off helplessly and Laura glanced doubtfully at the gothic gables looming amongst the beech trees, wondering whether Julia Graves was strong enough, or mad enough, to have beaten her husband to death.

'I'm not sure you could do much with the old place, the state it's in,' she said practically. 'Unless you're just into romantic ruins. And after what happened to your husband...'

Julia had by now furled up the banner and tucked it under her arm.

'Surely you don't believe in ghosts,' she said brightly. 'Believe me, Peter's not coming back.'

To Laura's surprise she found Thackeray at home when she got back from Woodlands Road, weary and depressed by the ill will she had uncovered there. When she unlocked the front door, he stood up and took her in his arms with unexpected force and kissed her so fiercely that she pushed him away, realising that perhaps there was as much anger as passion in his embrace.

'What did I do to deserve this?' she asked, with some

asperity. 'Last night you couldn't even be bothered to come home.'

Thackeray's face darkened and he moved away, taking a seat at the table by the window and watching her in brooding silence as she shrugged off her coat and dumped her handbag on a chair.

'We can't go on like this, Laura,' he said.

'Right,' she said cautiously. 'Could you not have rung me last night? I know better than to worry about you, but I was...' She hesitated, her usual felicity with words deserting her and leaving her tongue-tied.

'You were hurt?' he offered, knowing that was barely adequate as a description of what he seemed to have been doing to Laura now for a lifetime. She shrugged.

'I suppose,' she said, dully. Thackeray gazed down at his hands, which Laura could see where shaking slightly, before he lit a cigarette and inhaled deeply.

'I'm sorry,' he said. 'I went back to my own place. I had a lot of thinking to do.'

'About us? About work? What was so important that you couldn't call me?' Laura felt tears pricking the back of her eyes and she hated her impotence in the face of this man. It was as if the years they had spent circling round each other had been so much time wasted. She knew him no better now in these closed, angry moods, than she had ever done.

'Aileen is in hospital,' he said at last. 'Her heart's packed up. They think she won't recover.' His voice was distant, staccato, and Laura knew how much it cost him to say even that. But the news hit Laura like a blow to the stomach and she sat down abruptly opposite Thackeray and put her head in her hands.

'I'm sorry,' she said faintly. 'It's a bit of a shock, that's all.'

'That was the call I got last night,' he said. 'I stayed with her until very late and then I just wanted to be on my own.

I went back to my own place. I needed to come to terms with it. It brings everything back so clearly…' Laura took his hands in hers and for a moment they clung together wordlessly like casualties who have just escaped from some unimaginable horror.

'I'd no idea,' she said at last, through real tears now.

'You couldn't have.'

'But it'll be all over at last? Won't it? If she…when she's gone?'

'I don't know,' Thackeray said. 'I really don't know.' Then something else struck Laura like another sharp blow and she pulled away from Thackeray.

'Does anyone else know about her condition? Apart from you, I mean? Anyone in Arnedale?'

'I don't think so. I called her parents but they're in Newcastle. They're coming down to see her but not till tomorrow. Why do you ask?' And she told him exactly what Fergal Mackenzie had told her about DCI Hutton's speculations in the pub the day before.

'What the hell is Hutton playing at?' Thackeray said wearily.

'Fergal reckons he wants your job.'

'He can't possibly know about Aileen being rushed to the infirmary,' Thackeray said, trying to push his brain into something approaching working gear. 'He must have been listening to gossip in the Arnedale nick. There's a few people there who'll remember me. Maybe when Hutton got called down to Bradfield they filled him in and he's worked out that he can make some capital out of it. And of course when Aileen dies he may be right.' He recalled Jack Longley's warning about Hutton and watching his own back.

'It's old history, Michael,' Laura said. 'Surely it can't hurt you now.'

'Can't it?' Thackeray snapped. 'Think about it, Laura. You're the reporter. Her death won't be a secret, will it?

Someone will remember who she was and what happened. Someone will check the cuttings and run a story locally. I've enough enemies up there to make sure they do and Mackenzie is too sharp a journalist to hold back. Nor will Ted Grant. It'll be in the *Gazette*, then the tabloids will pick it up and my career could be on the line all over again. Can't you just see it splashed all over the *Globe*.'

Laura shivered because she could see it all too clearly. The death of a child killer would be unlikely to pass unnoticed and there was plenty of dirt to dig up if anyone took the trouble. There had been no trial because Aileen had never been fit to plead, but an inquest into Ian Thackeray's death was on the record and an equivocal open verdict returned because no one could be sure exactly what had happened. She had been able to find reports of it easily enough herself when she had delved into the cuttings when she had first met Thackeray and been infuriated by his elusiveness in the face of the visceral attraction between the two of them.

'Some people might think it's a good story,' she said reluctantly.

'Your editor for one,' Thackeray said. 'You might think it was a good story yourself if I wasn't involved. You might do it with a bit more sensitivity than the *Globe* but it would be just as intrusive. So where does that leave you if Hutton really stirs it up?'

'We'll have to work on some damage limitation to keep him at bay,' she said.

'That won't be so easy with Joyce and her cohorts rushing about complaining about miscarriages of justice and racism,' Thackeray said dismissively. 'Just about everything that can be set up in Bradfield to annoy so-called Len Hutton has been, as far as I can see. I'm going to end up hung out to dry in the middle of a fight that's not really mine. Terrific.'

His mobile rang before Laura could frame any sort of emollient reply to that, and Thackeray's face darkened again.

'I'll be right there,' he said.

Laura put a hand on his shoulder but he shrugged it off.

'She's worse,' he said, getting to his feet. 'I need to be there, and if possible get her parents there, too. It's not too far for them to drive down straightaway if it's as urgent as they say it is.'

'Of course,' she said, her face impassive.

'I'll be back when I can,' he said. 'Don't wait up.'

Would I? Laura thought to herself after he had gone as she wandered forlornly into the kitchen and began to prepare herself a sandwich. The news about Aileen should have been a liberation, she thought, but it now looked as if it had the potential to derail Michael Thackeray in new and dreadful ways. Eating her cold supper without tasting it, she determined to find a way of preventing that if she possibly could.

Chapter Twelve

In bed alone, Laura lay rigid in the certainty that something had wakened her. Her ears throbbed against the silence of the night, but she was quite sure that something was not right. She was not afraid, more puzzled. The night was stuffy with a hint of fog around the street lamps, which she could see through the half-drawn curtains and the bedroom window which she had left open at the top to let in whatever air it could. She had always felt safe here in her new home, even though it was on the ground floor and opened onto the overgrown garden. The sash windows were old and stiff and noisy, unlikely, she had thought, to be tackled by any but the most determined intruder if the place was occupied, and even now she did not think that the noise which had disturbed her was inside the flat.

She waited, listening to the murmur of her own heart and her regular breathing. At length, convinced that she must have been mistaken and had been wakened by a dream rather than reality, she rolled onto her side, aware that the other half of the bed was empty for the second night, and sighed. She wondered what was happening at the hospital and if her life with Thackeray would ever be the same again. Why was the past so impossible to shake off, she thought, feeling as helpless as she had ever done in the face of her lover's past.

She had just settled herself again for sleep, when the sound came again, clear and sharp in the quiet night air, the sound of metal on metal, and this time she knew without a doubt that it was real. Without switching on the light, she rolled out of bed and padded on bare feet to the window and pulled back the curtains.

Half of the garden was in pitch darkness but to one side a glimmer of light from the nearest street lamp flickered through the trees to cast a faint illumination on the unpruned shrubs and fading perennials of the overgrown communal garden to which none of the flats' owners gave more than fitful attention. Further away the trees had vanished into the mist and it was impossible to see any lights at all from the houses backing onto the garden. A wrought iron gate, supposedly kept locked, gave access to the rear from the side of the house and Laura knew now that it was the latch of this gate being lifted which she had heard. Carefully she eased open the window and leaned out. The knowledge that there was someone in the garden was more instinct than anything else, but as she waited, hardly daring to breath, she gradually became aware of a figure standing silently in the half-light to her right, a unmoving shape amongst the fluttering branches of the bushes.

'Who is it?' she asked quietly. The shape detached itself from its camouflage and stepped onto the pathway which ran beneath the windows.

'Miz Ackroyd? Stevie's mum said you wanted to talk to me.' The voice was young and hesitant, slightly gravelly with nerves.

'Dwayne?' Laura asked.

'I ain't talkin' to no policeman,' the voice said. Laura smiled faintly. If the boy had known that most nights he might have found a policeman right here in residence, he would have been away over the back fence and lost in the wilderness of foggy neglected gardens, haunt of foxes and owls at this time of night, which backed onto her own.

'Let me get dressed. I'll come to the door,' she said. She guessed that the boy would not consent to come in; nor was she at all inclined to invite him. She could vividly imagine Thackeray's horror if he found out that she had taken that sort of risk. She slipped into tracksuit pants and a sweater, tucked her tape recorder into one pocket, her keys and mobile phone into the other, and let herself quietly out of the flat, across the hall and out to the top of the stone steps outside the front door. That sharp click of the latch on the side gate made her jump again but she was ready and waiting as Dwayne Elton slid round the corner and stopped five feet below her and glanced up, his dark eyes gleaming in the light from the streetlamp outside the gate.

'Stevie's mum said you can get Stevie out of jail,' the boy said simply. 'Can you do that?'

For a fifteen-year-old, Laura thought, Dwayne was child-like in his directness and she wondered if perhaps the problems which had taken him to Woodlands school included some sort of learning difficulty. But she did not forget Mary Morris's suspicion that the boy was mentally ill either.

'I don't know,' she said quietly. Cautiously she went down a couple of steps and sat down on the top step, one hand firmly on her mobile phone, and safely beyond Dwayne's immediate reach. The house behind her was in complete darkness and she knew that her neighbour on the first floor was away, and that the other two slept, as she did herself, in bedrooms at the back of the house. She was, to all intents and purposes, completely alone.

The boy sidled round the side of the steps and stood looking up at her, his dark face impossible to read in the faint orange glow from the street. He was tall, at least as tall as she was herself, but skinny and not, she felt, a particularly menacing figure even though he wore a top with the hood pulled up in the fashion of the gangs of youths on the Heights.

'What do you know about the night Mr Graves was killed, Dwayne?' Laura asked, trying to keep her voice as calm as if she had been asking him about his history homework. With her left hand she switched on her tape recorder, although she was not at all sure that it would pick up reliably through the fabric of her pants.

'I went up the school with him,' Dwayne said.

'Did you?' Laura asked, not hiding the scepticism in her voice. 'Mr Davies saw Stevie, but he didn't see you, I don't think.'

'I met Stevie up there,' Dwayne said. 'I got there first.

Stevie came later.'

'To set the school on fire?'

'Nah,' the boy said fiercely. 'We weren't going to do owt like that. We wanted to get Stevie's Walkman and some other stuff he'd left there.'

'What other stuff, Dwayne?' Laura asked.

'Just stuff,' Dwayne said. He obviously was not going to satisfy her curiosity on this point, and Laura guessed that they had gone to retrieve something more illicit than a Walkman.

'So what happened?' Laura asked softly. 'Did Mr Graves catch you up there? Chase you, or something like that? Did he frighten you?' What she had been told about Peter Graves did not lead Laura to suppose that he would have been anything less than furious to find the two boys lurking round the school late at night.

'We never saw owt,' Dwayne said.

'You told Stevie's mother you didn't see Mr Graves. Is that really true?'

'I didn't see him. But I could hear him, no sweat. He were making enough noise before Stevie showed up.'

'What do you mean you could hear him? You overheard his meeting with Mr Davies, you mean?'

'Nah,' Dwayne said contemptuously. 'It were before Mr D arrived, an' before Stevie got there. He were having this big row with a woman, weren't he? A right ear-bashing she was giving him, shouting and screaming and everything. Just like my mum and dad, before dad went away.'

'Was it his wife? Do you know Mrs Graves?'

'Yeah, I know her,' the boy said, not bothering to disguise the giggle the memory of Julia seemed to evoke. 'We all know her. Daft cow. But it weren't her. It weren't anyone from t'school. She were calling him Peter and cussing fit to bust. I didn't know women knew all them words.'

Laura smiled faintly, secure in the knowledge that Dwayne could not see her face clearly.

'So let's get this straight,' she said, wanting to make sure that anything worth recording was picked up by the tape. 'You were waiting up there and heard all this going on: a woman and Mr Graves having a row? Then Mr Davies drove up?'

'Right,' Dwayne said. 'He got there just before Stevie.'

'OK, so Stevie turned up next. And what happened to the woman you heard shouting?' Laura wanted to get the sequence of events quite clear. 'Did you see her go?'

'Nah, I don't know where she went. Mr D weren't there long. We heard him talking to Mister Graves and then he drove off like he were two-ccing, like a bat out of hell.'

'So you were left up there with Mr Graves and possibly this woman. Did you hear them talking again?'

'Nah, we just hid and waited, like. He were in his office for a bit after Mr D left. That's at the back, right? So we hid in t'bushes at the front, until Mr D went, but Mr Graves did-n't switch the lights off or owt so we stayed there and kept shtum.'

'Could you hear what he and Mr Graves were talking about?'

'Nah,' Dwayne said. 'They were too quiet to hear.'

'And when Mr Davies drove off?'

'We heard the phone ring, and he was talking again so we guessed he'd be there for a bit so we went round to the side where Stevie reckoned he could get in through the door leading into the cloakrooms. He's good at opening locks, is Stevie.'

'And you got in?' Laura persisted.

'No, that's the point, innit? We could see the lights from Mr Graves's room, so we stayed back a bit. Then when the light went off Stevie tripped over this can which someone had left close to the door. We were right scared Gravesy would hear us but he didn't seem to.'

'Stevie picked it up? The can?'

'Yeah, well, we couldn't tell what it was at first. So Stevie unscrewed the top and we got this smell of petrol, and we got right worried. After the fires there'd been, you know? We dumped the can and got out of there as fast as we could.'

'You spilled the petrol?'

'Nah, I think Stevie screwed it back up. But it didn't half stink.'

'But you didn't see anyone else? Anyone who could have left the can there?'

'Nah,' Stevie said. 'But I reckon there must have been.'

'What do you mean?' Laura jumped on that.

'Someone else there, I mean. Because Mr Graves came to his window, just as we came round the corner, and I swear we hadn't made a sound. He just stood there, looking out, and it was as if he could see us although he couldn't of, it was too dark and we didn't move. Just froze till he turned back inside and switched the lights on at the front.'

'As if he was going home?'

'Yeah, well, I suppose so, yeah, that's what we thought. It were late, weren't it. Effing late to be at work, but that's like him, right?'

'But you didn't see him leave?' Laura persisted.

'Nah, we went over the fence at the side of the lodge sharpish and out onto the back road through the next-door garden. We didn't go down Woodlands Road again. Too dodgy. Thought we'd come back another night for Stevie's stuff.'

'But no one saw you.'

'I don't think so, though some of them bright lights, security lights, came on in one of the gardens. But we didn't see no one. No one at all.'

'Or hear anything else? No more shouting.'

'Nowt,' the boy said gloomily.

'I think,' Laura said carefully. 'I think that you know some things that the police don't know. For instance about the woman being up there that night, whoever she was. It would help Stevie if you told the police about that. Or his lawyer. How do you feel about that?'

'I ain't talking to no one,' Dwayne said, backing away slightly with a hand thrust aggressively in one pocket. Laura wondered anxiously what he kept there. 'They'll lock me up too. Stands to reason. They think Stevie did it so they'll think I helped him.'

'Not necessarily,' Laura said, trying to keep her voice calm. 'Stevie's not been telling the police very much apparently, maybe to protect you, I don't know. But if you come forward and tell them what really happened that night it might persuade him to be a bit more helpful. You can back each other up. Don't you see that?'

Dwayne took another step backwards, and Laura realised that if he was determined to run there would be very little she could do to stop him. He would no doubt be away again over fences and through back gardens just as he and Stevie had been on the night of the murder. She would not be able to catch him or even see where he went in the now thickening fog.

'Mrs Morris said to tell you that she wants to see you in school,' she said.

'I ain't going to no fucking school no more,' Dwayne said, sounding really angry for the first time. 'I got other things to do. And I ain't talking to no coppers and no lawyers either. Stevie's mum said you were all right. But that's it. I told you what I got to tell.'

Laura recognised finality when she heard it and guessed that whether or not the boy was involved in the murder of Peter Graves, he was lost to the world of order and legality. She shivered as the damp chill of the night penetrated right through her sweater.

'I'll see what I can do,' she said softly. 'But I think it'll be hard if you hide again. Stevie really needs you, in person.'

'Well, he can't have me,' Dwayne said, backing away now towards the side of the house.

'See you,' he said, and Laura thought she heard just a

touch of the wistful child in his voice before he vanished into the darkness.

Aileen Thackeray was declared dead at four-fifteen that morning. Her husband watched dumbly as the nurses finally removed the tubes which had been keeping her alive and tried to avoid the eyes of her parents who were sitting rigidly, hand in hand, on the other side of her bed. Aileen's heart had finally failed half an hour earlier but her parents had insisted that the medical team attempt resuscitation and Thackeray had not had the courage to object. He did not understand what the survival of this sad wreck of a human being meant to his father and mother-in-law whose religious faith he had long ago ceased to share but it cost him nothing at this stage, he thought, to respect it. They had called a priest when they had arrived at the hospital and he had given Aileen the last rites, a ritual from which Thackeray had removed himself as far as he decently could. But now, at the end, the vigorous application of electricity – a procedure Thackeray had seen before and hoped he would never have to watch again – had failed to revive her and eventually the doctor had been forced to admit defeat and declare his patient dead.

It was Duncan Mackie who finally broke the silence around Aileen's bloated corpse, decently covered now by a sheet up to her chin. He stood up determinedly, kissed his daughter awkwardly on the forehead, and took his wife's hand.

'I'll take mother back to the hotel for some rest now, Michael,' he said. Thackeray nodded, unable to speak.

'We'll need to talk about the funeral arrangements,' the old man continued. 'If you've no objection, we'd like to do that for her, take her home with us, and keep her close to us now.'

Thackeray nodded again and watched as the couple made their way slowly out of the ward, Duncan with one arm around his wife's shoulder and the other free to shake the hands of the nurses who were watching redundantly now from their station.   Simple courtesies from a simple, decent old man, Thackeray thought, who had not deserved the pain he had been caused, any more than his own parents had. How could he possibly object to anything they wanted?

When the Mackies had gone he gazed down at Aileen's pallid face himself. In repose now she was more like the young woman he had known in Arnedale, death smoothing out the spasms of violent emotion to which she had been prone while she was in Long Moor. He had loved her passionately once, until stress and long hours and the canteen culture of drowned sorrows had engulfed and almost drowned him, leaving Aileen adrift with a new baby and a depression which became steadily worse, unmentioned and unnoticed. He had never noticed, he thought bitterly. He simply had not seen it coming until that dreadful day, which he could still recall in all its banal detail, when he had found his son dead and Aileen hovering on the edge of oblivion. Memory, he thought, was a form of torture. He had heard people describe the slow-motion seconds before an accident, and women recall the cataclysmic moment of giving birth to a child as if it had happened yesterday. With him it was not birth but death which remained lit by a searchlight in his mind, the fronds of soft hair, the tiny bubbles around the mouth, the blue eyes of the drowned child imprinted on his retina forever. He knew it would never go away.

Twelve years he had waited for this final ending, hoping that at last it might all be over, finished at least, if not forgotten. But he knew now that this would not happen and that it never would. *Mea culpa:* the old half-remembered phrases came back, resurrected, he supposed, by the priest whose eye he had studiously avoided: my fault, all my fault from the start, he said softly to his wife. You're free but I won't ever be. I wish I could think you're with Ian now, but he's gone too, into the dark where we'll all end up alone. He turned abruptly on his heel, took his turn to thank the nurses on duty, and walked out of the hospital slowly, as if to his own execution.

Chapter Thirteen

DS Kevin Mower stood uncertainly in his boss's office at ten the next morning, wondering where Michael Thackeray might be. There was no coat hanging on the back of the door, no briefcase beside the desk and no cigarette butts in the ashtray which Thackeray kept determinedly beside him in spite of all attempts to ban smoking in the central police station. Mower had his typed report in his hand detailing the previous day's findings which he suspected might begin to unravel DCI Hutton's case against Stephen Fletcher. His faint satisfaction at that thought, though, was overlaid by some anxiety on Thackeray's behalf about the irascible Arnedale officer's likely reaction. And now Thackeray himself, most unusually, was not in his office at a time when Mower knew he was scheduled to see Superintendent Longley quite soon. He dialled Thackeray's mobile for the second time, and was told for the second time that it was switched off.

His anxiety increasing, he dialled Laura Ackroyd at work and got straight through.

'I've lost track of the boss,' he said. 'Is he ill or something? No one here seems to know.'

There was a long silence at the other end of the line and Mower could hear the faint clatter of keyboards and murmur of voices in the busy newsroom of the *Gazette*.

'He didn't tell you?' Laura asked eventually, obviously unsure of herself.

'He's due to see the Super in ten minutes and I need to know where he is,' Mower said.

'His wife's been taken to the infirmary,' Laura said. 'He went back there last night and I haven't heard from him since. She's has heart problems and I think she's dying.'

Mower drew a sharp breath. He knew little enough about Thackeray's wife's condition. It was a subject he never broached with Thackeray and Thackeray certainly never broached with him, although he knew that Mower had inadvertently uncovered what had happened to his family in Arnedale years before. But Mower understood now why Thackeray had been so distant for the last few days.

'I'll have to tell Jack Longley something,' he said. 'I'll be as discreet as I can.'

'People will have to know,' Laura said. 'He's not going to be able to keep it secret for long.'

'I suppose not,' Mower said. 'I'm sorry, Laura. If there's anything I can do to help let me know.'

'Thanks,' she said, and hung up abruptly.

Mower did not hesitate then. He called Bradfield Infirmary and bullied the nurse on the intensive care ward into admitting that Aileen Thackeray had died during the night, before calling Superintendent Longley's office and asking to see him urgently.

Longley looked up from his paperwork without much enthusiasm when Mower came in, but his eyes sharpened as soon as he heard what the sergeant had to say.

'I had a call from the DCI, sir,' Mower lied. 'His wife's died and I don't think he'll be in for a while…'

'When did this happen?' Longley asked.

'Last night, sir,' Mower said. Longley glanced at his phone.

'I'll call him, arrange some leave,' he said. 'Do you know where he is now?'

Mower shook his head.

'He sounded a bit spaced out. Shocked, I suppose. He didn't say where he was…'

'Leave it with me,' Longley said. 'I'll catch up with him. Now, what about this murder case? Is that all wrapped up, or will I have to get DCI Hutton back down here to sort out the loose ends.'

Mower glanced uncertainly at the report he still held in his hand.

'There are a couple of developments I think the CPS will

be interested in,' he said, and he told Longley how Ferdinand Boston had turned up on a garage videotape filling a petrol can, and about the arrival of a bloodstained hammer at police HQ the previous evening. Longley listened quietly enough, drumming his fingers on his desk as he worked through the implications of this new information.

'Have you sent the hammer to forensics?' he asked eventually.

'Yes, sir,' Mower said. 'And I've organised a fingertip search of Mrs Richards' front garden in case there's anything else there we should know about. We've never tracked down the clothes Stevie Fletcher must have got covered in blood if he was Graves's killer.'

'Good,' Longley said. 'And Boston?'

'I thought I'd go and have a chat with him about his lawnmower petrol this morning,' Mower said, cheerfully avoiding the fact that he had thought his trawl through garage videos a waste of time when Michael Thackeray had proposed it. 'We've got the forensic results on the can back, by the way. Fletcher's prints are on there, but there are others as well, very clear but so far unidentified. More than one person carried that can, probably that night, the lab says, so it's certainly not conclusive evidence that Fletcher took it up to the school. It's possible he did just find it, as he alleges.'

Longley looked thoughtfully at Mower for a moment.

'Let's just carry on with our own investigations for the moment, until we know if we've anything more definite to give the CPS,' he said. 'I'll contact DCI Hutton if and when I think it's appropriate.'

'Right, sir,' Mower said, feeling much happier than when he had entered the room.

'I gather you didn't get on too well with DCI Hutton when he was here,' Longley said abruptly. 'Is that right?'

Mower swallowed hard, startled by the question and unwilling to answer.

'I need to know what's going on in my nick, Sergeant,'

Longley said. 'Even if it's not what I really want to hear.'

'I found him uncomfortable to work with,' Mower said grudgingly. 'And he obviously took against DC Sharif.'

'For any good reason?'

'I didn't think so, sir,' Mower said. 'Sharif's a good officer. He's still got a lot to learn, but I think he'll do well.' The knowledge that Sharif intended giving evidence against DCI Hutton at a tribunal ticked like a time bomb at the back of his mind, but he wanted to talk that through with Thackeray before it exploded into the superintendent's consciousness.

'So Hutton's a racist? Is that what you're saying?' Longley persisted.

'I think Omar Sharif thinks so, sir,' Mower said.

'Right,' Longley said, evidently satisfied. 'Thank you, Sergeant; I'll bear that in mind. And Kevin…'

'Sir?'

'Keep me in touch, will you?'

'Sir.' Mower closed the door behind him with a sigh of relief. There might still be opportunity, he thought, to talk Omar out of self-destruct mode in time.

Laura found it almost impossible to concentrate at work that morning. Every time the phone on her desk rang she felt sick, although by lunchtime there was no word from Thackeray and in desperation she called Vicky Mendelson and invited herself to lunch. She desperately needed someone to talk to.

Vicky opened her front door to Laura with her usual welcoming smile and picked up her small daughter who was clinging to her left leg.

'Come on Naomi, my sweet,' she said. 'It's only Laura, you remember Laura?'

Laura held out her arms to the child but the little girl only buried her face in her mother's neck, overcome by shyness.

'It's just a phase, she'll come round in a minute,' Vicky

said. 'Come in and tell me all about it. You look stressed out.'

'Thanks,' Laura said wryly. 'That's a great comfort.' But she followed Vicky into the comfortable family kitchen where the table was set for two and a half eaten bowl of food stood on Naomi's high chair.

'Just let me see if I can persuade her to eat any more,' Vicky said, putting her daughter back into her chair. 'Why don't you get us both a G and T? You know where everything is.' Laura followed instructions and poured two drinks in the dining room. It was the room where she had first met Michael Thackeray at a dinner-party and been seriously intrigued by the unsmiling policeman's dour good-looks. It seemed like a life-time ago and she shivered slightly.

When Naomi was fed and changed and taken upstairs for her nap, Vicky eventually settled down opposite Laura at the kitchen table over bowls of soup and chunks of crusty bread.

'So tell me about it?' Vicky said quietly. After Laura had poured out her troubles, Vicky sat and stirred her soup with her spoon for a moment before she made any comment, her face veiled by her loose brown hair.

'It sounds an awful thing to say,' Vicky said eventually. 'But Aileen's death ought to make it easier for you and Michael. She's been hanging over you like a dark cloud ever since you met him. Surely he should be able to make a new start now.'

Laura shrugged slightly.

'He's never been able to talk about all that happened,' she said. 'And it doesn't look as though he's able to talk about what's happening now. I had to phone the hospital to find out that Aileen actually died early this morning. Now he's vanished. He's not at work, he's not answering his mobile and he's not answering the phone at his flat. What am I supposed to do, Vicky? He's in a crisis and he doesn't seem to want me anywhere near him. That's not how relationships are supposed to work. That's more like an end than a beginning.'

'He must be very shocked if this has all happened so quickly,' Vicky said. 'You should give him some time to come to terms with it. I'm sure he'll be in touch when he wants to be.'

Laura pushed her half empty bowl of soup away and gave her friend a despairing look.

'I'm frightened of what he'll do on his own,' she said. 'He's very afraid that Aileen's death will resurrect what happened when she tried to kill herself, and I have to admit he may be right. I know for a fact that he's got enemies in Arnedale, not least the DCI there, and someone may take it on themselves to blow it all up again. Even my grandmother and her friends on the Heights are adding to the brew. The campaign is virtually accusing DCI Hutton of being a racist; they're planning to demonstrate outside the magistrate's court again next week when the boy's case comes up. Even I think there's something dodgy about that murder investigation so I'm not much help there. In fact my being a reporter is a serious liability just now. I really don't know what to do, Vicky. I really don't.'

'Can't you at least persuade your grandmother to cool it down a bit on the Heights? It'll be months before the case comes to the crown court. They've got masses of time to find new evidence, if there's any to find.'

Laura shrugged.

'She's not exactly in charge of the campaign at her age. She's offering advice, I think, not much more than that. It's Stephen Fletcher's mother and some of the other women who are playing hell and planning the demo. There's nothing I can do about it.'

'And it'll get a fair amount of coverage in the *Gazette*, I guess?'

'You can bank on that,' Laura said.

'And what about Michael's wife? Would Ted Grant really dig up that old story again?'

'He might if someone in Arnedale started playing dirty tricks and provoked it,' Laura said gloomily. 'Michael hardly came out of the inquest on Ian's death smelling of roses when it happened. And it's damaged his career already. He was one of the fast-track graduates when he joined the police. Straight out of Oxford, destined for chief constable, all that high-flier stuff. And now? Fat chance.'

Vicky sighed.

'A bit of a mess all round,' she said. 'I'm so sorry, Laura. David and I feel a bit responsible for you two, you know. And more than anything we want to see you happy.'

Laura took her friend's hand and squeezed it hard.

'It's not your fault,' she said. 'I'd better get back to work. If I annoy Ted Grant much more this week I'll be out of a job. He's just looking for an opportunity to get rid of me.'

'Your little excursion into local radio didn't come to anything?'

'Not really. It was just a one off. I need to get out of Bradfield to push my career anywhere. Maybe if Michael's ditched me, I'll get my chance.' She gave Vicky a brilliant smile but couldn't hide the pain in her eyes.

'Oh, bugger men,' Vicky said.

'I do not believe this,' DS Kevin Mower said to DC Omar Sharif, the young detective constable he had taken with him on his trip to Southfield. So far their investigations had proved uneventful. Ferdinand Boston had welcomed them with impeccable politeness, if with some surprise, and readily agreed that he had bought petrol for his lawnmower on the night before the murder at the garage where his car had been recorded on videotape. He had then shown the police officers a can sitting innocently in his immaculately tidy garage still half-full, and seen them off again with many protestations of his willingness to help the police further in their inquiries in any way he could.

'Seems a harmless old boy,' Sharif had said as they drove another hundred yards or so up Woodlands Road.

'They're the sort who weave murderous fantasies on the quiet,' Mower said sourly. 'Neighbours from hell, driven berserk by recalcitrant kids playing their stereos too loud. Storms up there with a can of petrol to burn the place down, gets caught by the headteacher, bashes him over the head and bingo! He goes from respectable citizen to life sentence in thirty seconds of madness and all over the tabloids for his pains.'

Sharif looked at Mower suspiciously, not knowing whether to take him seriously or not. Mower had arrived in Bradfield from the Metropolitan force, trailing flamboyant rumours about his sex life and the stolid northerners he joined in Bradfield had still not quite assimilated his stylish clothes or his cynical veneer. Puritanically brought-up Muslims found him even more difficult to fathom.

'You think he could have simply bought another can to replace the one he left at the school?' he asked. Mower looked at him sharply.

'Worth checking out, Jim lad,' he said kindly. 'There were other prints on the original can, but no matches with anything on record. You could give it some thought. Meanwhile we'll call on the grieving widow.'

But when they pulled up outside the lodge, the tall goth-ic windows aflame in the westering sunshine, Mower did not get out of the car immediately. He sat and looked at his companion for a moment as if waiting for him to speak and when he didn't pick up on cue he broached the subject which was bothering him himself.

'You haven't told me what's happening with your Asian mate from Arnedale,' he said. 'Is he going ahead with his action against the deeply unpleasant DCI Hutton or not?'

'He is, as it happens, yes,' Sharif said reluctantly, staring out of the window of the car.

'And?' Mower pressed, knowing that there must be more.

'And I've decided I'll definitely give evidence at the tribunal if he wants me to. I'll tell them about the way Hutton treated me when he was in Bradfield.' He paused, still not meeting Mower's eye, and then turned to the sergeant angrily.

'I'm not going to be treated like that, sarge, not by Hutton, not by anyone. I was born in this country, raised in this country, schooled in this country. I belong here. I'll not be called a Paki bastard by anyone, whatever rank he claims. I've never even been to bloody Pakistan. I've told Achmed that I'll be there for him, if it helps.'

'I've told you before, it'll do your career no good,' Mower said. 'You're sticking your neck out.'

'I know that,' Sharif said. 'And I hate having to do it, because you and Mr Thackeray don't deserve the hassle, but I can't let it go. Bastards like Hutton have to be stopped. They may be able to get away with it in the Met but here it's different. Here there's enough of us to make sure everyone gets a fair deal.'

Mower winced slightly at the reference to the Metropolitan Police where he had started his own somewhat chequered career and where he was very aware that accusations of racism had been made by black officers right up to the exalted rank of commander.

'I hope you're right,' Mower said. 'But that doesn't mean the brass will thank you for it.'

'They'll have to get used to it,' Sharif said. 'Officers like me and Achmed aren't going away. We're the second generation. We won't lie down under it and we certainly won't go away.'

'Good luck, then,' Mower said, knowing Jack Longley would dislike what Sharif was planning as much as Hutton would, though for different reasons. 'So let's pop in and see the grieving widow while we're here shall we? See if she's remembered anything she should have told us about the night of the murder.'

But the grieving widow was not there. When they got to

the front of the lodge, they were puzzled to see the front door swinging open. Their calls gaining no response, the two detectives pushed the door wide and went in.

'Has she been burgled? Have those kids got in somehow?' Sharif asked no one in particular as they glanced into the empty living room and then into the kitchen where someone's lunch plate and coffee mug stood by the sink and a loaf of bread with a slice cut off it had been left to stale on its wooden board.

'No sign of that,' Mower said non-committally. He went to the bottom of the narrow stairs and looked up.

'Mrs Graves,' he called. 'Are you there?' When there was no response he led the way upstairs and went into each of the two bedrooms in turn. In one the double bed was neatly made, the wardrobe doors closed, the curtains pulled back. In the other, conventional furnishing gave way to a clutter of easels and shelves and a table top covered with brushes, palettes and paint.

'A bit of an artist, is she?' Sharif said uncertainly, as if the description itself might be in some way incriminating.

'Not too bad, either,' Mower said moving round an easel to take a long cool look at an impressionistic landscape in oils with the paint still gleaming and sticky. 'That's the school, look. I suppose it's quite a handsome building if you see it in some lights.' Sharif glanced over his shoulder and shrugged. Painting was evidently not something he would venture an opinion on.

Sure now that the house was empty, Mower led the way downstairs again and went back to the front door to examine the lock more carefully.

'It's not been forced,' he said. 'And if there've been intruders, they're certainly the tidiest I've ever seen.'

'Could still be kids from the school,' Sharif suggested. 'Little tearaways, most of them. They could have been in and then got scared for some reason.'

'Have a look outside, will you,' Mower said impatiently.

'Just in case. I want to give Mr Thackeray a call.' When the DC had gone he picked up Julia Graves's phone and dialled 1471 and made a note of the number the operator recited, before using his own phone to call Michael Thackeray, but again there was no reply from Thackeray's office or his mobile.

'Shit,' he said softly to himself. 'Where the hell is he?'

By the time he had hung up, Sharif had returned from his search of the garden with a shrug to indicate that there was no sign of Mrs Graves there either.

'She might have just gone shopping, sarge,' Sharif suggested tentatively.

'Perhaps, but with all those dubious kids on the doorstep, it seems very odd not to have locked the front door securely before she did. And I'll tell you something else that's very curious about this house. When we did the original inquiries I remember Julia Graves saying they had children, or a child maybe, at university. I thought it was strange at the time that the kids never turned up to be with their mother when their father died or not that I saw, anyway. What's even odder is that there's not a single photograph of kids in this house: not babies, not toddlers on the beach, not gawky teenagers, no school uniform pictures, no graduation pictures, zilch. Is that peculiar or what?'

'I wouldn't know, sarge,' Sharif confessed, as if children were a life form from another planet to which he had given little consideration.

'Believe me, it's very odd,' Mower said. 'Very odd indeed.'

At the end of the day Mower drove out of town to the utilitarian modern block where he knew DCI Thackeray owned a small flat. He rang the bell without much hope that he would get a answer, but after five minutes of fruitless leaning on the button he at last heard a muffled response on the door-phone and the front entrance buzzed open. There was no lift and he walked slowly up the four flights of stairs to the top, feeling that the hours he spent at his gym were not providing quite all he required of them. Thackeray's front door was open when he arrived and he walked straight into the living room, where the curtains were drawn and he had some difficulty in making out the figure of his boss slumped on the settee. The air was thick with cigarette smoke and the unmistakable smell of whisky. He turned on a lamp on a side table, which made Thackeray screw up his eyes in pain.

'Are you OK, guv?' Mower asked, picking up a bottle from the floor and turning it upside down. It was empty.

'What do you think?' Thackeray mumbled.

'I think you don't do things by halves,' Mower said, turning away with the bottle, to hide the anxiety he knew must be written on his face. He said nothing else but opened doors until he found the kitchen, put the kettle on and rummaged around for coffee and sugar. He went back into the sitting room with a pot and two mugs.

'You're on compassionate leave, by the way,' he said. 'Jack Longley's fixed it. I had to tell him something so I told him about your wife.'

'And how did you know about my bloody wife?' Thackeray snarled.

'Laura told me she was ill, the hospital told me she was dead. Easy,' Mower said. 'I am a bloody detective.'

Thackeray lay back on the settee again, closed his eyes and laughed hysterically.

'She's taken twelve years to die, my bloody wife,' he said

at last, tears in his eyes. 'Twelve bloody years. Can you believe that?'

'Drink the coffee,' Mower said.

'I'm glad she's dead, Kevin. Can you believe that?'

'Of course I can,' Mower said. 'I know you're glad. I'm glad, too. Laura will be glad. She wasn't a person any more, she was an incubus.'

Thackeray gazed at the sergeant with a glimmer of rationality in his eyes as the coffee began to clear his head.

'Good description,' he said. 'Very good. You're a good lad, Kevin, for a bloody Londoner.' And he laughed again until eventually his head fell to one side and he snored gently, fast asleep.

Mower watched him sleep for a long time, his own emotions in turmoil. Eventually he searched the flat for more alcohol and poured another bottle of Scotch he found in the kitchen down the sink. Then he rang Laura Ackroyd and told her where he was and described the state he had found Thackeray in.

'I'll come over,' Laura said.

'No, I'll bring him to you,' Mower said. 'Give him time to sleep it off a bit. But Laura, you must have booze in the house? Can you get rid of it?'

'All of it?' Laura sounded horrified.

'Every last drop,' Mower said firmly. 'He's back at square one here, you have to understand that. There's no halfway house. He's off the wagon big time and it's going to take both of us to get him back on again. Believe me.'

He could hear Laura crying at the other end of the phone before she hung up and he glanced at the snoring DCI with fury in his eyes. Why, he thought angrily, do good people do this to each other?

It was after two by the time Mower arrived at Laura's flat with a dazed looking Michael Thackeray in tow. He had chosen to wait until every pub, club and off-licence in the town

was likely to be shut before he woke Thackeray and then it
had taken all his powers of persuasion, and eventually a
modicum of brute force when Thackeray took an exhausted
swing at him, to get his boss out of his own flat and into his
car. On the doorstep of the tall Victorian house where Laura
owned the ground floor flat, Thackeray had leaned his head
against the rough stone of the doorframe and groaned.

'I need a drink,' he said.

'No you bloody don't,' Mower had answered, shoving
him roughly inside when eventually Laura came to the door
in a dressing-gown. She took Thackeray's arm and between
the two of them they steered him into the living room and
into a chair by the fireplace, where he slumped down and
buried his head in his hands.

Laura glanced inquiringly at Mower, her face pale and
her whole body so tense it hurt him to look at her.

'He needs to sleep it off,' Mower said. 'He'll feel like
death in the morning. And then you'll have to watch him,
maybe get him back to AA. I don't know how bad this is.
Only time will tell.'

Laura was astonished to wake around eight the next
morning to find Thackeray sitting on the side of the bed
with a mug of coffee in his hand and another on the bedside
table beside her. She had slept heavily after Mower had
helped her get Thackeray to bed. Now he glanced at her with
heavy eyes which she found difficult to read. Apart from
looking exhausted, he appeared unscathed.

'I'm sorry, Laura,' he said quietly. 'That was unforgiv-
able.'

'We'll get over it,' she said, without total conviction. 'I
do understand what you're going through, you know. Come
back to bed. I don't need to be in until ten.'

Thackeray shook his head, although the sudden movement obviously hurt.

'I'm going into work,' he said. 'Hanging around doing
nothing's not an option.'

Laura sat up sharply.

'You can't,' she said. 'You're not fit.'

'Fit enough,' he said. 'It's what's going on my head that matters, and that won't be helped by mooching around all day crucifying myself.'

She made to object but he put a restraining hand on her arm.

'Believe me,' he said gently. 'I need to go to work. Then I need to go and see my father. Then it will be over.'

'The funeral?' she hazarded.

'My parents-in-law will organise that. They want her buried near them. I've no problem with that.'

'But you'll go?' She knew that would be an ordeal she could barely begin to imagine.

'Maybe,' he said turning away again. 'I'm not sure.' He drained his cup and stood up, wincing slightly as he stretched, and she watched him dress in silence. Somewhere where her stomach used to be there was a hollow pit this morning. When he was ready, he came back into the bedroom and leaned over to kiss her but she took hold of his hand and pulled him down.

'If you're going back to work there's something I need to tell you about,' she said. Thackeray groaned slightly.

'Oh God, what have you done now?' he asked, his voice light but his anxiety was more real than he pretended. Laura took an audio tape out of the drawer of her bedside table and slipped it into the radio-cassette.

'You need to listen to this. It's very fuzzy,' she said. 'I had the recorder in my pocket. But you can get the gist of it.'

Thackeray listened in silence and when the tape petered out into a hiss of static he leaned forward and closed his eyes for a moment.

'I take it that's Stephen Fletcher's friend? What's his name? Dwayne? The one who's run off rather than make a statement? So how did you find him?' he asked eventually.

'I didn't,' Laura said slowly. 'He found me. He came here

the night before last. I would have given it to you yesterday if I'd ever caught up with you.'

Thackeray was evidently startled by that and sat up, his whole body suddenly alert.

'He came here?' he asked incredulously. 'How the hell did he find you here? Who told him your address?'

'I think Stevie's mother must have found out where I lived. It's not as if it's a secret is it? I'm in the phone book.'

'Good God, woman,' Thackeray said. 'Perhaps after this you'd better get yourself out of the wretched phone book. You can't have kids from Wuthering knocking on your door in the middle of the night. It's not safe. You could have been...'

'What? Killed? Raped? What makes you think that? The fact that he's black? People like Mary Morris deal with these kids every day and come to no harm. She never gave me to believe that Dwayne was dangerous.' Some of Laura's pent-up anger found an outlet now in defending Dwayne.

'No, he just has a best friend who hits people over the head with blunt instruments and he comes round to tell you he was there at the material time. Laura! I suppose you invited him in for tea and sympathy?'

'I didn't invite him in,' Laura said, more quietly. 'I talked to him outside in the garden.'

'Oh, wonderful, a really good place for an assault and a quick getaway in the dark.'

Laura turned away, very aware that she had thought exactly the same when Dwayne had become agitated, and had found herself shaking and faint when she had finally come back inside and closed her front door on the world again. But she did not think it wise to go into that just now.

'Can you use the tape?' she asked. 'Can you get it cleaned up so that it's clearer?'

'Oh, I expect so, though as evidence it's worthless without Dwayne himself,' Thackeray said dismissively.

'Well, that's up to you,' Laura said. She turned away and sipped her coffee in silence until Thackeray could stand it no more. He leaned over and took the mug out of her hand and pulled her towards him in a fierce embrace.

'You take too many chances,' he said. 'Too many risks. Don't you know what it would do to me if I lost you too?'

When Thackeray got to his office, he listened to the muffled tape of Dwayne Elton's conversation with Laura again, drinking more coffee to assuage his thumping head. Before it had finished, a startled Kevin Mower put his head round the door.

'Are you OK, guv?' he asked. 'I didn't expect to see you...'

'I'm fine,' Thackeray said curtly, his tone allowing the sergeant no further space for questions about his health. 'Listen to this,' he said, spooling the tape back and starting it again.

'Dwayne Elton?' Mower asked when the tape hissed to an end.

'Exactly,' Thackeray said sharply, sliding the cassette across the desk towards him. 'First of all see what the technical folk can do to sharpen it up. It's Dwayne and Laura having a heart-to-heart. And second, find the little bastard! He admits on the tape that he was at the school that night. I want him brought in.'

'Perhaps Dwayne was the reason Stephen clammed up so comprehensively when we interviewed him,' Mower said thoughtfully. 'Perhaps Laura and her gran are right after all: Stevie's innocent but he's covering up for his mate. Though we won't win any brownie points from the anti-racist brigade if we go after Dwayne instead of Stephen. I don't think substituting one black suspect for another is quite what they have in mind.'

'We follow the leads where they take us,' Thackeray snapped. 'You know that. And if Fletcher's innocent we let him go. There are too many loose ends in this case, whatever DCI Hutton and the CPS reckon. I want you to tie some of them up properly and you can start by finding Dwayne Elton.'

'And the Volvo driver and the petrol can, guv?' Mower said. 'I guessed you'd want me to chase that up yesterday. I've talked to Ferdinand Boston and he doesn't deny being the man at the garage. And I've passed the hammer to forensics, though I've had nothing back yet. There's nothing to show it's the murder weapon, although Amos Atherton did suggest after the post-mortem that a hammer might have been used. We found nothing else of interest where it was found, though. And we need more fingerprints to cross-check. Shall I bring Boston in for questioning here?'

'Not yet,' Thackeray said. 'We've not enough to go on. We'll concentrate on the Elton and Fletcher angles first. If either of their fingerprints are on the hammer we've got them.'

'Guv,' Mower said. He hesitated for a second, sorting out in his mind a few edited highlights of the previous day's trip to Southfield which bothered him.

'While I was up there yesterday I tried to see Graves's wife again, but she wasn't in. It was strange, actually, because she'd left the front door open, and I went in just in case there'd been a break-in, but I couldn't see any sign. I locked the door and asked uniform to keep an eye on the place. A bit odd. In fact the whole house is a bit odd, I reckoned. I thought the Graves's were supposed to have kids, but there's not a single photograph of a child there – not babies, not toddlers, not teenagers.'

Thackeray hoped that Mower could not see how that casual observation hit him in the hollow pit which passed for his stomach these days. When Ian had died, he remembered going round the house and collecting every cherished photograph of his son and hurling them into a bonfire in the back garden. It was only much later, when he discovered that his parents had kept their own collection out of his sight, that he could bear to look at images of the dead child again.

'I'd keep quiet about any unauthorised searches you've been conducting,' Thackeray said. 'But try to catch up with Mrs Graves today. Go over her statement to see if she remembers anything more. And call in on the school and talk to the acting head, Mary Morris. It's possible Graves met someone else that night apart from Gareth Davies. If we're to believe Dwayne Elton, he had a furious row with someone, probably a woman. Find out where both of them were at the material time and whether either of them knows whom else he could have been rowing with at around nine, nine-thirty, before Gareth Davies arrived at the school. Laura says his wife is sure Graves had a lover.'

'Laura says? Has she been talking to Julia Graves as well?' Mower risked a raised eyebrow at that but Thackeray did not respond.

'Laura's been asking questions,' he said irritably. 'You know that. But she's trying to prove Stephen Fletcher's innocent. I'm trying to confirm that there's enough evidence for the CPS to make a case. There's a difference.'

'If you say so, guv,' Mower agreed. 'Anything else?'

'There's been enough speculation about this case,' Thackeray said. 'Before I report to Jack Longley about it again I want some facts to back up the theories. I'm not sticking my neck out for anything less.' In fact, he thought, given the threat DCI Hutton might pose, he would really rather not stick it out at all.

Laura drove up the long hill to the Heights that lunchtime, forcing herself to concentrate on the traffic as it ground its way out of town. She had been unable to concentrate at work all morning and was finding it no easier now she had decided to visit her grandmother again for a quick lunch. She parked outside the tiny bungalow in the shadow of the flats where Joyce insisted on remaining in spite of the growing problems of vandalism and violence all around her, and took her usual Marks and Spencer's bag of goodies from the passenger seat beside her. Her grandmother lived the life she had learned to live in the 1940s, shopping locally and often, and keeping very little in the house with which to entertain unexpected visitors. She responded slowly to Laura's tap on the flimsy front door. Laura knew her grandmother's arthritis was getting worse, although she seldom complained. Soon, Laura thought, she would have to accept the help she had resolutely refused now for years. But when Joyce eventually opened the door her eyes lit up.

'Come in, love,' she said. 'You're just the person I wanted to see.'

Laura smiled, in spite of her own anxieties. She knew that her assistance was about to be demanded for one or other of Joyce's campaigns, and she guessed that it would probably be on behalf of Stephen Fletcher again.

'I brought us lunch,' she said, dumping her carrier bag on the coffee table and going into the kitchen for plates and glasses.

'Now then,' Joyce said when she had graciously accepted a salmon and cucumber sandwich with no more than a mildly raised eyebrow. The extravagance of the younger generation never ceased to amaze her. 'About this black lad they've got locked up. Is there anything new that we could give his solicitor for the court case next week? Anything you've picked up from that man of yours.'

'Nan, you're incorrigible. And you underestimate how discreet Michael can be when he chooses, anyway.' And especially when his mind is as far from his work as it is currently, she thought.

'But I do know one thing for sure,' she conceded, cautiously. After Thackeray's furious reaction she definitely did not intend to tell her grandmother about her nocturnal interview in the garden with Dwayne Elton. 'I told you about his friend Dwayne Elton, didn't I? I'm sure he knows as much as anyone about what went on at the school the night Peter Graves was killed. My guess is that he was up there with Fletcher. But he still hasn't turned up at school or spoken to the police. No one seems to know where he is. You said you'd try to find out where the Eltons went when they pulled Brontë House down, didn't you? If you really want to help Stevie Fletcher that's where you should concentrate your efforts. He's the one with some of the answers.'

'Do the police think Dwayne did it then?' Joyce asked sharply. 'There's not much point getting one black lad off if the police have another one lined up to take his place.'

'Nan, one of them may well have done it,' Laura said mildly. 'Just because they're black doesn't mean they're necessarily innocent any more than it means they're always guilty.'

'I made some inquiries about DCI Hutton,' Joyce said.

'And?' Laura asked, but her grandmother just shook her head, lips pursed in disapproval.

'So you haven't tracked down the Eltons then?' Laura persisted.

'As a matter of fact I have,' Joyce said. 'At least I found out where his mother and sisters are. They were moved into a flat in Priestley House when the Bronte came down. But Dwayne's not there. They haven't seen him since the night of the murder either.'

'That doesn't sound good,' Laura said, wondering whether Dwayne had taken refuge in the labyrinth of empty flats on the estate which were best known as the haunt of drug dealers. If so, the police would have their work cut out finding him without provoking major violence and, given recent events, quite possibly gunfire as well. The Heights, she thought, was another world and an increasingly frightening one. Laura shrugged eventually and gave her grandmother a hug.

'Let's not spoil our lunch,' she said, handing Joyce a calorie laden dessert that she had not been able to resist in the shop and, judging by the gleam in her eyes, Joyce would not be able to turn down now. 'You're far too thin,' Laura said. 'And now tell me about this holiday you're supposed to be having in Portugal with dad. Have you booked a flight yet, or do you want me to do it for you?'

Twenty minutes later she had examined her car carefully for the sort of lightning vandalism some of the estate kids indulged in for kicks and, finding nothing amiss, unlocked the doors to begin her journey back into town. Joyce stood at her door watching her granddaughter leave when both women were startled by two sharp sounds coming from somewhere in the complex of flats on the other side of the road.

Laura looked at Joyce in alarm.

'Was that what I think it was?' she asked urgently. 'Were those gunshots?'

'It'd not be the first time,' Joyce said, backing further into her doorway. 'The gangs have got weapons now. The police know that.'

Laura hurried her grandmother back into the house, her expression determined.

'You can't stay up here,' she said. 'You'll have to think about moving, and soon. It's not safe any longer.'

Joyce shook her head, but Laura could see there were tears in her eyes.

'Maybe,' she said, her voice so low that Laura could barely hear it. 'We'll see.'

Laura finally tore herself away from her grandmother's house, after they had called the police and reported what they had heard, her anxiety turning into fury as she drove back into town far too fast. What were the police doing, she wondered, leaving elderly people terrorised by youngsters apparently using guns with impunity in broad daylight? It was another issue she could take up with Michael Thackeray, she thought, although she knew that more issues between them was the last thing their relationship needed right now.

She stormed into the office and glanced around the busy newsroom to locate the paper's crime reporter, Bob Baker, and found him pounding his keyboard intently in the far corner of the room. He glanced up distractedly as she approached.

'Hi,' he said cheerfully enough. 'What can I do for you, darling?' But when she told him what had happened on the Heights she could see his eyes glaze over slightly. Eventually he shrugged.

'It's been going on for weeks,' he said. 'What I'm waiting for is the police to organise a serious raid up there.'

'And is there any prospect of that soon?' Laura asked.

'Not that I've heard,' he said.

'Somebody's going to get killed,' Laura said. 'And it may well be somebody completely innocent – like my grandmother.'

'Yeah, right,' Baker said. 'I'll look into it. But right now I'm back on the dead headmaster case. A little bird tells me the kid they've got banged up is no longer in the frame and there's much more to the whole affair than meets the eye. Did you hear anything like that from your contacts?' He emphasised the last word of his question suggestively.

'No, I didn't,' Laura snapped.

'I'll tell you someone who won't be best pleased,' Baker said, ignoring Laura's obvious annoyance. 'And that's DCI Hutton – the one who stood in for your bloke. He was sure he had that lad Fletcher bang to rights.'

'I think you're pushing your luck as usual, Bob,' Laura said tartly but Baker just laughed.

'We'll see,' he said.

Chapter Fifteen

Thackeray had insisted that it was too early to put out a missing person call for Julia Graves when Mower called in to say that she was still not at home. There was no evidence that she had come to any harm, he had said, but it might be worth checking out the school to see if anyone had seen her. Mower had agreed with that readily enough and walked the length of the school drive thoughtfully, still sure in his own mind that there was something odd about Julia Graves's disappearance and worried that Thackeray had seemed to be only half listening to what he had to say.

Mary Morris had looked at Mower curiously as she showed him into her office and even more quizzically when he told her that he wanted to know everything that she knew about where Julia might be.

'I've not seen her this week,' she said. 'But then it's unlikely I would. It's quite possible not to see Julia for weeks at a time. I think she shuts herself up painting for days and then the garden is mainly at the back of the house and she spends a lot of time there, pottering about. She's not the sort of housewife you see bustling off to the shops or taking a dog for a walk. I suppose she's a bit of a recluse really.'

'We're concerned for her safety. She seems to have gone out yesterday, leaving the house unlocked...'

'That's unusual,' Mary admitted. 'Julia's always very careful about security, I do know that much. I think if the truth is known Julia's a bit scared of the kids here. They're not above the odd jeer as they pass the lodge. That's one reason she keeps herself so much to herself.'

'I can imagine,' Mower said. 'They seem to have upset most of your neighbours.'

'Unjustifiably, in most cases,' Mary came back quickly. 'Most of them never get further than the pavement outside school where the buses pick them up. The idea that they're roaming around terrorising the local community is just non-sense. I'm sure the police would know about it, in lurid detail, if it wasn't. The neighbours here wouldn't be shy about calling up your colleagues in uniform at the slightest infraction.'

'Will you talk to your staff and the kids. See if anyone else has seen her?' Mower asked.

'Of course,' Mary said briskly. 'No problem.' Mower hesitated. It was obvious that Mary Morris was anxious to get on with her day. She looked tense and slightly ill at ease and Mower wondered how far recent events had made her afraid for her own safety. Losing your predecessor to a violent student could not inspire much confidence in the rest of the youngsters in a school like this, he thought. But he decided to pursue his inquiries regardless of how uncomfortable Mary Morris appeared. In spite of DCI Thackeray's apparent unconcern, he was sure that Julia Graves's absence was significant in some way, although he had no idea how.

'I'm told Julia thought her husband was interested in another woman,' he said carefully, and was surprised when Mary Morris smiled a faintly satisfied smile.

'D'you know anything about that?' he pressed.

'You've discovered Peter was not the paragon of virtue he cracked himself up to be, have you?' she asked. 'Does this mean you're having doubts about Stevie's involvement? Join the club!'

'Not necessarily,' Mower said quickly.

Mary Morris looked at the policeman speculatively.

'You could say Peter fancied himself with women,' she said. 'One of my younger colleagues was thinking of taking out a sexual harassment case against him. He'd never touched her. But I knew what she meant. He had that sexually predatory presence at times, always watching, always too close, breathing down your bra.'

'But a lover?'

'I don't know. If Julia said he had, then I would guess she

knew.' Mary Morris's pale, finely lined face had clouded over as if the very thought of her former boss haunted her.

'Could it be someone at the school?' Mower pressed.

'I can't think of anyone who would give him the time of day, let alone jump into bed with him,' she said. 'Which doesn't mean, as I say, he didn't try his luck. He created such bad feeling here.' She sighed. 'I don't think there was anyone he hadn't outraged in some way at some time, particularly the women members of staff.'

'Including the pupils?' Mower asked quickly.

'Oh, some of them,' she admitted. 'He was the last person who should have been in charge of vulnerable, volatile kids. But how many of them were big and strong enough to hit a tall man over the head and kill him? It never looked like a child's crime to me. Stevie's not very tall, you know.' But Dwayne Elton might be, Mower thought.

'How tall is the lad who's gone missing? What's his name? Dwayne?'

'Taller than Stevie,' Mary Morris said cautiously.

'And with a history of violence?'

Mary's lips tightened and she suddenly looked much older.

'I'll let you know if he turns up,' she said wearily. 'But I'm sure he won't. I think we've lost Dwayne as well as Stevie. Now, if you don't mind, I have my chief inspector coming in ten minutes to talk about a report which he says he never wrote, if you can believe that...?' She looked inquiringly at Mower, almost willing him out of his chair. He gave in and got to his feet.

'You'll ask the staff if they've seen the reclusive Julia?'

'Of course,' Mary said. Then she drew a sharp breath. 'There is one thing you probably don't know. I'd forgotten till just now. I think she went to classes at the old art school. It's part of the college of technology now, of course. They might have seen her, I suppose.'

'Right, I'll check that out if she doesn't turn up soon,'

Mower said. 'The other thing that puzzled us was that we were told she and Peter Graves had children, but there's absolutely no sign in that house of children. Nothing they might have left behind, no spare room they might stay in when they come home, not a single photograph. Are you sure they had a family?'

'Peter never spoke about his children but I do remember when he first came here that he said there was someone away at university.'

'You've no idea where? If Julia really has disappeared we'll need to contact them.'

Mary Morris shook her head.

'I can't help you there, I'm afraid,' she said. 'And now I really must get on.'

Superintendent Jack Longley opened his DCI's office door without knocking and eased his bulk into the room. He found Thackeray in semi-darkness sitting with his chair swivelled round towards the window apparently gazing out at the rainswept trees whose last leaves where spiralling around the town hall square. Unable to see Thackeray's face, Longley cleared his throat before switching the light on.

'They told me you were in, Michael,' he said. 'D'you think you should be? In the circumstances?'

Thackeray spun round to face his boss, his face like stone, his eyes chilly and unreadable.

'I'm fine,' he said. 'I'm just waiting for Mower to report back.'

Longley sank into a chair himself and nervously brushed near non-existent hair across his bald head.

'I was sorry to hear...' he began.

'It's the best thing that could have happened,' Thackeray interrupted him. 'She was never going to recover.'

'Aye, well, God moves in mysterious ways,' Longley said and instantly regretted it as he saw the flash of anger in the DCI's eyes.

'Well, you must take what time off you need, Michael,' he said quickly.

'The funeral will be in the north east,' Thackeray said. 'Her parents are arranging that but I don't know when yet.'

'Aye, well, let me know.' He leaned back in his chair and made a tent of his hands before speaking again.

'DC Sharif,' he said eventually. 'Did you know he was involved in some tribunal case being taken out by an Asian DC in Arnedale?'

Thackeray stiffened slightly but shook his head.

'Who told you that? He's not mentioned it to me,' he said. Nor, he thought angrily, had Mower, on whom he could usually rely as his eyes and ears in CID.

'I picked it up at county,' Longley said. 'I wasn't best pleased, I can tell you. Bloody nightmare that looks like becoming. We want to be plastered all over the papers for bad race relations in this town like we want to light the blue touch-paper.'

'Have you talked to Sharif?' Thackeray asked.

'Not yet, but I will, don't you fret. If he's got a gripe he should come to you first off, or to me, not go rushing off to a bloody tribunal.'

'They're both complaining about DCI Hutton, I assume,' Thackeray said, with sudden foreboding.

'Oh aye. Mower said he was a racist bastard, but I'd no idea anyone would take it this far.'

Thackeray nodded slowly, his mind flashing back to Arnedale and the man he had never met who was allegedly asking questions about his own past. He had half hoped that the fact that Aileen's parents had arranged for her body to be taken to an undertaker's close to their own home might mean her death was less likely to register in the town where they had spent their married life, but he had not really convinced himself. He still feared that when Aileen's death became public knowledge the embers of old scandals would be vigorously fanned back into life by his enemies old and new. But that was an eventuality he did not want to discuss with Longley. And there was just the possibility that an attack on Hutton's own integrity might deter him from attacking Thackeray's.

'There've been reports of more shots on the Heights,' he said, changing the subject decisively. 'Laura actually heard them. Someone up there's going to get killed if we don't get to grips with these drug gangs.'

'I'm not disagreeing with you,' Longley said. 'But the drug squad's got some on-going operation up there, as per usual, so we're supposed to keep a low profile.'

'So what do we tell the community association when they come demanding action again? As they will.'

'I'll deal with the community association,' Longley said. 'You concentrate on the dead headteacher, if there's really still some mileage in that. They're as incensed up there about the arrest of Stephen Fletcher as they are by guns right now. Make sure the case stands up before the lad comes to court again, if you can. Or get it thrown out. I'm not bothered which, to be perfectly honest, but we do need some certainty.'

'Right,' Thackeray said. 'Mower reckons that Graves's wife has done a runner, which raises some interesting questions. At the very least we'll have to track her down. And as far as the Heights is concerned, I'm keen to find Fletcher's mate Dwayne Elton. It's quite likely he's gone to ground up there in that rabbit warren of empty flats.'

'I'll talk to the drug squad about that,' Longley said. 'Leave it with me.'

He got up to go and Thackeray nodded numbly. His head felt as if it was about to explode with the effort of concentrating on what the superintendent was saying.

'Take it easy,' Longley said again.

'Sir,' Thackeray just about managed as the door closed behind Longley. He knew that the superintendent was right. He should not be here trying to function normally. His problem was simply that he didn't know where else he could function at all.

Ella Ferenc was tidying up tubes of paint in a large empty studio when Mower tracked her down at the school of art. She was a tall, well-built woman with luxuriant dark hair which she wore in a dense tumbling mass down her back and she glanced up with liquid brown eyes which were openly appraising as the sergeant came in.

'Can I help?' Ella asked. The accent was faint but distinct. Probably from somewhere in middle Europe, Mower thought, which possibly explained the slight wariness with which she looked at his warrant card.

'I was looking for one of your students, Julia Graves,' Mower said. 'They told me in the office that she was due in for a class today.'

'She was, but she didn't turn up,' Ella said. 'She's not in any trouble, is she?' Again, that slight caution overlaid the friendliness of the inquiry.

'Not at all,' Mower reassured her. 'I need to talk to her about her husband's death, but she wasn't at home earlier today, or yesterday when I called in.'

'I was surprised when she didn't come in this afternoon. It's not like her. She's very keen as a rule, though to be perfectly honest, she's not very good. A chocolate box sort of painter, not exactly modernist, let alone post-modern.'

'I thought you'd all given up painting in favour of chopped up cows and displaying dirty knickers,' Mower said sceptically, glancing round at some of the fairly conventional work on the walls.

Ella threw back her head and laughed uproariously.

'Oh, that old thing. It's not true, you know. In fact, I paint myself. But abstracts. But you get all sorts in these non-exam classes. They're all adults and they pays their money and takes their choice. It's amazing how many Monet clones we get, all fiddly foliage and bloody water lilies.' She tossed her hair out of her eyes and waited for Mower to continue with a faint smile on her full lips.

'So Julia Graves was one of the amateurs then?'

'I don't think she'd claim anything else,' her teacher said. 'Though funnily enough she bought one of my paintings. I've been meaning to ask her to loan me it back. She bought it a while ago and I'd like to include it in the exhibition I'm having in London next month.'

'I noticed it when I was at the lodge a little while ago,' Mower said.

'She said she used to hide it away when Peter was alive. He didn't like abstract art.'

'How well did you know the Graves's?' Mower asked. Ella hesitated for a moment.

'I liked Julia,' she said. 'Though I thought she was a wimp as far as Peter was concerned. She should have left him years ago. We sometimes went for a drink after class, me and some of the students. I got to know her a bit then. She never bitched about him openly, but it was obvious that she was frightened of him. Odd things came out, about how demanding he was.'

'Did you ever go to the house?'

'No, I didn't. I don't think Julia invited people there much.'

'And what about the kids? I can't make out whether the Graves's had a family or not,' Mower said. The missing child or children, he knew, worried DCI Thackeray more than anything else about Julia Graves. Ella looked doubtful.

'They didn't have any children, did they? I never heard Julia mention kids, ever.'

'And Peter himself? Did you know him?'

'Well, I certainly felt I knew him from the way Julia went on about him. In fact I did see him once, from a distance. It was the day I took the painting Julia bought up there for her. I dropped in with it to the Lodge just as the kids were coming out of school and I saw Peter – at least I thought it was

Peter – on the steps watching them go. Keeping some sort of order I suppose.'

'But not to speak to?'

'No, no. I wasn't sure it was him at the time. And I had my work cut out fending off the attentions of some of the lads as I pushed my way in with this bloody great canvas.' She gave Mower a slightly complicit smile, as if he would appreciate the picture

'I thought the wolf whistle had gone out of fashion years ago,' she said. 'But apparently not.'

'How long ago was this visit to the school?' Mower asked, keen to move away from thoughts of sex. Ella thought for a moment.

'Last summer,' she said. 'May or early June.'

'And you'd already had Julia in your class sometime by then?'

'Oh, yes, she signed on here almost as soon as they moved to Bradfield, about eighteen months ago.'

'And Julia never talked about her family?' Mower returned to his previous question. 'A child, or children, at university? Left home and working somewhere else, maybe?'

Ella finished stacking away the paints and flopped down on the edge of table, running a hand through the tousled hair.

'She didn't talk much, and certainly not about having a family,' she said. 'But I'm sure there was something awful there that she would have liked to talk about. Of course, in a large class, or even in the pub, you can't have personal conversations, but it was just something about her, the way she looked when other students talked about their kids. I'm sure there was something awfully wrong in the past. But she never said anything specific. Nothing at all.'

'Do you think she could have become depressed after Peter's death? Any evidence that we should be seriously worried that she seems to have disappeared?' Mower asked, knowing that he was becoming seriously worried regardless of the evidence.

Ella laughed again.

'She didn't seem the least depressed to me,' she said. 'Not about that anyway. More relieved, really. She actually started painting better last week, as if someone had taken a great weight off her mind. Which maybe they had?'

Tearing himself away from Ella Ferenc with more reluctance than he would admit to, Mower drove back to the central police station without any real hope that DCI Thackeray would still be there. It was a wet and windy evening and the main CID office was deserted, but after he had hung up his dripping leather jacket he noticed a thin line of light under Thackeray's door. No one responded to his knock and he eventually opened the door and stuck his head inside. Thackeray was sitting at his desk with a bottle of whisky in front of him and a face so ravaged that Mower stepped inside quickly and closed the door behind him.

'Guv,' he said quietly. 'It's time to go home.' Thackeray looked at him silently as if he did not know him. His eyes had sunk so far into their sockets that it seemed as if he was trying to escape from the harsh fluorescent light of the office into another world entirely. Mower took the almost empty bottle, dodging a half-hearted attempt to stop him, and screwed the top on. He took Thackeray's coat from its hanger on the back of the door, went round to the far side of the desk and helped him into it.

'Come on,' he said. 'I'll drive you.' Thackeray shrugged but stood up without protest and allowed himself to be half led, half carried into the main CID office where Mower rescued his own coat. On the way out of the building he took time to go into one of the men's lavatories where he poured Thackeray's remaining Scotch down the drain, and hurled the bottle into the waste bin.

'Hell and damnation,' he said softly to himself, before

resuming their slow progress out of the back door of the building and across the swamped car park to his car.

From the car, he called Laura and told her tersely what to expect. She was waiting at the front door when Mower helped his boss out of the car, up the steps and into Laura's flat.

'I'll help you to put him to bed,' he said quietly to Laura in the kitchen after they had left Thackeray slumped on the sofa, apparently unable to move. 'And get him back to AA. If you don't we'll lose him. Believe me. I've seen it happen so many times in this bloody job. I almost went there too, after Rita was killed. He's on a slippery slope and he won't be able to claw himself back up on his own. He needs help. Fast.'

Laura looked at Mower with her eyes full of tears.

'And if I can't get him back on track?' she asked.

'Then dump him,' Mower said brutally. 'Otherwise he'll take you down with him.'

Superintendent Jack Longley put the phone down in his office and sighed heavily. The call had been an unwelcome one and he did not think he had handled it at all well. He was not a man much given to self-doubt but DCI Charles Hutton had taken him by surprise with the vehemence of his assault on Bradfield division in general, DCI Michael Thackeray in particular, and the unlikelihood of his ever having made a significant mistake in his entire career. Off balance, Longley had initially tried to placate the irate officer from Arnedale but that had got him nowhere. Hutton evidently took Bradfield's tentative efforts to take a fresh look at the Graves murder case – Longley did not know how he had obtained so much detail but instantly determined to find out – as a personal insult.

'The Crown Prosecution Service was entirely happy with the case against Fletcher,' Hutton had claimed loudly, although Longley knew that this was not strictly true. 'You seem to take more notice of the hysterical rent-a-mob up on bloody Wuthering than you do of the evidence on the file. And you know why that is, don't you? It's because Michael bloody Thackeray's hand-in-glove with the protesters, and listens to the Ackroyd women, wishy-washy liberals with more axes to grind than Lizzy bloody Borden, both of them. We'll get to the stage soon where we can't stop a bloody ethnic carrying a sub-machine gun down Kirkgate for fear of being accused of racism. It's political correctness run riot, and Thackeray's going along with it, as far as I can see. He's in a conflict of interest situation with that hack he lives with. The man should have more sense with his background. He leans over backwards to look caring and sharing, does Thackeray; in the hope people will forget what happened to his wife and kid. There wasn't much caring and sharing there, from what I hear. Drunken rages and a bit of wife battering is more like it, according to folk who knew him in Arnedale. It's no wonder his wife flipped.'

'That's uncalled for,' Longley had protested. 'It was years ago. Water under the bridge.'

'With his wife still in hospital, her whole life buggered up? I don't think so. There's people in Arnedale haven't forgotten that, and won't either.'

'His wife has died,' Longley said and instantly wished he had not. There was a long silence at the other end of the line. 'DCI Thackeray's on compassionate leave and I'm overseeing the Graves investigation personally,' Longley broke in eventually and not strictly accurately. 'If I need any additional help from you, Charles, I'll let you know, but I reckon it's only a question of tying up a few loose ends. Nothing significant has emerged so far to worry the CPS, though it does look as if we might have found the murder weapon.'

'That's good,' Hutton said, but the heat in his voice seemed to have dissipated suddenly and he sounded preoccupied.

'I'll keep you in touch, shall I?' Longley asked.

'Aye, I'd be grateful, sir,' Hutton said. 'But there is one other thing.'

'Oh yes?' Longley asked, his voice cold again as he guessed what was coming next.

'Your young Asian DC, Sharif. I hear he's making some sort of complaint against me.'

'He hasn't made any approach to me,' Longley said truthfully.

'Aye, well, there something going on. I've just lost a useless apology for a DC, Asian as well, and he reckons he's taking me to a tribunal. I hope Sharif hasn't got himself involved in that because I'll tell you for nothing, I intend to hang Hussain bloody Achmed out to dry. Lazy, vindictive and I reckon criminal as well. I'm working on that and things are coming out of the woodwork you wouldn't believe. Or maybe you would. You must have enough experience of these beggars in Bradfield. Stick together like shit to a blanket, of course. You want to watch Sharif. I wasn't impressed, I can tell you.'

'I think that's all I need to hear about my officers, thank you, DCI Hutton,' Longley had said, feeling himself redden with fury. 'All I can say is that my experience doesn't seem to mesh with yours.'

'Well, sir, I hope you're right and I'm wrong,' Hutton said. 'But you'll keep me in touch with any developments in the Graves case, won't you? I wouldn't like to see all my hard work for you go down the tubes.'

Longley hung up and wiped the sweat from his face and neck before hauling his considerable bulk down the stairs to Michael Thackeray's office. But the DCI was not there and Longley stood for a moment, breathing heavily and gazing at Thackeray's empty desk.

'He's gone to see his parents-in-law. Something about the funeral,' Sergeant Mower said. His sharp eyes had spotted the superintendent coming down the stairs.

'Thank you, sergeant,' Longley said. 'Ask him to pop in to see me when he next comes in. Is Sharif in today?'

'Not just now, sir,' Mower said. 'He's gone to see an informant on the Heights.'

'I'd like to see him, too,' Longley said shortly and turned on his heel. Mower watched him go with a sense of anxiety which gripped his stomach like a clenched fist. Longley had unease written all over him, he thought, and he would have good reason when he discovered the truth: that his DCI was sleeping off a massive hangover and DC Sharif was intending to meet Hussain Achmed again on his way back from Wuthering. If things got much worse, Mower thought, there was no way he was going to be able to protect either of them from Longley and the wrath of more senior officers still. He was like the Dutch boy with his finger in the dyke, only he knew that this high tide was likely to overwhelm him and sweep him out to sea.

Laura had lain rigidly wide awake for a long time that morning beside a comatose and snoring Michael Thackeray before finally sliding out of bed and calling in sick to the *Gazette*. She had inevitably slept badly and felt drained as she desultorily tidied the place up and waited for him to wake. When he eventually did he took her by surprise and she wondered just how long he had been standing fully dressed in the bedroom doorway behind her. He looked pale and haggard.

'Shouldn't you be at work?' he asked.

'Not until I'm sure you're OK.'

'I'm fine.' That was so obviously untrue that she could not help a faint smile.

'We need to talk,' she said.

He flung himself into a chair and sat silently for a long time staring at the floor, hands hanging limply between his knees.

'Michael?' Laura ventured at last. 'Please?'

'It never goes away, you know? The craving, it never goes away. You're never cured. You have to understand that.'

'Kevin Mower says you should go to AA. Get some help,' Laura said.

'Yes, he's probably right.'

'Can I do anything?' Laura asked. Suddenly he was angry.

'I can't ask you to put up with this, Laura. Not any of it. You need to understand that the last couple of days were nothing, a minor incident, a tiny binge. It can be much, much worse. Aileen bore the brunt of it and it killed her. I can't do that again. I mustn't.'

'You've survived all these years,' Laura said. 'You can do it again.'

'I can't guarantee it,' Thackeray said. 'No one can guarantee that.'

Laura felt very cold but quite clear-headed. She got up and knelt on the floor in front of Thackeray, taking both his hands in hers.

'I'm not giving up on you, Michael Thackeray, so don't imagine I am. An appalling thing happened to you but you didn't just survive. You succeeded. You hauled yourself back on track. This is just a glitch. You can do it again. We can both do it, together. What sort of a wife would I make if I gave up on you the first time the going got tough?'

She put her arms around him and her cheek against his and felt rather than saw the tears as they clung together for a long time.

Later, when Thackeray had gone, showered and shaved and swallowing coffee and painkillers until he felt about twenty-five per cent normal, and decided that for the sake of his sanity and his career he needed to go into work, Laura answered a call on her mobile and found the fragile hope she had rekindled instantly shattered again.

'There you are, Princess,' Fergal Mackenzie said. 'I tried you at the office.'

'I get a nasty feeling when I hear your voice, Fergal,' Laura said.

'Ach, well, that's what it's like in our filthy business, Princess. But I have to ask you something. We've had a death notice in, one Aileen Thackeray, passed away after a long illness. Would that be your Bonnie Prince's wife, by any chance?'

Her mouth dry, Laura had to admit that it would be.

'Aye, I thought so. She sounded about the right age although the notice doesn't mention a husband. It's been submitted by her parents apparently. A bit unusual, that, for a married lady.'

'So it'll appear on Thursday?'

'That's right. It was submitted in time. Perhaps you'd best warn your man what's coming?' Laura's stomach tightened at that. The last thing Thackeray needed was more bad news, she thought. She remembered his real fear of being pilloried by the Press if and when Aileen died. And Mackenzie had not finished yet.

'Is there going to be an inquest, do you know?' he asked. Laura's horror grew.

'She died of heart problems, natural causes,' she said. 'Why should there be?'

'It was just a thought,' he said. 'If that happened I'd have to run a story. I couldn't ignore it. It's a possibility if some vindictive beggar decides she really died because of a suicide attempt twelve years ago and tries to prod the coroner into action.'

'And we know there's at least one vindictive beggar in Arnedale who might do just that,' Laura said despairingly.

'Aye, well, I'll keep my ears open for you, Princess. But it looks to me like you're headed for a rough ride. Take care.'

Laura gazed at her silent mobile for a long time. Suddenly there seemed to be more wolves in the shadows of her life than she had ever known before. All she could hope was that she and Michael were strong enough to defeat them.

The autumn evening was already closing in when DCI Thackeray and Sergeant Mower drove up the steep hill to the Heights, followed by a dozen uniformed officers, in a police van and a patrol car. Thackeray, pale and exhausted and anxious to get back to the relative calm of Laura's flat, had been on the point of calling it a day when Mower and Sharif had come into his office, full of suppressed excitement.

'You're sure your informant's reliable?' Thackeray had asked Sharif when he explained how his informant, whom he had been urging to come up with something useful that very morning, had called him five minutes ago to say that she had seen Dwayne Elton outside a squat in Holtby House, the even more dilapidated tower block which faced her own.

'She said there've been kids coming and going on that landing all week,' Sharif had said enthusiastically. 'And she knows Dwayne by sight. She's quite sure it was him.'

'Going in, not coming out?'

'That's what she said. She said if we're quick enough we'll catch him.'

Thackeray had hesitated for no more than a moment. He knew that Superintendent Longley was at a meeting at county HQ. Contacting him would take time they might not have.

'I want that lad,' Thackeray said, more decisively than he had really felt, and within half an hour his squad of cars, the occupants in body armour under their jackets, was on the road. As the convoy swung onto the estate it passed Joyce Ackroyd's tiny bungalow, one of a row built in the shadow of the flats on the assumption that it would keep families in touch with their grandparents, an assumption that Thackeray felt had been optimistic in the 1960s and hopelessly over-optimistic now.

'Isn't that Laura's car?' Mower asked, nodding at the Golf parked under a streetlight close to Joyce's garden gate.

'She must be visiting Joyce,' Thackeray said dismissively. 'They're up to their eyes in this protest about the Fletcher boy.'

'You're still not convinced it wasn't him?' Mower ventured.

'Not convinced enough,' Thackeray said. 'But let's see what young Dwayne has to say for himself, shall we?'

The police vehicles parked close to the entrance to Holtby House and some of the uniformed officers took up stations at the two entrances while Mower and Thackeray and the rest pounded up the narrow concrete stairs to the fourth floor, cursing the perennially inoperative lifts as they went.

'There's been plenty of activity up here,' Mower said grimly, kicking aside a clutter of used syringes and other rubbish on the top landing. 'Perhaps we should have waited for armed back-up, guv?'

'They're on their way,' Thackeray snapped. 'Is Stephen Fletcher a drug user?'

'Not as far as I know,' Mower said. 'There was no suggestion of that when we interviewed him. Nothing hard, anyway.

They all smoke cannabis up here. Goes without saying.'

'And Elton?'

'I don't know,' Mower admitted. 'If this is where he hangs out it looks like it's a distinct possibility.'

The top landing was ill-lit and deserted as the police officers made their way along to the third front door, one of the few which was not boarded up.

'None of these flats is occupied officially,' Mower said as the uniformed officers looked at the detectives and waited for instructions. 'Do we go in, guv?' he asked Thackeray.

Thackeray nodded and the burliest of the officers swung a battering ram at the door, which splintered under the impact, but did not give way.

'They've reinforced it,' the officer wielding the ram grunted, as he took another swing. This time the door lurched drunkenly on its hinges and the shouts of alarm from inside intensified. The flat appeared to be in total darkness which the policemen's torches lit up only fitfully as they pushed one after the other through the narrow entrance.

Looking back on what followed, neither Thackeray nor Mower could come up with more than a jumbled impression of total confusion as what seemed like an enormous number of people erupted into a violent melee in the confined space of the flat. Several of those inside tried to push their way out onto the walkway as the police pushed in but they were soon overpowered. Inside others slugged it out with the officers who had ventured furthest into the darkness.

'Dwayne Elton, we're looking for Dwayne Elton,' Thackeray shouted above the brawl that had broken out around them as he and Mower stepped inside the narrow hallway. His answer was a heavy blow to the head which swung him back against the wall and temporarily dazed him. He heard one of the uniformed officers summoning urgent assistance before Mower appeared at his elbow again.

'You all right, guv?' the sergeant asked. 'There's a whole

crew of them in here.'

Thackeray shook his head to clear it and grabbed at a young man wearing boxer shorts and very little else who was trying to push his way forcibly past him towards the shattered door.

'You're nicked,' Thackeray said, bundling his prey out onto the landing where heavy footfalls told him that help was on its way in the shape of more uniformed officers from the armed response unit, one of whom grabbed his prisoner and secured his hands behind his back while the others surged into the free-for-all inside the flat.

'Some of them got away, guv,' Mower said anxiously. He leaned over the rail in an attempt to see what was happening at ground level. 'They've knocked holes in the walls to give themselves the run of the whole landing.' Down below the flashing blue alarms of the police vehicles cast a flickering light around the concrete car park and revealed small huddles of spectators on balconies watching the police in sullen silence.

'Jesus, what's she doing here,' Mower said suddenly.

'Who?' Thackeray asked, still feeling groggy and aware of the stickiness of blood on his forehead. He pulled out a handkerchief and dabbed at the damage irritably.

'Laura and some other woman,' Mower said, pointing to two figures hurrying towards the action. 'They're going to get caught up in the bundle if they're not careful.' Even as he spoke an overflow of bodies from the flat, both official and unofficial, raced out of the entrance to Holtby house, catching the two women unawares and knocking one of them to the ground.

Pausing only to make sure that uniformed officers now had the situation under control in the squat, Thackeray thundered back down the concrete stairs to find that the uniformed officers and their still struggling prisoners had by now moved over to the police vans, leaving Laura leaning over her companion, who was sitting on the floor in a smart business suit which was now somewhat the worse for wear and struggling to get her breath back.

'What the hell are you doing here?' Thackeray asked both women. Laura glanced up at him ruefully.

'This is Jenny Sweetman, Stevie Fletcher's solicitor. We came to see Dwayne Elton, as it happens, but it looks as if we're too late.'

'It didn't cross Miss Sweetman's mind, I suppose, that before coming up here she might have told the police what was going on,' Thackeray said, helping Jenny to her feet and dusting her down peremptorily. He did not look at Laura again. 'We've only been searching for Dwayne Elton for about a week.'

'I was intending to persuade Dwayne to come to the police station with me, as it goes,' Jenny said breathlessly.

'When he's ready to be questioned about possession of Class A drugs, affray, carrying an offensive weapon, assaulting a police officer and whatever else I can think of to throw at him, you'll be able to see your client,' Thackeray said curtly. He turned away from the two women and Mower risked offering Laura a sympathetic smile which gained him no more than an angry glare in return.

'I think you'll find that you've got lots of people there you can throw charges at, but Dwayne Elton isn't among them,' Laura shot at Thackeray's retreating back. He spun round.

'What do you mean?'

'You obviously didn't see that a couple of them got away. We were looking up at the top walkway as you bashed the door down. Two lads came out of a door further down the landing and swung down onto the balcony below. When your men left the doors unattended, they ran out that way. I'm pretty sure one of them was Dwayne.'

Mower held his breath as Laura faced Thackeray for a long moment, before the DCI turned on his heel again and went back to the car without a word.

Chapter Seventeen

Thackeray sat in his office late that evening contemplating his uncertain future. Laura had been right. After the cut on his head had been cleaned and dressed by the medical officer, and he had swallowed as many painkillers as he dared, he had checked on the arrested young men and discovered that Elton was not amongst them.

'We've picked up enough gear to send them all down for a while,' Mower reported back to the DCI. 'But no firearms, thankfully. And no one's saying whether Elton was actually there let alone where he might have gone now. So we're back to square one, guv.' In fact it was worse than that. Almost as soon as Thackeray had got back to the police station, Longley had been on the phone demanding to know why he had launched a raid on the Heights without his, and the drug squad's, approval.

'It seemed like too good a lead to miss,' Thackeray had said, but he knew that while he would have been garnering congratulations from county HQ if the tip-off had borne fruit, the failure to find Elton would not impress.

'We'll discuss it tomorrow morning,' Longley had said before hanging up abruptly.

'Sir,' Thackeray had acquiesced gloomily. He wondered how many more tomorrows like this one threatened to be he could survive, how many more days he could sustain the belief that what he and his officers offered the Heights, or multi-racial Aysgarth Lane, offered any sort of improvement in the day-to-day lives of the people who lived there. A few more young men with a heroin or crack addiction would be locked up as a result of today's exercise, but he doubted that many of them would be cured in overcrowded prisons where drugs were almost as readily available as they were on the street. A few more dealers would be put temporarily out of action, replaced by the end of the week by the next generation of young, ill-educated men and youths looking for an

easier supply of cash and the good things of life than conventional employment would ever offer them. And so the
cycle would continue, with no obvious end in sight.

The need for a drink swept over him, as it had the previous day. What difference was there, he wondered, between
his own sickness and that of the kids he had just arrested?
He put on his coat, switched out lights as he went through
the deserted CID office, and left the building to be assailed
by a sharp wind and sleety rain as he crossed the town hall
square. A pub door swung open and closed again and for a
second he hesitated outside, his whole being assailed by the
smell of alcohol and cigarette smoke and the insidious
promise of some sort of oblivion. Reluctantly he moved on
and made his way up one of the steep hills leading away from
the town centre to a narrow anonymous doorway between a
shoe shop and a take-away curry restaurant. Up a dark flight
of stairs he pushed open the door giving onto a badly lit
room where a number of men and women sat in a circle of
chairs in total silence.

'Come in, come in, if we can help,' someone said quietly. Thackeray took a chair and glanced round the circle. Few
eyes met his. Most people present seemed to prefer to gaze
at the floor or at a point above the newcomer's head.
Eventually one of the circle spoke, his voice barely audible,
and his unshaven chin sunk into the turned up collar of his
grubby duffle coat. Thackeray had heard it all before: the
litany of effort and backsliding, the occasional optimism and
the all-pervading guilt. For half an hour he listened to Pam
and George and Aiden reveal their daily struggle to stay
sober, until he could listen no more. He got to his feet
abruptly and hurried out of the room, allowing the door to
close behind him with a thud which reverberated down the
stairwell. He leaned against the wall, ran a shaking hand
through his dark hair and swore softly to himself.

'I can't do all that again,' he said aloud as he walked slowly down the stairs, holding onto the banister tightly as if

afraid he would fall. 'I won't do all that again.' Out on the
street someone was laughing hysterically, a young girlish
voice made shrill and in no way attractive by drink. He
opened the door and the icy wind caught him and made him
shudder. 'I can't and I won't,' he said. 'It's over.'

As he stood watching the girl and her companions stag-
ger into the door of the next pub down the hill his mobile
rang. It was David Mendelson and for a moment he hesitated, sure that Laura must have asked the lawyer to call him.
He was certain that his friend's concern and advice was not
what he wanted to hear in his present desperation. This was
an abyss he had to climb out of himself. In the end he let the
call transfer to voice mail, and after a minute he picked up
the message. Mendelson did not offer the sympathy which
Thackeray expected. His voice was sharp with anxiety.

'Michael, can you call me?' he said. 'I heard on the
grapevine today that there's some pressure on the coroner to
order a post-mortem on Aileen and convene an inquest. I
don't know who's behind it but the official request seems to
have come from the Arnedale coroner. She died outside his
jurisdiction of course, but I suppose he thinks he has an
interest as he conducted the inquest on your son. It seems
completely out of order to me but I think we should talk, or
maybe you should talk to your own solicitor. It could all get
very messy.'

Thackeray groaned as the implications of what
Mendelson was saying sank in. David might not know who
was behind the pressure from Arnedale, but he thought he
had a very good idea. He did not call Mendelson back.
Instead he walked slowly down the hill back into the town
centre and picked up his car. Back at his own flat, without
the carrier bag of booze he had been almost irresistibly
tempted to buy on the way, he lay fully dressed on the bed
and gazed at the ceiling for a long time, smoking and half listening to a Billie Holiday CD. When the music eventually
stopped he called Laura.

'It's me,' he said when she picked up. 'I thought I should let you know I won't come back tonight.'

'Right,' she said and he could tell that she was still angry.

'I'm sorry,' he said.

'Right,' Laura said, her voice strained. 'Are you drinking again?'

'No, I promise you, I'm not. But I have to do this my way,' he said.

'No place for me then, when things get tough?'

'There's not a lot you can do,' he said. 'I can beat it, Laura. Believe me.'

'Did David contact you? He called here…'

'Yes, I got his message.'

'And can you beat that too? On your own?'

'I don't know,' he said. 'Can we talk tomorrow? Lunch maybe?'

'Call me in the morning,' she said. 'I'll see how I'm fixed.' She hung up. It was as if, he thought, she was making an appointment with a stranger.

He lay down on the bed again and eventually fell into an uneasy sleep, plagued by dreams in which he made love to a woman he could barely identify as Laura or Aileen or a complete stranger. He woke early, before daylight, showered and dressed and drove into work faster than was safe or legal. He felt, he thought, even worse than he had the day before and faced battalions of new problems which needed to be dealt with decisively before the day was over. After coffee and a cigarette he slumped at his desk, still wondering if he could really cope with anything any more.

'The drug squad aren't happy with that little escapade,' Superintendent Jack Longley said with rather less venom than Thackeray had expected when he went into his office later that morning. 'Apparently they'd had that flat under surveillance for weeks waiting for Mr Big to turn up. But you took a hell of a chance. You know there are firearms up there. I'd have thought you'd have had more sense.'

A slight shiver went down Thackeray's spine at that. He had lost a colleague to unexpected gunfire once and the memory haunted him still. He had been very lucky the previous night. He knew it, and he knew Longley knew it.

'We were misinformed about the flat we raided,' Thackeray said. 'Our informant told us it was occupied by a black family who were harbouring Dwayne Elton. If the drug squad knew anything different they should at least have kept us in the picture. How can anyone do a risk assessment if there's information available we're not privy to?'

'Exactly what I told them,' Longley said. 'And now you want to get up Charles Hutton's nose as well, do you?'

If only Longley knew how little enthusiasm he had for that project, Thackeray thought. But he could see no way round launching a thorough discussion with the Crown Prosecution Service about the now less than compelling case against Stephen Fletcher.

'D'you really think this other boy, what's his name, Dwayne, is involved in the murder, then?' Longley asked.

'Up to his neck,' Thackeray said flatly. 'He pretty well confessed to being there when he spoke to Laura Ackroyd.'

'Exceeding her brief a bit, isn't she, your friend Laura?' Longley had never approved of Thackeray's relationship with a journalist, and Thackeray knew that this latest episode of freelance investigation on her part might add yet more fuel to the bonfire he seemed to be making of his career.

'More by accident than design in this case, I think,' he said with more reassurance in his voice than he felt. 'Don't worry. I'll keep an eye on her.' Which, he thought, glancing out of the window at the hazy sunshine outside, was one of his vainer promises.

'So I suppose you want to reopen the investigation officially,' Longley said heavily.

'If we don't I guess the defence will try to get the case thrown out before it even gets to the Crown court,'

Thackeray said. 'There are too many loose ends: Dwayne Elton, no proper investigation done on where that blasted petrol can came from, a possible weapon turning up now. Why now, after all this time, for God's sake?'

'And the grieving widow taking off without a by-your-leave.'

'Yes, there's Julia Graves. I'll put a missing person call out for her this afternoon, if there's no more news,' Thackeray said. 'Fears growing for her safety will do as an excuse.'

'Could she have killed her old man? Some domestic row got too much for her?'

'Apparently there might have been another woman,' Thackeray said, carefully avoiding connecting another item of information to Laura's researches. 'I've got Mower making some discreet inquiries about that.'

Longley sighed heavily.

'Messy,' he said. 'And there's political dimensions to this one, Michael. All the fuss that's going on about that school, the attempts to get it closed, the council under pressure from the residents. Just get it cleared up quick, will you, before we get complaints to the chief constable from the Southfield nimbies. You know they think they should be exempt from owt as common as police inquiries, and if we've harassed them and then find it really is the yobbos from the Height's who're to blame, we'll end up deep in the mire.'

'There's a few other dimensions to it, as well,' Thackeray said unhelpfully, as his brain ground very slowly into gear. 'Like why our colleague from Arnedale didn't widen the investigation the first time around. He's left more leads trailing than Agatha Christie. A quick arrest was convenient, maybe? Or did a black lad just fit his prejudices, which is what Kevin Mower thinks. If Stevie Fletcher is banged up for no good reason, those questions aren't going to go away. Jenny Sweetman's going to want some pretty convincing answers. So's the boy's mother and all her friends on the Heights.'

'Aye, well, we don't know that Stevie Fletcher is banged up for no good reason quite yet, do we? So let's not jump our fences before the Grand National's bloody started. The defence has already played the race card once and much good it's done them because contrary to what all those bleeding-heart *Guardian* readers think, black lads do occasionally commit crime. I know that, you know that, even Jenny bloody Sweetman knows that. And no one knows that better than the custody sergeant who's minding all those junkies you nicked last night.'

'Apparently our stock on the Heights is off the floor for once after the raid,' Thackeray said with a faint smile. 'They won't do anything to help us up there but they're happy enough when we clear out a dealer's squat for them. It's a good job they don't know it was all such a cock-up.'

'It won't go down as a cock-up in the clear-up figures, so I shouldn't fash yourself,' Longley said dismissively. 'Or about the drug squad. Mr Big, my backside!' He shifted his bulk in his chair contemptuously. 'All that's bugging them is that we'll take the credit for last night's little enterprise, not them.'

Thackeray made his way back to his own office looking grim. He had not spoken to Laura again after their chilly conversation the previous night but he knew that she would not have suspended her own inquiries and that Longley's go-ahead for further investigation of Peter Graves's murder could put them on a collision course again. He knew he should call her, not just for that reason but because he feared that with the unpredictable Dwayne Elton still at large, and now forced out of his safe haven on the Heights, perhaps even suspecting that Laura had something to do with the police raid on his hiding-place, he might approach Laura again. And the results of that might be less benign than they were the first time she and Dwayne had met.

But before he could call the *Gazette* to try to persuade Laura to have lunch with him, as a first step to mending fences and pleading with her to take more care, there was a tap on the door and DC Mohammed Sharif put his head round.

'Can I have a word, guv?' he asked, looking sufficiently desperate for Thackeray to nod him in.

'I've got about two minutes, Omar,' he said.

Sharif fiddled with his tie as if it was too tight.

'It's a bit difficult,' he said at last after a couple of false starts. 'I was going to talk to Sergeant Mower but he's not around…'

'On inquiries,' Thackeray said shortly.

'Yeah, right, well, I expect he's told you that I agreed to give evidence at a tribunal for a mate at Arnedale nick – except he's not at Arnedale any more, he's resigned, that's what it's all about…'

'Kevin Mower told me briefly,' Thackeray said. 'I told him to say you were sticking your neck out.'

'Yeah, well, it's even worse now,' Sharif said, looking even more uncomfortable. 'My mate's brother just called me and said Hussain's been arrested. They came to the house this morning with a search warrant and took him back to Arnedale with some stuff they found in his room. Said he'd nicked it.'

Thackeray sat very still, feeling cold. Sharif was watching him with tension in every inch of him and fear in his eyes.

'This was here, in Bradfield?' Thackeray asked.

'Yeah, Hussain Achmed went back to his family. He joined the police in Leeds first off, before he went to Arnedale. I don't know why. But his parents are here in Bradfield. They live just off Aysgarth Lane.'

'Did his brother say how he reacted? Did he say anything before they took him away?'

'Ali said he was in tears,' Sharif said, not far from tears himself. 'He said he'd never stolen anything in his life.'

'And you believe him?'

'I don't know, do I? I think he went to my school but he's

older than me and I don't remember him at all. I didn't know he existed till this business with DCI Hutton came up.'

Thackeray sighed.

'There's no reason why any of this should affect you here,' he said. 'Kevin Mower knows that DCI Hutton upset you while he was working here and you agreed to help another officer for the best of motives, so don't worry about it. Leave it with me. I'll try to find out what's going on up in Arnedale and let you know.'

'Sir,' Sharif agreed, reluctantly.

'If you get rattled the first time things go wrong you won't survive in this job, Omar,' Thackeray said, suddenly feeling his years. 'You're doing fine. Just keep cool.' Sharif relaxed slightly and managed a tentative smile.

'Thanks,' he said.

But when he had gone Thackeray cursed under his breath, picked up the phone and relayed to Superintendent Longley what Sharif had told him.

'Did you know Hutton was planning a search and an arrest on our turf?' he asked.

'I didn't,' Longley said. 'And I've not been told official-ly yet. Don't worry. I'll get straight onto the Super in Arnedale and find out what the hell's going on.'

'Are you thinking what I'm thinking?' Thackeray asked.

'What? That Hutton's getting his retaliation in first? That's an extremely serious allegation, Michael, even as a passing thought.'

'I never said a word, sir,' Thackeray said grimly. He put the phone down but before he could damp down his anger enough to try Laura's number it rang again.

'You'd better get up here sharpish, guv,' Sergeant Kevin Mower said. 'I'm at the school and all hell's let loose.'

DS Mower had arrived at Woodlands School soon after lessons began for the day. As he stood in the hallway, gazing up at the stained-glass window which filtered the light down the broad Victorian staircase in broad splashes of gold and aquamarine, he was surprised at how quiet the building seemed. The occasional sound of a teacher's voice filtered through the closed doors, then a ripple of laughter, the faint clatter of a keyboard, a waft of music which he could not identify. Whatever the problems the school faced, both inherent in its clientele or in the dispute over its future, it gave every impression of running sweetly this morning.

He was waiting for Mary Morris, who eventually hurried down the stairs, her full black skirt lifting to reveal surprisingly shapely legs, Mower thought. He had never been one to let an opportunity to appreciate the female form pass him by. The deputy head had a faintly irritated look of interrogation on her face and ran anxious fingers through her hair.

'What can I do for you, sergeant? I thought we'd covered everything yesterday?'

Mower glanced around the tiled hall.

'I think we should talk in private,' he said. Mary shrugged and led him into her office. She listened impassively as Mower told her about the police failure to arrest Dwayne Elton the previous night.

'Poor Dwayne,' she said. 'He and Stevie may have been up here that night, but I still can't believe they committed murder.'

'We thought you should know he's on the loose and may be feeling desperate. You did say he was unpredictable,' Mower countered.

'Unpredictable, yes, but not vicious. I've never felt threatened by Dwayne.'

'Are those two lads on hard drugs?' Mower asked flatly.

Mary Morris shook her head emphatically.

'Naturally we watch out for that,' she said. 'I've no evidence that either Dwayne or Stevie are addicts. Though like all these kids with problems of one sort and another, they're at risk all the time. I can understand that sometimes it looks like an easy way out.'

'You're sure nothing was stolen that night?' he said, more for confirmation than information.

'Your people didn't find any sign of a forced entry. Peter seemed to have locked up and put the alarms on before he was attacked. And nothing was taken, as far as we could see.'

'So you wouldn't expect Stevie or Dwayne to have come up here looking something to nick to fund their habit. And they're not violent. It sounds too good to be true,' Mower said.

'Don't get me wrong,' the deputy head came back quickly. 'There's hardly a child in this school who's any sort of an angel. They all unpredictable, highly emotional, can throw the most alarming tantrums. We've a special system for firefighting if anyone throws a serious wobbly. But neither of them is amongst the most difficult. Dwayne is seriously disturbed and does bear a grudge sometimes. There was one younger boy who crossed him somehow, and he made his life a misery until I put a stop to it.'

'I'll pass that on,' Mower said, wondering if Dwayne would try to work out who had betrayed his hiding place to the police. That would bear checking out as well, whether he jumped to the right conclusion or the wrong one.

'But that's not the only reason I'm here,' Mower went on. 'I know you said yesterday that you had no idea whether or not Peter Graves had a lover.' Mower looked at her speculatively. 'It wasn't you by any chance, was it?'

Mary shook her head vigorously.

'At my age, I'll take that as a compliment but it's still a stupid question, sergeant,' she said briskly. 'My relationship with Peter was confrontational all right, but not in the sexual sense. I despised the man.'

'Just checking,' Mower said with a small smile.

'Why is it so important to find out who he was sleeping with?'

'Because that sort of relationship can lead to violence,' Mower said. 'Also we have reason to believe that there was a woman in school that night, before Gareth Davies arrived.'

'Was there now,' Mary Morris said thoughtfully. 'I wonder who that could have been.'

'So do we,' Mower said. 'In fact we have to find out. It could have been Graves's wife, of course, but as we don't know where she is, we can't ask her. In the meantime, I need to talk to all your women staff, if only to eliminate them from our inquiries.'

'Well, I'm pleased to hear there are now some more inquiries, for Stevie's sake. But it won't take you long. There are only four other women teachers here, unless you want to include the dinner ladies, of course, but I think you'll find most of them are long past the age where seducing a head-teacher is a very practical proposition. They're more into comparing snapshots of their grandchildren.'

'You'd be surprised by some of the grannies we meet,' Mower said grimly.

'And there's Ella Ferenc, I suppose. She comes in sometimes to help.'

'Ella Ferenc?' Mower asked. 'The art teacher? I've already talked to her. She did tell me she visited…'

'It's only occasionally, as the kids come up to their GCSEs. It was Gareth's idea of course.'

'Gareth?' Mower repeated, feeling that he was stepping into a swamp he did not even know existed.

'Ella's Gareth Davies's wife, though she uses her own name professionally…'

'She didn't tell me that,' Mower said, angry now. 'Perhaps because that gives her just as much motive for murder as he had.'

'They must both be furious at the way Gareth was treated,'

Mary Morris said. 'But murder? I can't imagine that. Anyway, you'll have to track her down at home or at college. She not been in here for months.'

'We'll have Davies's address on file,' Mower said.

'I suppose I can ask the female staff to talk to you at break,' she offered. 'I don't want to drag them out of their classes. Disruption of any sort isn't good for these kids and they've had more than their fair share lately.'

But Mary Morris's concern for her flock was dashed almost as soon as she had expressed it. Mower had not realised how effectively the high, tiled hallway acted as an amplifier for noise, but when a young girl ran into it screaming as loudly as her lungs would allow, there could have been no one in the school or even in the houses immediately beyond who did not hear her and feel their blood chill. Mary Morris was out of her chair even quicker than Mower.

'Josie, what is it?' she said, as she flung open her office door, seized the girl by the shoulders and clutched her tightly to her chest. 'Whatever's happened? Have you hurt yourself?' Even with the screams muffled now, Mower was aware of the growing murmur of concern swelling behind the classroom doors, as if a sleeping lion had been aroused from its midday doze.

'Take her into my office,' Mary Morris said sharply to Mower. 'I'll have the whole school in uproar again. I'll be back in a minute when I've calmed everyone down.'

Mower took hold of the girl's thin arm and pulled her firmly into the office and shut the door. Her screams had subsided now to hysterical sobbing and he sat her in a low chair and held her close.

'It's OK, sweetheart,' he said, as if he had been comforting hysterical children for years. 'It's OK now. Take your time and tell me what the problem is.'

'There's a dead body,' the girl said between hiccups and sobs. 'Down at the end of the garden. There's a woman lying there dead.'

Mower's mind switched into overdrive at that and he had called an ambulance and Michael Thackeray by the time Mary Morris returned.

'Take over here, and don't let any of the kids into the gardens,' he instructed the startled headteacher before he ran, following Josie's somewhat garbled instructions, to the back of the school. The old house stood on raised ground, with blocks of modern temporary classrooms to one side. The gardens fell in terraces towards a long-disused railway line. The first level had been tarmacked over as a playground, but below that rambling and neglected fruit trees grew at strange angles in an area of roughly mown grass and an over-grown pathway led across the site from a dilapidated gate in the side wall to a derelict block which must have once been stables and the servants' quarters for the big house.

Mower took the stone steps to the playground two at a time and then jumped from the terrace wall into the old orchard, dodging between the trees and glancing behind every overgrown bush until he reached a matted shrubbery beyond the stables. Julia Graves was lying there, her long golden hair spread out in a cloud which obscured her face, her light dress torn, and crumpled beneath her, and one hand clenched on what looked like a handful of leaves.

He knelt beside her and brushed the hair away from her neck and felt for a pulse and relief flooded through him as he realised that she was still alive, although very cold. Gently, he turned her onto her side and made sure her airways were clear. He could see no signs of external injury but a small dribble of saliva had run from her mouth and when he put his head close to hers he could hear that she was breathing with a slightly guttural noise in her throat, almost snoring. Carefully he lifted one eye-lid and recognised the pinpoint pupil he half expected. He could hear the ambulance siren now, and stood up. Mary Morris was standing outside the back entrance to the school and he raised one hand.

'Tell the paramedics to hurry up,' he called. 'She's alive.'

As he watched anxiously, she turned away to meet the hurrying ambulance crew and led them down the slope and through the trees.

'It looks like an overdose,' Mower said curtly as they began to examine her. 'But she may have been here since yesterday.' He and the headteacher watched anxiously as the paramedics set to work, and then followed the stretcher back to the ambulance, which was parked, blue lights still flashing, on the drive in front of the school.

'What do you reckon?' Mower asked the driver as he closed the back doors on his patient and colleague. The paramedic, a stolid man, bulky in his green fluorescent overalls, shrugged slightly.

'She's a long way under,' he said. 'It may be too late.'

As the ambulance pulled away, Mower watched DCI Thackeray's car come up the drive and swing into the space it had vacated. They stood in the golden autumn sunshine while Mower filled in the details of what had happened.

'A suicide attempt?' Thackeray asked. Mower shrugged.

'Impossible to tell,' he said. 'I suppose it could be an accident. They want us to look in the lodge to see if we can find out what she's taken.'

'Right, I'll see to that,' Thackeray said. 'You follow the ambulance down to the infirmary and let me know what happens. If I find anything useful I'll call you.'

Thackeray drove quickly back down to the main gates of the school and tucked his car in by the lodge gate, which had been left swinging open. He got out, feeling deflated after the adrenaline rush of a fast drive up to the school. But as he closed the gate behind him he was startled by a shrill voice from behind him.

'What is it this time?' Alicia Boston asked, striding in through the school gateway like some avenging valkyrie. She was wearing cord gardening trousers, a floral shirt and still carried a heavy garden fork in her right hand which she jabbed into the ground too close to Thackeray's feet for comfort.

'What is it this time? Another murder? One of those lit-tle hooligans stabbed someone, have they? Set someone on fire? Used a hammer on someone else?'

'I'm sorry, madam,' Thackeray said, his look frosty enough to stop Brunnhilde in her tracks, but not, apparent-ly, this suburban version. 'I don't think we've met.'

'Neighbourhood Watch, Alicia Boston,' Alicia said firmly, one hand on the handle of her fork. 'And you? I sup-pose you have authority to go into the lodge?' Thackeray showed her his warrant card grimly.

'There's nothing here for the Neighbourhood Watch to be concerned about,' he said. 'Everything is under control. Simply an unfortunate accident, we think.'

'Nothing at this place is ever an accident,' Alicia snapped back quickly. 'I sometimes think the council keep the school up here deliberately to keep the property values down. It's a disgrace. Police cars, ambulances, fire engines, all hours of the day and night...'

'If you could excuse me, I have some urgent matters to attend to,' Thackeray said, his patience quickly exhausted. 'It's really the council you should raise your complaints with, not the police.'

'Useless,' she said angrily. 'It's all been useless. No one takes a blind bit of notice. How much more aggravation do we have to put up with before they close the place down?'

As she turned away a dark blue BMW pulled up by the kerb and the driver wound down the window.

'Problems, Alicia?' he asked.

'One crisis after another,' Alicia Boston said, turning with a warm smile towards the newcomer. 'Ambulances screaming up the road, police here by the minutes...'

'Jump in, I'll drop you at home,' the driver said. As Mrs Boston made her way to the passenger door he glanced at Thackeray who was still standing by the gate to the lodge.

'Mark Oliver, part of the campaign to close this place down,' he said, his expression deeply unfriendly. 'Do keep us informed, won't you, Chief Inspector? This is really getting out of hand.' With that, he accelerated away with a squeal of overstressed tyres, leaving Michael Thackeray to wonder how he knew who he was. As he turned back to the lodge gate he almost fell over Alicia Boston's garden fork. With a faint smile, he took a paper tissue out of his pocket and wrapped it carefully around the handle, picked the fork up and stowed it in the boot of his car.

'Purely for purposes of elimination,' he said to himself as he slammed the boot lid down. 'Something my esteemed colleague from Arnedale should have done weeks ago.'

DCI Charles Hutton was obviously doing his best to be civil but his barely controlled fury almost hummed against Superintendent Jack Longley's ear.

'How do you know what's going on anyway?' Longley demanded of the man on the other end of the phone in Arnedale, glad that Hutton could not see the beads of sweat he felt on his forehead.

'I spoke to Mendelson at the CPS,' Hutton said, his voice full of self-righteousness. 'Nowt wrong with that is there? I like to know how my cases are progressing. He said you've reopened inquiries.'

'Just tying up some loose ends,' Longley said. 'Your lad will be in court as planned as far as I know.'

'I should bloody well think so,' Hutton said.

'We do have one complicating factor, though. Graves's wife tried to top herself yesterday, and I'd like to know exactly what that's all about. Nobody seems to think she shed many tears for her old man. What was your impression?'

'A bit ga-ga if you ask me,' Hutton said. 'All kaftans and fairies at the bottom of the garden. But everything she said about that night tied in with what the other witnesses said. I'd no reason to think she might be lying. She'd be hard put to bash anyone over the head with that amount of force, any road. She's a frail little thing.'

'Well, she's come round this morning and Michael Thackeray's gone up to the hospital to interview her, so I've no doubt that'll be cleared up shortly,' Longley said. 'But I'm glad you called, Len. I wanted to talk to you about yesterday's little cock-up.'

'Cock-up? What cock-up?' The receiver seemed to shudder with the force of Hutton's question.

'Well, you did intend to let me know you wanted to arrest someone in Bradfield, I take it?' Longley responded far more mildly than he felt. 'I assumed the message must have got lost in the works somewhere, because I certainly never got it. Pity, that. It would have been better to have someone who knows Aysgarth Lane on hand. We have our problems up there, as you know, without strange coppers rushing in there mob handed.'

'Stirring up the natives, you mean?' Hutton's tone was contemptuous now. 'I've no time for no-go areas myself. And no time for bent coppers, come to that, whatever bloody colour they are. We'd no difficulty picking up Hussain Achmed. No problems at all. I've already charged him and he'll be in court later this morning. I reckon I'll need to be having words wi'that lad of yours, as well. What's his name? Sharif is it?'

'Why's that then?' Longley asked, his voice icy. 'I've no problems with DS Sharif.'

'Thick as thieves wi'my lad Achmed, isn't he?' Hutton said. 'Thieves likely being the operative word. Jumped in with both feet, didn't he, as soon as he realised Achmed was in trouble. I don't like that. But then it's typical of that lot, isn't it?'

'I'll ask Michael Thackeray to have a word with Sharif, find out how well he knows your lad,' Longley said and if Hutton had been able to see his face he might not have wanted to continue the conversation. As it was he ploughed on.

'Still hanging in there, is he, Thackeray?' Hutton asked.

'Any reason why he shouldn't be?'

'Well, you're in a better position to know that than I am, sir,' Hutton said. 'But a mate of mine did happen to mention he'd seen your colleague coming out of an AA meeting looking a bit the worse for wear. Wouldn't be the first time, would it? He's still something of a legend in the pubs and clubs of Arnedale, you know. And losing his wife just now must have rattled a few skeletons. But I dare say he'll cope – one way or another.'

Before Longley could curb his fury and think of a suitable

answer to that, Hutton had hung up. The superintendent sat gazing at the buzzing receiver in his hand for a long time before he hung up himself. The flood of poison Hutton had unleashed could not be unsaid, he thought, and he guessed that it was based on at least an element of truth or Hutton would not have risked putting his allegations into words. But what worried him much more than his witch-hunt against the two young Asian officers, was the almost casual way he had flung mud in Michael Thackeray's direction, mud Longley knew that he could not afford to ignore, however maliciously it had been thrown.

'I suppose you think it's all my fault,' the young pregnant woman said to DCI Michael Thackeray. 'I should have told her earlier I was expecting the baby.' They were sitting in a visitor's room outside the intensive care unit at Bradfield Infirmary and Thackeray was not in fact thinking anything of the sort.

With a slightly abstracted air he was trying very hard to concentrate on what the young woman opposite him was saying rather than his own obsession with the power of genetic inheritance. Marianne Graves was the image of her mother, more than twenty years younger, give or take, and with her straw-coloured hair cut short rather than flowing around her shoulders, but still an uncanny duplicate of the pale faced, light eyed woman who was lying just yards away fighting for her life.

He knew that his own young son had been unnervingly like him too, and he could not clear his mind of an obsessive suspicion that the boy would have matured even closer to his father's image had he lived. He would willingly have given the rest of his own life to have confirmed that belief, and he wondered what could have driven this woman and her mother so comprehensively apart.

They had traced Marianne Graves by way of the 1471 number Mower had carefully written down when he first entered the lodge and had found Julia Graves missing. They had found the same number, with no name beside it, record-ed on the flyleaf of her mother's address book when they had searched the lodge more thoroughly. There were no photographs of children in the house, nor any letters. Not even a birthday card hinted that Julia Graves's two children, Marianne and her brother Jonathan, might be alive. But Marianne had answered the telephone herself at her home in Luton, and had driven to Bradfield within hours.

'If I'd known she was on antidepressants, I'd have been more careful telling her about the baby,' Marianne said, breaking into the chief inspector's thoughts impatiently. 'I thought she'd be thrilled. How was I to know she's gone a bit funny? I've not spoken to her for years until the last cou-ple of months.'

'Did you know your father was dead?' Thackeray asked.

'No, I didn't. There was a message from Mum on the answer machine about a week ago but when I rang back I never got a reply. Not from her or Dad. If Dad used to answer I always hung up, of course. There was no way I wanted to talk to him.'

'Tell me how you came to be estranged from your par-ents,' Thackeray found the strength to ask quietly at last.

'We were taken into care, weren't we?' Marianne said. 'I was twelve and Jonathan was ten.'

Thackeray paused, his normal imperturbability shaken not only by the answer but also by the coolness with which it was offered. He could only guess at the trauma which must have accompanied that removal of two children from their parents.

'And why was that?' he asked, at length.

'Child abuse, of course,' Marianne said, refusing to meet Thackeray's eyes. 'We were fostered, and then adopted. We didn't want to go back. But Jon wasn't very happy and he ran away in the end. I haven't seen him for six years.' Her eyes were full of unshed tears.

'And who abused you? Your mother?'

The young woman shrugged wearily.

'It's a long story,' she said. 'Officially, it was supposed to be Mummy. But that was a story she concocted to protect my father. He was the one who hit us. He broke Jon's arm once, twisting it up his back. But there was a lot of awful stuff. But when social services came snooping around she told them it was her. And she told us that if we blamed my father it would ruin his career and we'd all be homeless and living on the streets. We were young enough to believe that, so we went along with what happened. In the end they took us away anyway, so it didn't make any difference. It was what we wanted by then. And sorting out the truth was too complicated. No one would have believed us if we'd changed our story. He was a deeply frightening man, my father. I don't think either of us ever wanted to go back.'

'So you lost touch?' Thackeray said, trying to keep his sense of outrage out of his voice.

'We had our own lives,' Marianne said. 'Our new parents were very sweet, not inspiring, but they did their best. As I say, Jon did a runner in the end. And I got married last year. The baby's due in two months.'

'And you didn't tell your mother any of that?'

Marianne glanced away, twisting her hands together in her lap.

'She must have found out,' she said. 'I think my adopted mother must have let her know, because she called me about two months ago. She'd got my phone number from somewhere and she said she wanted us to meet.'

'And did you?'

'No,' Marianne said so quietly that Thackeray could barely hear her. 'I told her she and my father had ruined Jon's life and I wasn't in the mood to let her back into mine. She didn't call again until she left this message the other day. She must have wanted to tell me what had happened to dad, I suppose.'

Thackeray stared at the institutional vinyl on the relatives' room floor and shuddered silently. He knew only too well how easy it was to destroy the thing you loved, but this was a variation on a familiar theme he had not heard before.

'I suppose I should have tried harder to call her back,' Marianne said. 'I suppose you think it's my fault she's taken an overdose, because I wouldn't see her, even though the baby was on the way. I suppose I was the last straw or something. I'm sorry.'

'Did she ever give you any indication she might try to kill herself?' Thackeray asked.

'Of course not,' Marianne said angrily. 'If she had I'd have done something about it. I'm not completely stupid. She said that she understood that I felt I'd been let down. She said she'd been let down too.'

'By your father?'

Marianne shrugged.

'By people, I think she said. Do you think she tried to kill herself?'

'She doesn't seem to have left any sort of note,' Thackeray said, more robustly than he felt. 'I don't think we can jump to any conclusions about her motives at this stage. In any case, she may regain consciousness again, the doctors say. She came round a bit this morning, which is why I came up in the hope of talking to her. She may recover, you know.'

Marianne looked at him with deep scepticism in her eyes.

'And pigs might fly,' she said dismissively.

'There's one thing I'd like to ask you, although it's not a question you'll like,' Thackeray said. 'Nor even one I can insist on your answering.'

Peter Graves's daughter looked at him with a mocking glint in her eyes.

'Oh, I know what you want to know, Chief Inspector,' she said. 'You want to know if I think my mother could have killed my father, don't you?'

He nodded his acknowledgement and she looked him straight in the eye, a pale chilly gaze which told him that she had been damaged as much as her brother by Peter Graves's failures as a father. He wondered how her own baby would fare.

'I can tell you one thing,' Marianne said. 'I could have killed him, apart from the fact that on the night in question I was two hundred miles away in the company of about fifty people at a birthday party. I could easily have killed him. But my mother? No chance. You hear of worms turning, but not that worm. His family had all the reasons in the world to hit him over the head, but neither the opportunity nor the means nor, in my mother's case, when it comes down to it, the guts. Sorry. You'll have to look somewhere else for your murderer. Maybe it was the boy you've got locked up after all. I don't think it's that unlikely one of those kids turned on him, do you?'

Julia Graves's daughter sounded totally convinced by her case but Thackeray was not. He knew only too well how apparently normal people could suddenly snap, and Julia seemed to have suffered far longer than most would at the hands of an abusive husband. Everyone has a breaking point, he thought, and it was not impossible that Julia Graves had reached hers and then decided to end her own life. It sounded only too familiar to him.

On an impulse, Thackeray turned away from the town centre when he left the infirmary and turned the car up Aysgarth Lane, past the bustling Asian shops, out into the quiet suburbs, then along the main road to the north and his home town of Arnedale which he had avoided as far as he could for more than ten years. His father, Joe, lived in discontented retirement in a small bungalow with his ageing sheepdog and a deep sense of grievance that he had been unable to end his days on the hill farm where he had spent almost his entire life. The old man must have seen Thackeray's car draw up on the hill outside the house because he was at the door almost before Thackeray had pulled on the handbrake.

'Are you reet?' he asked without warmth as his son held out a conciliatory hand, which was ignored.

'Not too bad, considering,' Thackeray conceded, following his father into the small stuffy living room and taking off his coat.

'I was sorry to hear she'd gone,' the old man began awkwardly.

'Don't be,' Thackeray said. 'It was for the best'

'Aye, maybe, God rest her soul.' The two men stood looking at each other in mutual incomprehension for a moment and Thackeray knew that there was no bridging the gap between them, the gap between belief and unbelief, Joe's faith that Aileen had gone to a better place and his own certainty that she had gone into the dark that would swallow them all eventually.

'When's t'funeral then?' Joe asked.

'I'm not sure yet. Her parents are arranging it at their local church. Do you want to go?'

'It'd be a funny sort of father-in-law didn't go to his own daughter-in-law's funeral,' Joe said, his face flushing with sudden anger.

'I'll take you up there,' Thackeray said, suddenly overcome by an immense weariness. 'We'll go together.'

'Aye, that'd be best,' Joe said. 'I suppose her parents think the Sacred Heart would bring back too many memories.' Memories of Ian's tiny coffin being carried into the Roman Catholic church in Arnedale were obviously as sharp for his father as they were for him, Thackeray thought, and maybe as painful. Joe said nothing more and busied himself in the tiny kitchen making tea and digging out a packet of biscuits from a cupboard.

'I had a friend o'yours from t'local police round yesterday,' he said eventually, as he poured two mugs of the inky brew. 'Offering condolences. Name of Hutton?'

Thackeray felt himself freeze and hoped that his father did not pick up the panic which he was sure must be visible in his eyes.

'Hutton?' he said. 'DCI Hutton? I wouldn't call him a friend exactly. What did he want?'

'Just to know when Aileen's funeral was,' Joe said. 'I thought he must have known her.'

'Not that I'm aware of,' Thackeray said.

'Seemed to know all about what happened, any road,' Joe said.

'Did he, now?' Thackeray said, his face grim now. 'I'll give him a call.'

'People are bound to rake it all up, when they know Aileen's gone. Stands to reason. Folk have long memories in Arnedale.'

'Too long,' Thackeray said. 'If you want to do me a favour, Dad, I'd be grateful if you didn't talk about Aileen and Ian to anyone you don't know well. It isn't going to do me any good to have it all dragged up again.'

'No, I don't suppose it is,' Joe said waspishly. 'Nor your drinking. I hear you've started that again.' Thackeray stared at his father close to a state of shock.

'What did you say?' he asked, his mouth dry.

'Boozing,' Joe said. 'Does this lass you're supposed to be marrying know about that?'

'I'm not boozing, as you call it,' Thackeray lied between gritted teeth, realising fully for the first time the malevolence of an enemy he barely knew, and wondering if this sort of bile had been directed at his father, who had no power over him, how far Hutton had gone or might be prepared to go, with people who had. There was, he thought, only one person in Arnedale who might be able to answer that question for him. He finished his tea as quickly as he dared and, promising to call him with the time and date of the funeral, took his leave of his father, who watched him go with brooding, anxious eyes.

He drove down the steep hill into the town centre where, because it was not market day, he was able to park in the broad high street right under the windows of the *Arnedale Observer*. Fergal Mackenzie, he discovered, was not only in the office but more than willing to see him. He took the seat the small, red-bearded Scotsman waved him to in his cluttered editor's office and met the not unfriendly but searching blue gaze full on.

'Whatever you've heard, it's probably not true,' Thackeray said flatly. 'You seem to have a pretty effective character assassin loose up here.'

'Aye, well, I guessed that much,' Mackenzie said thoughtfully. 'I'm just wondering what he has to gain, Mr Thackeray?'

'I'm not sure,' Thackeray said. 'I seem to have annoyed him by digging a bit deeper than he likes into the murder case in Bradfield that he claimed to have had all sewn up. So there's some professional tension there. Not that I'm totally convinced yet he got it wrong. And then one of my Asian officers has annoyed him...'

'The man's a raving Nazi,' Mackenzie said, explosively. 'I only found out this morning that he's charged his only Asian officer – or ex-officer, rather, because the lad had already resigned – he's now charged him with theft. In the magistrate's court this morning, he was, looking completely shell-shocked.'

'So I've been told,' Thackeray said.

'That would be easy enough to set up?' Mackenzie suggested, raising a spiky red eyebrow in interrogation.

'Easy to set up, and difficult to knock down if the man's determined enough,' Thackeray said. 'But I never said that. Perhaps you should talk to the detective constable himself, or his solicitor. I assume they granted bail?'

Mackenzie looked at his guest thoughtfully.

'I might well do that,' he said. 'They granted bail, though the police solicitor objected vehemently, as it goes.'

He hesitated for a moment before going on. 'I don't like your DCI colleague much,' he said. 'And I happen to know he's made quite a few enemies in the short time he's been in Arnedale. You know better than I do what a conservative little town this is, but on the whole, since you helped clear out those bastards Barry Moore and Les Thorpe, the people running the place, including the police, seem to have been straight enough. But Hutton's bad news and the best place for bad news is on the front page of the *Observer*. I'll do a bit of digging, see what I can turn up.'

'Be careful,' Thackeray said.

'Oh, I'll be careful,' Mackenzie said. 'And I'll say to you what I said to your bonnie Princess: you should mind your own back. The wolves seem to be out in force.'

'Thanks,' Thackeray said. 'But it's not so easy when a lot of the dirt he's chucking about is true.'

'We all make mistakes, man,' Mackenzie said. 'You're not expected to go on paying for them forever.'

'Are you not?' Thackeray asked with a faint smile. 'I can think of a few folk who'd disagree with that. Most of my own family for a start.'

Kevin Mower never did get to meet the girl he had spotted across a crowded bar the previous night again, as planned. As he was leaving the central police station and turning up his coat collar to keep off the spitting rain and sharp wind, DC Mohammed Sharif fell into step beside him.

'Have you got a minute, Sarge?' the younger man asked. Mower glanced at his colleague and recognised the slow burning anger in his dark eyes.

'Sure,' he said. 'What's the problem?'

'I need back-up,' Sharif said. 'You know what's happened to Hussain Achmed, don't you? He's on bail?'

Mower nodded cautiously.

'What exactly have they charged him with?' he asked.

'Theft,' Sharif said. 'They claim a wallet went missing at

the nick and they found one of the credit cards out of it at Hussain's place.'

'Nasty,' Mower said. 'Did he do it?'

'Of course he didn't bloody do it,' Sharif said. 'He's been set up to get DCI Hutton off the hook with this tribunal, hasn't he?'

'Difficult to prove,' Mower said quietly. 'What does Achmed say about the card?'

'He says he remembers the wallet going missing. Belonged to a DC called Brian Metcalf, not a particular friend of his, but OK, he thought. But as far as Hussain knew the wallet turned up again in the locker room and that was the end of it. Now Metcalf's saying one of the cards was missing, though he didn't notice till much later. And then it turns up in Hussain's room. Magic, or what?'

'Convenient, anyway,' Mower said. 'Had the card been used?'

'Apparently it had, and Metcalf says it wasn't by him. More than a grand's gone missing – in cash withdrawals.'

'So no indication of what the money was used for? That's convenient too, isn't it?'

'That's what I thought,' Sharif said. He hesitated. 'Could we get a look at the card statement, do you think? If we knew where the withdrawals were made Hussain might have a chance of proving he didn't make them.'

'His solicitor should be doing that, surely.'

'He says his solicitor's not being very energetic, not very interested,' Sharif said, an edge of anger in his voice again. 'He's a local man, Arnedale local, I mean, and he hasn't even managed to get a copy of the statement out of Arnedale CID yet and Hussain's in court again next week. I thought I might be a bit more persistent actually, and quicker, but I don't have any contacts...'

Mower whistled under his breath. They both knew that there were ways of obtaining the information Hussain needed, but those ways were not strictly legal.

'Do you have the card details?' Mower asked. Sharif reached into an inside pocket and handed Mower a piece of paper.

'The solicitor's got that far,' he said. Mower held the sheet of paper for a second between finger and thumb, as if it were contaminated by a deadly virus, and considered his own reasons for wanting to wrong foot DCI Hutton before he folded the paper in two and put it in his pocket.

'I'll see what I can do,' he said. 'No promises – and certainly no guarantees.' He glanced at his watch and swore softly. Already late, he guessed his date would have given him up by now.

Chapter Twenty

Laura Ackroyd stared at her computer screen, seeing nothing but flickering images which made no sense. She hoped none of her colleagues could see that her eyes were full of unshed tears. Thackeray had finally come home the previous night, looking grey and weary. She had cooked him a meal but he had said little, throwing himself into a chair and watching television, although she doubted that he was concentrating then on what was on the screen in front of him any more than she was now.

'Michael,' she had said tentatively. 'Are you all right? Can't you tell me about it?'

He had shrugged and told her briefly about his trip to Arnedale.

'It's the uncertainty that's getting to me,' he said. 'I don't know what that bastard in Arnedale's up to, or why, except that he's stirring up as much trouble for me as he can. And Aileen's death gives him the perfect opportunity to drag all that happened into the open again.'

'Is there going to be an inquest?' she had asked quietly, knowing as well as he did that if there was the *Gazette*, as well as the *Arnedale Observer*, would be bound to cover it.

'The coroner's asked for a post-mortem. If he's satisfied that she died from natural causes there doesn't need to be an inquest.' The statement was non-committal but she had never seen him look so defeated.

They had fallen into bed early and gone to sleep in each others' arms, but she had been aware of him moving round the flat before dawn the next morning, and when her alarm finally went off, she found that he had already left. She picked up the post in the hall and glanced idly at a letter with a typed address, half inclined to leave it until she came home from work, but then stuffed the whole lot into her handbag to look at later.

It was not until she had logged onto her computer and

into the Internet to continue her research into the mysteries surrounding Woodlands School, that she remembered the letters she had stuffed into her bag. She glanced at a couple of bills and then opened the small plain envelope with a typed address and no indication of its origin except an Arnedale postmark. It contained a single sheet of photocopy paper which she smoothed out on her desk and read slowly, with increasing disbelief.

The page was obviously taken from a medical report prepared, she guessed, for the coroner who had held the inquest on Michael Thackeray's baby son twelve years earlier. But the subject was not the baby himself, but his mother Aileen, who had survived after being rushed to the local hospital emergency department. It detailed the coma she had fallen into after her suicide attempt, gave an estimate of the horrifying number of anti-depressants and painkillers she had ingested, and listed a number of unexplained bruises on her body. Laura knew that by the time the inquest on Ian had been held, Aileen had recovered sufficiently for her life no longer to be in immediate danger, although her brain had been irretrievably damaged. This medical assessment had not been disclosed at the inquest, or at least not mentioned in the *Arnedale Observer*, whose reports she had read. But she presumed that it was the reason that the Bradfield coroner was now taking an interest in Aileen's death, and she knew with just how much malice it had been sent to her. And she guessed that somewhere in the archives at Arnedale police station there were probably more lurid details about exactly what had happened when Michael Thackeray had found his baby son drowned in the bath.

She folded the page carefully and put it back in its envelope, with a sudden vision of vultures circling around a wounded animal, and glanced again round the newsroom, hoping no one could see her distress.

'Oh, Michael,' she whispered to herself. 'The knives are really out.'

She picked up the phone and got Kevin Mower on his mobile.

'Meet me at lunchtime, could you?' she asked quietly. 'It's really important.' To her immense relief Mower agreed, as Laura became conscious of a looming presence at her elbow.

'Owt or nowt in this stuff about the school?' Ted Grant asked.

With an immense effort of will, Laura pulled her attention back to the computer screen in front of her, although she felt sick with anxiety.

'Give me till lunchtime,' she said. 'I think I'm getting somewhere.'

'No longer than that, though,' Grant said. 'You've wasted enough time on it already.'

And in fact by mid-morning, the tumblers in her brain had fallen into place and unlocked at least one of the mysteries surrounding Woodlands School. She had been surfing the Internet again trying to discover exactly what Freeland Properties were planning to do with the Woodlands site when the school eventually moved, as councillor Jeremy Waite had assured her it must. Suddenly, a name leapt out at her from the company's website.

'What an idiot I am, I should have guessed,' she said to herself as she took on board the fact that Mark Oliver, the stylish and wealthy leader of the anti-school campaign, was also a director of Freeland.

'No wonder he's so happy to spend his precious time helping the wrinklies get the place closed down. The only question then is why Freeland are so anxious to get the school off the site ahead of the lease running out,' she muttered to herself, gaining a few curious looks from nearby colleagues. And the answer to that question, she thought, probably lay in a small paragraph in the business section of the *West Yorkshire Press*, which her search engine had also located, anticipating extremely bad financial results for the

Leeds-based company. Building on the prime site in Southfield, she guessed, might be the lifeline Mark Oliver's company desperately needed.

She printed out the pages of information she wanted, logged off her computer and added the sheets to the file in her bottom drawer. There was one more thread she wanted to tease out before she felt that she had a story that would get past the libel lawyers and justify the front page lead she thought her suspicions deserved. Assuring Ted Grant that she was on to something good, she drove up to the Heights and tapped on her grandmother's front door.

'Jeremy Waite,' she said to Joyce when they were settled over a cup of tea. 'Tell me everything you know about Jeremy Waite, and then tell me who can tell me a bit more.'

Joyce looked at her quizzically.

'He'd have had sight of the inspectors' report,' she said shrewdly. 'We know we didn't leak it, and Mary Morris at the school would hardly let it out, even if it was genuine. And much as I dislike the idea of privatised inspectors I don't think they'd allow themselves to be regarded as unreliable with confidential information.'

'But why would Waite want to pass a bad report to the school closure campaigners, whether or not it was bogus?' Laura asked. 'There's no advantage to the council in moving the school any sooner than they're legally obliged to. It's going to cause them more problems than it solves.'

'Perhaps there's an advantage to our young Jeremy then,' Joyce said. 'Perhaps this task force he's set up will provide the answer Mark Oliver wants to hear in exchange for a nice little boost to Jeremy Waite's bank account from the developers. He's an ambitious lad, is Jeremy, and maybe greedy with it. And if the school's been undermined by all this bad publicity, so much the better. If the genuine report's not so bad after all, the chances are the public will never take that on board. What space would your Ted give it in the *Gazette* for a start. The damage has been done.'

Laura looked at her grandmother for a long moment.

'You're saying Jeremy Waite's corrupt?'

'I'm saying it's a possibility,' she said. 'It wouldn't be the first time, more's the pity. There were a few in my day, though on the whole we eased them out without a great hoo-ha in the newspapers. Other places had much bigger scandals in the sixties and seventies. There's no reason why it shouldn't happen now. I doubt if folk are any more honest or less greedy.'

'If the report's a fake anyway, I suppose Mark Oliver could have written it himself,' Laura said doubtfully.

'Whoever wrote that report knew the jargon,' Joyce said with total certainty. Laura grinned.

'It certainly had the ring of truth about it, all that stuff about learning styles and unsatisfactory modes of teaching and falling behind national norms, whatever they are.'

'Did it look right?' Joyce asked.

'What do you mean?'

'Did it look like a proper Ofsted report? Mary Morris will know. If it looked right, then you can bet it was done by an insider. An amateur wouldn't get the detail right. And if it was done by an insider you'll probably find it somewhere in the town hall. Jeremy Waite could easily have done it himself or maybe he even persuaded one of the inspectors to do it for him...'

'It would be done on a computer,' Laura said quietly. 'Difficult to trace.'

'You may never prove anything,' Joyce said wearily. 'He's a canny lad, is Jeremy Waite. If he's been paid to help Freeland you can bank on it he's had untraceable notes in plain brown envelopes.'

'Just like the plain brown envelope the report came to the *Gazette* in.'

'There'll be nowt obvious,' Joyce said. 'You can bank on that.'

'The police could still turn the place over,' Laura said

reluctantly, seeing her front page story disappearing into the middle distance as another police inquiry was launched which might take months to complete.

'Aye, well, if you're going to get your man onto the case you'd better get him to move a bit sharpish,' Joyce said. 'If you give them any warning you're onto them the evidence will disappear faster than frost on midsummer morning.' She hesitated for a moment, apparently deep in thought.

'You could talk to Fred Stevenson, the union rep. He works in Waite's department, or he used to. He must be coming up to retirement but I'm sure he's not gone yet. He'd have invited me to the do if he had. He was a good lad years ago when he worked for me. If there's owt funny going on he might have heard a whisper.'

'I'll give it a try,' Laura said doubtfully.

She drove back to the office thoughtfully and persuaded Martin Bates to let her photocopy the first few pages of the report on the Woodlands School.

'With a bit of luck I may be able to find out if this damn thing's genuine,' she said to the uncertain young reporter. 'You'll be Ted's blue-eyed boy again if it is. Just leave it with me till the end of the day.' Bates did not look convinced but he let her take her photocopy anyway.

At the Town Hall it was not difficult to prise Fred Stevenson out of his office for a cup of tea and a bun in the canteen, where she explained exactly what information she wanted.

'It could have been done on a home computer, of course, in which case we'll probably never find out who wrote it,' she said, handing him the first few pages of the report. 'But my guess is it was done by someone here, and most likely in the office, because this will be where all the previous reports will be filed. They'd be handy for getting the layout and the language right. What d'you think are the chances of tracking it down if it was.'

Stevenson was a small lugubrious man, with lines and

creases of disappointment written across a face almost as
grey as the sparse hair which covered his scalp. But his eyes
were sharp enough and had sparkled with anticipation as
soon as Laura had explained who had sent her and what she
and her grandmother wanted.

'There's a lad I know in the IT department can find out
owt about owt inside a computer. Never mind you think
you've deleted it, young Jason can turn it up again like a rabbit out of a hat. I'll put him on t'job. A bit of routine computer maintenance in the education offices. No problem.'

'You're sure he won't get into any trouble?' Laura cau-
tioned.

'Jason knows more about computers than Jeremy Waite
knows about stabbing folk in t'back, and I reckon he learned
that at his mother's knee. Don't you fret. If it's there, he'll
find it, will Jason, and no beggar will ever know he's even
looked.'

Thoughtfully she walked back down the broad stone
steps of the town hall, and headed towards the café bar where
she had arranged to meet Kevin Mower and persuade him to
try to find out just how and why someone was trying so hard
to derail Michael Thackeray's career. Later, she thought, feeling sick, there would be an even harder task to undertake.
Although she knew she was being manipulated, she could not
see how she could not show the document from Arnedale to
Michael Thackeray himself and ask him to tell her, at last,
exactly what had happened on the day his son died.

Later that afternoon, DS Kevin Mower put down the phone
and returned to the forensic reports on his desk in bewilder-
ment. In the end he picked up the sheaf of documents and
walked the short distance down the corridor to the DCI's
office.

'It makes no sense, guv,' he said as he dropped the bundle onto Thackeray's desk. It was late, he was tired, he was
deeply depressed and at a loss over what Laura had told him

at lunchtime. His boss's office was thick with cigarette smoke, always an indication that Thackeray too was feeling the pressure. He glanced round the office, looking for signs that Thackeray had been drinking again but saw none. But the fury in Thackeray's eyes told him that he knew precisely what he was thinking.

With an effort he wrenched his mind back to the murder inquiry. He did not think that he had missed anything important as far as the re-investigation of Peter Graves's death was concerned.

'The boy, Elton?' Thackeray asked. 'Any sightings?'

'No one's seen him since our near miss, guv,' Mower said. 'We've got someone keeping an eye on his mother's place and around Wuthering generally, but so far nothing.'

'He's big enough and strong enough to have killed Graves on his own,' Thackeray said. 'And his school records indicate episodes of extreme violence. 'Volatile' that silly woman at Woodlands called him. I think homicidal might be nearer the mark.'

'You're worried about Laura,' Mower hazarded, recognising the fear in Thackeray's eyes for more than professional concern.

'I've spoken to her,' Thackeray said. 'She called, full of some tale about corruption over the school site. I'll talk to her about it tonight and if it stands up I'll get her to come in tomorrow with everything she's got, though it hardly sounds strong enough to me to warrant an investigation. Jack Longley will want cast-iron reasons to start digging into council affairs.'

'Why don't you get off home, guv,' Mower suggested, knowing he was overstepping unspoken boundaries. He was not surprised when Thackeray shook his head grimly.

'Shortly,' he said, lighting another cigarette. 'Tell me what forensics have come up with first'

'The hammer,' Mower said, shuffling through his reports. 'Hadn't been in the open long – too clean, not enough mould or rust, and we know for a fact that the murder weapon was rusty. So that suggests it was dumped much more recently than the night of the killing. There's been a lot of rain since then but the bloodstains were miraculously intact, so it had probably not been under the hedge much longer than a day. But in any case the blood's not Peter Graves's. In fact it's not even human. If that hammer hit anything it was nothing more suspicious than a pound of rump steak.'

Thackeray nodded, as if not surprised at this unexpected scientific conclusion.

'Then there's the fingerprints,' Mower said.

'On the hammer?'

'On the hammer. On the petrol can. And on the garden fork we so conveniently acquired. All the same.'

'Alicia Boston's?'

'Precisely.'

'So the lads may have tripped over the petrol can after all, just as they said they did,' Thackeray said reluctantly. 'I think Mrs Boston has some explaining to do, don't you?'

'Now, guv?' Mower asked cautiously, resisting the temptation to glance at his watch. But Thackeray got to his feet and shook his head as he reached for his jacket.

'I think Mrs Boston'll keep till the morning. I don't think she's our killer, though there's a lot she's not been telling us,' he said. 'Tomorrow we'll tackle her about the can she handled and the hammer that didn't kill Graves. Now, get out of here, Kevin. I can always tell when you've got a date. As it happens there's something I want to do this evening too, so you're off the hook. But I'll see you here at eight in the morning, and if you're late I'll have you back on traffic duty before your feet touch the ground.' Mower wondered just how volcanic Thackeray's reaction would be if he knew where he was really going that evening.

'Oh, by the way.' Mower said over his shoulder as he opened the door. 'Gareth Davies, the sacked teacher, called as well. Something he's left out of his statement, he said. I agreed to see him in the morning too. I'll catch up with his wife while I'm at it. Turns out she may have been a bit economical with the truth as well.'

It was dark by the time Sergeant Kevin Mower and DC Omar Sharif drove into Arnedale and found a place to park in the main street amongst the scattered litter and half dismantled stalls of that day's open air market. Mower glanced at his watch.

'We should just catch them,' he said.

They dodged across the road, busy with home-going traffic, and went into an office on the ground floor of one of the Georgian buildings which lined both sides of the broad street. Mower flashed his warrant card at the startled receptionist, who was struggling into her heavy coat, and demanded to see Simon Atkin, one of the solicitors who worked there. He turned out to be a tall, skinny young man in a cheap sharp suit who, Mower reckoned, could not have qualified much more than a couple of months earlier. He had dark circles under his eyes and a slightly hunted look as the police officers walked in.

'You're handling the case of Hussain Achmed?' Mower asked, showing his warrant card again, and when Atkin nodded he took a seat in front of his desk uninvited.

'We're here to help,' he said, with a smile which held no warmth at all.

'Why would the police help?' Atkins asked, reasonably enough and when they explained he sat down again at his desk looking bemused.

Ten minutes later the two officers were sitting in one of Arnedale's many pubs, attracting unfriendly glances beneath an array of photographs of the town's cricket teams going back half a century. They were studying two similar sheets of paper spread on the table in front of them. One was the credit card statement the police had belatedly supplied to

Hussain Achmed's solicitor, the other the statement with the same dates and transactions on it that Mower had coaxed out of one of his contacts who had access to the card company's own computers. If he felt any guilt at this highly illicit transaction he showed no sign of it. The two statements were not identical.

'It's a forgery,' Sharif said. 'See there, everything's the same except for where the cash was withdrawn. After the 15th, all the withdrawals on Atkins's version are made in Bradfield but on the genuine statement they're made in Arnedale or, look here, in Eckersley.'

'They must be pretty sure Achmed was in Bradfield on those dates and could have withdrawn the money,' Mower said. 'They must have checked up on his movements and know he didn't come back to Arnedale over those few days. He's been quite efficiently set up.'

'How are they going to explain how he got hold of the pin number to use the card?' Sharif asked doubtfully.

'Some people keep the numbers with the cards: bloody stupid but they still do it. It only needs Brian Metcalf to say he did that and Achmed is stuffed. Metcalf'll look a bit of a fool in court but if he's decided he's going to vouch for the forged statement one more lie isn't going to bother him one way or the other, is it?'

'They hate Hussain Achmed that much?' Sharif asked with quiet horror.

'He's become a threat,' Mower said. 'Forcing him to resign was a triumph for these bastards. Getting taken to a tribunal could be a disaster.' He drank the rest of his lager and put the papers away carefully, his face set and his eyes very cold.

'Shall we see if we can find the charming DC Metcalf?' he asked, getting to his feet. 'And avoid that bastard Hutton if we can.'

Sharif drained his orange juice and followed the sergeant, wondering how he could keep the rage which threatened to engulf him in check. Casual insults he was used to, but this poisonous plot shook his limited faith in the police force to the core. How long would it be in his career, he wondered, before he met someone as bigoted as Hutton again. A year? A month? Or just a week?

The two men parked their car immediately outside Arnedale police station and watched as officers came off duty, slouching down the stone steps tiredly, or in cheerful groups obviously heading for the pub. Michael Thackeray would have been amongst the latter, Mower thought grimly, when he worked here as a detective sergeant. After five minutes or so they saw DCI Charles Hutton come down the steps alone and drive off. Mower put a hand on Sharif's arm and turned away from the senior officer as he passed their car but the DCI did not glance in their direction.

'The last thing we want is for Hutton to know we're around before we've got this thing pinned down,' he whispered.

'Can we get the bastard booted out of the job, Sarge?' Sharif asked. Mower shrugged.

'Metcalf's the crucial one. It was his card, his statement and the case will fall apart if he withdraws his evidence. It'll be much harder to prove Hutton was behind it.'

'We'll have to get him at the tribunal, then,' Sharif said. 'I want him, one way or the other.' Mower glanced at the younger man and recognised the rage in his eyes.

'You won't make many friends down that road,' he said.

'And nothing will change unless someone stands up to these bastards,' Sharif said.

'Right, but let me do the talking to Metcalf. I need you there as a witness but I don't want you stirring up a race riot. That's just counter-productive.' They watched in edgy silence for another five minutes before Mower stiffened.

'That's him,' he said. 'I met him in Bradfield once when he came down for some briefing or other. Let's go, shall we?'

The two men got out of the car and fell into step one on

each side of Brian Metcalf.

'Hello, Brian,' Mower said in as friendly a voice as he could muster. 'Kevin Mower. You remember me from Bradfield CID? And this is Mohammed Sharif, commonly known as Omar.'

Metcalf looked flustered.

'Can I help you?' he said.

'Oh, I think so,' Mower said kindly, taking Metcalf's arm. 'Why don't we pop in here for a quick half.' And he steered their quarry into a quiet pub down a narrow alleyway of cottages, well away from the Bull where he knew Arnedale CID normally drank. They took a table in a shadowy corner and when Mower had set up the drinks, he took the documents they had collected out of his pocket.

'We're a bit worried, Brian,' he said, as the Arnedale officer took what looked like a much needed gulp of his pint. 'Omar's particularly worried about this theft charge against his mate Hussain Achmed.'

Metcalf put his pint down jerkily and slopped beer across the table but he said nothing. He was a broad, burly man with sandy hair and a high colour but he looked pale now.

'You see, when we started to look into it, we came across something very odd,' Mower went on, with Metcalf looking visibly sicker by the minute. 'You know what we unearthed?'

Metcalf shook his head.

'We found two different versions of your credit card statement. There's the statement the CPS disclosed to Achmed's solicitor, which looks incriminating because there's a series of withdrawals made in Bradfield, allegedly by Achmed. That presumably came from you. And then there's the statement the credit card company says it sent to you and which shows those cash withdrawals were made in Arnedale after all. Now how do you account for that?'

Metcalf shook his head wildly and made to get up from the table but Mower put an iron hard arm across his shoulder and pressed him relentlessly back into his seat.

'Let's keep this friendly, shall we?' he said. 'Otherwise I may feel obliged to go straight to county HQ with my worries.'

Metcalf subsided again, looking hunted.

'I assume there's absolutely no evidence that Achmed was in Arnedale when those genuine withdrawals were made? In other words, he has an alibi? What did you do? Have him followed so that you could make the statement fit his movements?'

Metcalf shrugged and said nothing.

'The credit card company will swear that the statement I've got a copy of here is the genuine one,' Mower pressed and Metcalf shrugged again, his lower lip trembling slightly as he sipped half-heartedly at his beer.

'Did you set him up, Brian?' Mower whispered fiercely, although the bar was empty enough for no one to be in earshot. 'You don't like Asian coppers any more than your boss does, do you? So you set him up to get him off DCI Hutton's back over the tribunal complaint? Is that it? Got you well in with Mr Hutton, did it?'

'It wasn't my idea,' Metcalf muttered. Sharif drew a sharp breath of satisfaction at that.

'But you went along with it? And you checked out where Achmed had been the days you made the withdrawals, waited for the statement to turn up and then altered it to fit?'

Metcalf nodded, and wiped his face with the back of his hand. He was sweating heavily.

'And you had the credit card in your possession all the time? Achmed never had it at all?'

'The wallet was found at the nick after a couple of days. Everything was intact,' Metcalf muttered. 'Achmed had left by then.'

'So it all fell into place – you could plant it on him and fiddle the statement so that he couldn't claim an alibi in defence? He was where the statement implied he was at the relevant times?' Mower pressed. Metcalf nodded miserably.

'It wasn't my idea,' he said again.

'So whose idea was it to pervert the course of justice?' Mower asked.

'I can't tell you that,' he said.

'So you'll carry the can for Mr Hutton, will you?' Sharif asked. Metcalf threw him a poisonous look.

'Stick together, you lot, don't you?' he said.

Mower banged the two credit card statements down on the table.

'Listen to me very carefully, Brian,' he said. 'I'll tell you what's going to happen. Achmed's solicitor and the CPS will get copies of your genuine credit card statement in the morning. The company will vouch for it, obviously, and dismiss your crude little forgery. The CPS will then either let the case go to court next week, and your nasty little set-up will be revealed publicly in Achmed's defence, or they'll withdraw the charge beforehand. Either way they'll be asking you and your boss some pretty searching questions. Achmed will then be free to continue his tribunal case, in which I've decided I'll give evidence too, as your boss very foolishly included me in his racist banter when he was in Bradfield. And Achmed may well make a complaint to the Police Complaints Authority about the way he was charged, in which case I sincerely hope they throw the book at you and Hutton and you both end up in court.'

Metcalf stared at Mower and Sharif with undisguised hatred.

'The BNP's got it about right,' he hissed, as he got to his feet. 'Me, I'd see you all in hell, bloody terrorists.'

Thackeray's conversation with Laura earlier that afternoon had been cool, brief and unsatisfactory, leaving both of them edgy and deflated. She had called in to police HQ to pass on what she and Joyce Ackroyd suspected was behind the campaign to close down Woodlands School and been shown up to his office. But she had been disappointed when he made it plain that their suspicions about corruption at the town hall came pretty low on the CID agenda. He was much more interested, it seemed, in Dwayne Elton and the possibility that he might try to contact Laura again.

'I hear what you're saying,' Laura said irritably. 'But I'll be OK. I promised to babysit for David and Vicky Mendelson tonight. No one will find me there.'

Thackeray had hesitated, on the point of asking whether he should join her later at their friends' house, but he did not make the suggestion. He found it hard to watch Laura with the baby daughter the Mendelsons had named after her. It reminded him too acutely of what he had lost and what he found it almost impossible to envisage ever sharing with Laura herself.

'I'll see you at home about eleven,' she said. 'They said they won't be late back.'

'Be careful,' he had said lamely and the silence as she turned to leave his office told him more than words could how much she was hurt by his coolness. As the afternoon wore on he had become more and more anxious about Laura and the threat to her safety that he believed Dwayne Elton posed.

He pressed on with his paperwork after most of his detectives had gone home, before finally closing his files and making his way down the stairs and out of the building. It was already seven-thirty and he drove quickly the mile out of town towards Laura's flat, parking fifty yards down the road where he hoped she would not be able to see him. To his relief, her car was still parked outside in its usual place and he knew that he was not too late to undertake the self-appointed task of making sure she arrived safely at the Mendelsons, a precaution which he knew would infuriate Laura as much as it reassured him.

He sat in his car smoking and listening to a Billie Holiday album on the stereo for what seemed like an hour but was probably no more than five minutes before he saw the lights in the flat go off. A couple of seconds later he watched as she closed the front door behind her and walked round to the driver's door on the side of the car furthest away from the kerb. He turned the music down and heard the car door slam reassuringly.

What happened next had him shouting aloud in alarm. As the Golf's lights came on and Laura eased away from the curb, what seemed like no more than a dark shadow detached itself from the bushes beside the road, pulled open the passenger door and got in. For a second or two the car braked and slowed, but before Thackeray could even get his own door open it had accelerated away again down the street, the tail lights disappearing round a bend.

'Hell and damnation,' Thackeray said, slamming his own car into gear and giving chase, though cautiously. With the Golf in sight again he held a steady distance and pulled out his mobile phone to contact police HQ.

'I need back-up urgently,' he said and his mouth was almost too dry to spell out the details of where he was and what had happened.

'Don't approach the VW,' he said at last. 'I've reason to believe Dwayne Elton's dangerous. He could be armed.'

Laura knew as soon as Dwayne hurled himself into the passenger seat beside her that she had made a mistake and that if she ever saw Michael Thackeray again he would have every reason to ask why she had not asked him to come with her to the Mendelsons. The invitation had been on the tip of her tongue when they had discussed her plans but she had dismissed it. There was a narrow line, she thought bitterly, between her much cherished freedom to pursue her own life and the impulsiveness which had got her into risky situations before, and she had just crossed it again.

She glanced at Dwayne, who was huddled against the passenger door, with one hand firmly lodged in the pocket of his black hooded jacket. It was impossible to read any expression in his face in the fitful light and she risked a smile.

'How's things?' she asked. 'If you'd said you wanted a lift you'd have been very welcome. You didn't have to ambush me.'

The boy looked at her, and she could see as the lights outside brightened slightly that his jaw was clamped shut and there was no sign of friendliness in his dark eyes. She glanced at her mobile phone on a shelf near the gear lever but his eyes followed hers and he reached out quickly for the receiver.

'Don't even think about it,' he said. 'Was it you told the pigs where I was the other night?' He put a hand on her arm and pointed her in the direction of the road which led up the long winding hill to Southfield. She signalled a right turn and followed his instructions.

'I didn't know where you were,' she said mildly and truthfully.

'You was there. On the Heights. I fucking saw you.'

'Someone had told Stevie Fletcher's lawyer where she might find you. She wanted to persuade you to talk to the police, to help Stevie. Which is just what I wanted you to do the last time you came round to my place, remember? I was just along for the ride.'

It was an effort to keep her voice calm as she saw the boy tense again, the right hand still invisible in his pocket. If he had a concealed weapon, and there were enough guns on the Heights to make that a distinct possibility, then the odds on her getting out of the car unscathed if he decided to use it were very slim.

'Where are we going?' she asked, her mouth dry, although as the road wound up the hill and the houses became larger and more widely spaced in their landscaped gardens, she thought she already knew the answer.

'School,' Dwayne said.

'There'll be no one there at this time of night,' Laura said and then realised that this was an occasion when a lie might have been advisable. The notion of a school for some reason brimming with teachers and parents might just possibly have deterred Dwayne.

'I want to show you summat,' the boy said.

'Right,' Laura said faintly. At the next junction she looked left and then right, turning her head deliberately towards her companion, and was not reassured by the glazed look in his eyes.

The school gates were closed when they arrived, and Laura parked outside, pulling gently into the kerb and taking the time to look up and down the dimly lit avenue in the hope that she might find help, but apart from a few parked cars the road was deserted. The lodge and the buildings beyond were in complete darkness and she tried to estimate her chances of outrunning Dwayne if she took off down the road and tried to seek sanctuary at one of the secluded houses, where lights shone faintly through the trees, but even as she pulled on the handbrake he proved himself to quick for her. He was out of the car and round at her door before she had unfastened her seatbelt.

'I want to show you summat,' he said again. 'I won't hurt you.' But he grabbed her arm nonetheless and half-dragged her from the car and through the school gates, closing them carefully behind them. Holding her by the left arm in a fierce grip he finally took his hand out of his coat pocket and to Laura's immense relief switched on a small torch.

Unwillingly she allowed herself to be pulled down the side of the school and into the grounds at the back, across the tarmac of the playground and down some steep stone steps, slippery in the night air, where eventually they stumbled to a halt as Dwayne tried to penetrate the darkness ahead of them with the thin beam. Laura was acutely aware that they had moved some considerable distance from the road and that even if she cried out it was unlikely anyone would hear her. Overhead an owl screeched and made them both jump.

'I hid in the old garages back there last night,' Dwayne said, pulling her further into the trees through long sodden grass and invisible bushes which snagged on her jeans .

'We used to go in there for a drag at breaktime. It were right dark but this morning I found it. Just down here. Back o'them old buildings.' At last the beam of his torch found what he had been seeking and Laura picked out the ruin of the painting which she had last seen hanging on Julia Graves's sitting room wall. It had been slashed to ribbons and then set on fire. Beneath it a bundle of what looked like old clothes had also been blackened by the flames but not totally destroyed.

'It were Ella's picture,' the boy said. 'She showed us how she painted them when she came to t'school. It were her who were here that night. It were her voice yelling at Mr Graves. When I saw the picture I realised who it was.'

Laura digested this piece of information slowly. There could only be one reason for Peter Graves and Ella Ferenc to be having a blazing row, she thought, and that was a relationship much closer that anyone apparently knew about. Had the row ended in violence, she wondered. Or had Ella's husband or Peter's wife also overheard the lovers' quarrel and taken a terrible revenge?

Dwayne seemed to be waiting for her to offer some comment but before she could speak the darkness of the night exploded around them. She had hardly been aware until that moment that a faint red glow had begun to illuminate the trees, casting flickering shadows in the leaves above

them, but even as she turned to look at the old house looming above and behind them and take in the flames which
were clearly visible at the upper windows, the fire roared
through the roof like a wild animal suddenly released from
its cage. In the sudden glare, the dark figures which raced
towards them and crashed past her as Dwayne cried out in
alarm and ran further into the trees seemed like demons
summoned from hell.

Horrified Laura heard Thackeray's familiar voice, hard-
edged with anger, reciting the police caution to Dwayne as
he dragged him roughly back from the shadows into the
light of the inferno above them.

'No, Michael,' she cried, against the roar of the flames
and the shouts of police officers who had followed
Thackeray down the slope from the school. 'You've got it
wrong. It wasn't Dwayne either.'

Thackeray glanced at her briefly, his eyes furious, as he
went through the boy's pockets before letting a uniformed
officer handcuff his wrists behind his back.

'Abduction will do to be going on with,' he said. Laura
looked from the blazing school to the cowed teenager in
despair.

'No,' she insisted. 'You've got it all terribly wrong.'

Dragged back on duty later from a serious bit of chatting up
in one of Bradfield's shiny new bars, Sergeant Kevin Mower
could not understand why DCI Thackeray was insisting on
pursuing his inquiries into Peter Graves's murder with such
manic determination this late in the evening. But his suggestion that they defer the questioning of witnesses until early
the next morning was peremptorily dismissed and Mower
shrugged and followed instructions, assembled a small team
of officers from that evening's duty roster and drove his
boss out of town.

It was after midnight and Ella Ferenc and Gareth Davies
were already in bed when the police knocked on their door

insistently. Davies, still tying his dressing gown, nodded DCI Thackeray and DS Mower into the house without seeming unduly surprised to see them. His wife, her hair dishevelled and eyes wide and bright, was wearing only a nightdress, and watched from the top of the stairs before coming down a few steps.

'Perhaps you'd like to get dressed, Mrs Davies, while we talk to your husband,' Thackeray said. She nodded and turned back up the stairs.

'Keep an eye on her,' Thackeray said to the uniformed woman officer who was standing in the hall behind them before he and Mower followed Ella's husband into the cluttered living room.

'Mr Davies, you said you wanted to change your statement. Just what is it exactly you want to tell us that you didn't tell us before?' Thackeray asked. He looked exhausted and his voice was harsh.

Davies slumped in a chair in the small sitting room, still stacked with his wife's paintings, and buried his face in his hands briefly. Then he grabbed his pipe from its ashtray and chewed on it, unlit, for a few moments before he replied. He looked haggard and there was a barely healed graze across his cheek and a dark bruise on his forehead. His eyes flickered nervously from Thackeray to Mower and back.

'I won't pretend I wasn't glad when Graves was killed,' he said. 'The man was a menace and he was wrecking lives. I told him that the night he died. He just laughed at me and called me a sad loser.'

'Did you go back to the school again later that night?' Thackeray asked.

'No, I didn't,' he said. 'I came home, just like I said I did, and Ella came in from college about half an hour later and we were both here for the rest of the night. I was so fed up that I drank about half a bottle of Scotch, if you must know. I couldn't have gone anywhere later.'

'Ella teaches on Monday evenings?'

'Yes,' Davies said, gazing at the bowl of his unlit pipe as if it would provide an answer for him.

'So what did you want to tell us, Mr Davies?' Thackeray's voice was as cold as the Arctic.

Davies put his pipe down, looking miserable, and took a deep breath.

'When I was with Peter he seemed uneasy, anxious even, and I couldn't understand why. It was as if he was waiting for something that he didn't want to tell me about.'

'You mean he was expecting someone else?' Thackeray asked.

'I think maybe there was someone already there, in the school, keeping out of the way while we had our discussion. As I came out I could smell perfume.'

'A woman then?' Thackeray snapped. 'Your wife? Or Graves's wife?'

Davies shrugged helplessly and glanced towards the door where Ella now stood, fully dressed, with the woman PC close behind her.

'I can't let those kids take the blame,' he said, turning away from his wife and gazing at his pipe again.

'Was there any indication who else might have been in the school?' Thackeray persisted harshly.

'Not really,' Davies said, his eyes flickering back towards Ella. 'I can't be sure.'

'I think you can make an educated guess,' Thackeray said. Davies looked at his wife again and for a second the space between them crackled with ferocity and Thackeray noticed her fists clench and he realised suddenly that there were reserves of violence in Ella Ferenc that someone should have noticed before now. He turned back to Davies and took in his bruised forehead with sudden comprehension. Davies, he thought, certainly knew.

'I'm sure you can guess who it was,' Thackeray said again.

'It smelt like Ella's perfume,' he said very quietly, turning away and gazing into space. 'Very like the one she wears, heavy and a bit musky...'

Thackeray swung round towards Ella Ferenc, who was gazing at her husband's hunched shoulders in horror.

'We found some bloodstained clothes at the school tonight,' he said. 'Would you know anything about that, Mrs Davies?' Ella stared at him silently for a long time.

'I suppose you'll be able to find out who they belong to? DNA and all that stuff?' she asked.

'Forensics should be able to tell us whose blood is on the clothes and quite probably who wore them,' Thackeray said. 'I should caution you, Mrs Davies, that anything you say may be taken down and used in evidence in court. What I'd like you to do now is to come down to the police station where I'd like to continue this interview there.' He sounded weary, all the veiled ferocity gone now as he watched the brightness disappear from Ella Ferenc's liquid eyes. She was silent again for a moment and then shrugged, and all vitality seemed to drain out of her like dirty water swirling out of a basin.

'Never mind all that,' she said quietly. 'It was me. I was there. My class was cancelled that night because there was no heating at college. So I went up to talk to Peter and simply kept out of the way when Gareth turned up. After it happened, I knew there was someone else around in the gardens. It must have been the boys, I suppose. I panicked and hid the clothes I'd been wearing behind the old stables where I'd parked the car. I always parked down there out of sight when I went to see Peter. There's a back way out so Julia could never see me coming and going. I had a coat in the car so I drove home in that, meaning to go back to collect the clothes I'd been wearing and burn them. But there's been so much activity around the school, police in and out, fire brigade in and out, I've not been able to get near to do what needed to be done. It amazed me that the police didn't find them sooner.'

'We've just been talking to Julia Graves,' Thackeray said.

'She found the blood-stained clothing buried in the bushes. You do dress quite distinctively. She recognised them and tried to burn them herself – along with your painting. She seems to have been torn apart with jealousy and a desire to protect you. She made a very poor job of it.'

Ella Davies nodded.

'Poor Julia,' she said. 'Neither of us seems to have been very efficient. And in the end I knew I couldn't let that poor boy be blamed for it either.' She flashed a look of contempt at her husband. 'I would have come to you in the end, even if Gareth hadn't worked it out for himself. When my class was cancelled I decided to go to see Peter to beg him not to end our affair. I sat in the staffroom while he talked to Gareth and then went back to his office. We had the most awful row and in the end he walked out and I followed him. I screamed at him and he turned and hit me and we both stumbled and half fell and I picked up whatever it was he'd tripped over. It turned out to be a heavy spanner thing, all rusty. And I hit him with it, and once I'd started I couldn't stop. Then I ran. You'll find the spanner somewhere near where the clothes were. I threw it into the bushes. I was surprised you hadn't found that either.'

That could be because no one was looking hard enough, Thackeray thought bleakly as he arrested Ella Davies and the police woman escorted her out of the house. He was not the only one who would find it hard to forgive the damage Charles Hutton had inflicted with his botched investigation of the murder of Peter Graves.

'We'll need a fresh statement from you too, Mr Davies,' he said to her husband finally. 'If you come down to the station tomorrow morning, that will do.' And he and Mower left him shivering in his chair and fumbling with his empty pipe.

'She beat him up,' Thackeray said, as they got into his car.

'He'll never admit that. They never do,' Mower said.

'She should have known that he wouldn't be able to live

with himself if the lad was convicted,' Thackeray said. 'The trouble is, he probably won't be able to live with himself now he's dropped her in it either, poor beggar.'

It was almost three in the morning as Thackeray hesitated before putting his key into the lock of Laura's flat. He was dog tired, but satisfied at least that Ella Davies had been charged with Peter Graves's murder before he left police headquarters, after she had defied her solicitor's advice and persisted in her confession. The flat was in darkness and there was no sound from the bedroom. Thackeray undressed in the bathroom, leaving his clothes on the floor, before slipping into bed beside Laura. She moved sleepily and flung an arm round him but said nothing. The next day was Saturday, he thought, and he had no doubt that there would be enough time for words then.

She was already up and dressed when he woke from an exhausted sleep at eight thirty and his heart skipped a beat when he caught her unawares in the kitchen with the sunlight shining through her tangle of copper hair. He went to kiss her but she pulled away quickly.

'You were very late,' she said, coolly. 'I thought you weren't coming – again. What happened?'

'Ella Ferenc has confessed to the murder,' he said.

'Ella?' Laura said, obviously surprised. 'I thought it might have been Gareth.'

'So did I when he said he wanted to change his statement. I thought he might have wanted to put his hands up. But what he wanted to tell us was that he thought his wife had been there that night. She didn't get home until half an hour or more after him and it turns out the class she should have been teaching had been cancelled. He must have been riddled with guilt at the prospect of Stephen Fletcher being convicted. I have to go in to question him later.'

'So you'll let Stephen go?'

'The charges will be withdrawn. We even know now who took the petrol can up there that night, and it wasn't Stevie.

It was just the first attempt Mark Oliver and his friends made to put the school out of action permanently. We caught him red-handed last night. The last thing he was expecting was an armed response unit to turn up out of the blue minutes after he torched the place. He's in custody too.'

'You'll be interested in the stuff I dug up about his business affairs now, I suppose,' Laura said dryly, and Thackeray nodded.

'And Dwayne?' she asked. 'You were very rough with him last night.'

Thackeray hesitated for a second. He brushed a finger lightly down Laura's cheek and was surprised when she pulled away from him sharply. He shrugged.

'I'm sorry,' he said. 'I thought he had a gun. I don't suppose you want to make a complaint about what he did last night.'

'No, I don't,' Laura said flatly. 'I was only ten minutes late for my babysitting in the end, in spite of all your histrionics. I was fine.' Thackeray looked at the faint purple shadows under her eyes and did not believe her.

'What I don't understand was why you didn't know Ella Ferenc was Gareth Davies's wife,' she said, returning to the attack.

'It would have helped if you'd told me earlier,' Thackeray said. 'Charles Hutton's sloppy investigation hadn't worked it out, so we had no idea who she was or that she was connected to the school. Anyway it seems Peter Graves chose that night to finish the relationship with Ella. That's what the boys overheard. Which could have given Gareth a motive to kill Graves, but he swears he knew nothing about the affair until that night when he guessed there was someone else at the school and smelled a perfume he recognised. But Julia really did see him leave and Peter Graves was still alive then. Of course, he could have come back but in fact it seems that it was Ella who hung around, hoping to carry on the argument with Graves when her husband had gone. The row carried on outside and when Graves stumbled she picked up an old spanner and hit him with it. It's there somewhere in the bushes, apparently. I've got people doing a thorough search this morning. Something else Hutton failed to do properly.'

'I thought the burnt clothes must be Julia's,' Laura said. 'I thought she must have tried to kill herself in some sort of fit of remorse because she'd killed her husband. That seems to be what she wanted us to think, though I don't understand why if she knew that Ella had done it.'

'You think she tried to cover up for her?' Thackeray asked. 'She's conscious now and recovering, apparently. I'll be talking to her again soon.'

'Ella was her friend,' Laura said slowly. 'She was everything Julia would have liked to be: attractive, successful, a painter heading for her own exhibition. Perhaps she just decided that there's been enough destruction of people's lives and she'd rather Ella got away with it. It's not as if anyone's shedding any tears for Peter Graves.'

Laura toyed with her cup of coffee, thinking of the exuberant, angry woman she had met so briefly and thought she could have liked.

'So Julia's going to be all right?'

'Apparently she's sitting up in bed holding her daughter's hand,' Thackeray said. 'I think she's looking forward to being a grandmother.' He did not admit how pleased that had made him.

'And you'll be charging Mark Oliver as well?'

'Oh, yes, he chose a very bad moment to torch the school,' Thackeray said, knowing that this would satisfy Laura as much as anything. 'He ran straight into my back-up team as he left the premises, with enough petrol on his hands to have gone up in flames himself.'

'But it wasn't him the first time?'

'No, it was Alicia Boston who made the first attempt to set the place on fire. And she dumped a hammer up near the

Heights just in case we missed the point that one of the pupils must have been to blame. She turned out to be Oliver's poodle, and a pretty ineffective one at that.'

'Oliver bought another poodle as well,' Laura said. 'I discovered after I spoke to you yesterday afternoon that the report on the school which someone leaked to the *Gazette* was actually written on Jeremy Waite's computer. How convenient was that for Oliver?'

'You think we should interview Waite?'

'Oh, nothing would please me more, Chief Inspector,' Laura said with a faint smile. But her eyes soon clouded again.

'It won't help the kids from Woodlands though,' Laura said quietly. 'I called Mary Morris just now. After everything that's happened, she says that she thinks the council won't try to reopen the school. They'll just try to integrate the kids into normal schools and she's sure that will be a complete disaster for most of them. They'll get thrown out within weeks and end up in trouble. Joyce will be heartbroken.'

'And you?' Thackeray said, reaching across the table for Laura's hand. 'Are you heartbroken?'

Laura's attempt at a smile was less than convincing.

'What about the poisonous DCI Hutton?' she asked. 'He seems quite determined to damage you.'

'Ah, I almost forgot to tell you,' Thackeray said quickly. 'I heard yesterday afternoon that there'll be no inquest into Aileen's death. As for the rest of it, this outcome will do his reputation no good at county. He made a complete mess of the murder investigation, largely as a result of his own prejudices. He decided who'd done it before he'd done even a basic investigation. And the discrimination allegations will go to a tribunal, Mower says. He reckons the charges against the Arnedale detective won't stand up and he'll give evidence at the tribunal himself.'

'Kevin's a good friend to you,' Laura said, wondering just how Kevin had defused at least some of the threat from Arnedale.

'I reckon Hutton will have to resign,' Thackeray said. 'And a good thing too.'

'But the damage he's done won't go away,' Laura said quietly. 'I think he must have sent me this.' And she pulled a crumpled sheet of paper from her pocket and handed it to Thackeray. He smoothed it out on the table top and read it slowly and Laura could see his expression grow bleak. Finally he screwed it up again and turned back to Laura.

'What do you want me to tell you?' he asked.

'The truth,' Laura said. 'I want you to tell me what you've never told me properly, what happened that day. We can't go on with this hanging between us for ever.'

Thackeray sat silently for a long time until Laura thought that she had finally pushed him too far into territory that was too painful. But in the end he took a deep breath as if about to lower himself into icy water.

'When Ian died there were some of my colleagues, and some of Aileen's friends, who called me a murderer,' he said at last. 'And that's what I've felt like ever since. But what they meant, I think, was that I'd pushed her into what she did. Which is certainly true. I didn't notice her depression because most of the time I wasn't capable of noticing anything much. But that day I noticed everything. It's still as clear to me as if it happened yesterday.'

He swallowed hard and hesitated for a moment as if willing her not to want to go on, but she was still looking at him with a seriousness in her eyes that she seldom showed and he nodded almost imperceptibly as if in surrender.

'That day, I got home quite early for once,' he said. 'And quite sober. The house was very quiet, which I thought was strange, and there was no one downstairs. I went upstairs quickly because by now I felt that something was wrong and I went into the bathroom first. Ian was floating just below the surface of the water, with his eyes open. He looked quite peaceful and I knew he was dead but I still grabbed him and tried to revive him. But there was nothing there, not a spark.

I wrapped him in a towel and took him into his room and put him in his cot, tucked him up to keep him warm, ridiculous, I know, but I still did it.'

He stopped with his eyes full of tears and Laura put a hand over his.

'Then I went to look for Aileen. I was mad now, full of rage and hate, and when I found her on the bed, unconscious, I grabbed her and hit her, I don't know how many times. I wasn't sure even whether she was alive or dead but what I wanted was her dead. I've never had any doubt about that.'

'The bruises?' Laura said quietly. 'But she survived.'

'I realised eventually she was still alive,' Thackeray said. 'I had my hands round her throat and some instinct made me stop. It might have been better for her if I hadn't, when you think of all those years since.'

'But you could have been charged with murder, manslaughter at least,'

Thackeray shrugged.

'I wouldn't have cared,' he said. 'Then.'

'How did you explain the bruising?'

'I told the doctors her heart had stopped and I'd revived her, thumped her chest, you know? I don't think they really believed me but in the circumstances, with a dead child brought in by the same ambulance, they let it go.'

Laura looked at him for a long time, her eyes full of tears.

'You've locked that up for twelve years,' she said. 'Can you let it go now?'

'I don't know,' he said. 'Can you?'

She put a hand over his again.

'I don't know either,' she said.